IF

ONLY

IF
ONLY

Susan Pennock

Matador
Unit E2 Airfield Business Park,
Harrison Road, Market Harborough,
Leicestershire. LE16 7UL
Tel: 0116 2792299
Email: books@troubador.co.uk
Web: www.troubador.co.uk/matador
Twitter: @matadorbooks

ISBN 978 1805140 313

British Library Cataloguing in Publication Data.
A catalogue record for this book is available from the British Library.

Printed and bound in Great Britain by 4edge Limited
Typeset in 10.5pt Adobe Garamond Pro by Troubador Publishing Ltd, Leicester, UK

Matador is an imprint of Troubador Publishing Ltd

For;
Sally, Sandra, Hazel and Roger

Prologue

She worked hard to keep her demeanour welcoming while at the same time clasping tight to the hammer held behind her back. Ushering her visitor inside, she swung it upwards and brought the heavyweight down with a satisfying thud. The sight of the bloody and broken head ignited her rage as she rained down frenzied blows onto the body, which now lay at her feet. As blood and brains sprayed out like a fountain of gore, her breathe became ragged; she slowly began to tire. Finally, she calmed. Her face settled, a smile twitched at the corners of her mouth.

1

JANUARY

A question Angela often asked herself was? Could she murder without getting caught? While daydreaming, her imagination would enjoy full reign on how she could achieve it. This would usually pop into her head on the coattails of another. One which, all her life, she had been asking herself, why does my family, and especially my mother, hate me? When the question flared, she would tamp it down by making excuses for their behaviour. Today something inside her snapped. Everyone knew that Christmas was supposed to be about coming together to celebrate. Her family had arranged to go away for the festivities, and even knowing that she would be on her own, none of them had been bothered enough to ask if she would like to go with them.

Angela knew she had never been easy to get on with as a child by the way her mother constantly moaned at her that she took offense too quickly, and she never tried to fit in. The phrase – odd, was often used to describe her. Fed up with the label, on a bad day, she demanded to know what she meant by it. Her mother's short temper exploded with the details of her daughter's many faults.

'You make everyone else feel uncomfortable with your staring and constant questions. The silent approach you have taken to adopting is unnerving. Creeping about not knowing where you will pop up next puts us all on edge. The unkempt appearance you manage to foster makes me and your father despair. Your jealousy of Mark and Judy is unwarranted, yet, you use it like a stick to beat us all.'

As the list went on, the tirade got more and more outlandish. Since then, every day spent in each other's company grew even more toxic than usual. Seething in her room, growing tired of the constant daily battles, Angela decided that she had no other choice but to make plans to leave home. Fortunately, thanks to a conversation she overheard on the bus, she found a flat to rent in Ipswich, a few miles away from her parents. Her mother's disappointment that Angela wasn't moving further away was evident in her snort of disgust. Keen for the arguments to stop and for Angela to be able to leave as soon as possible, her father offered to pay not only for the first month's rent but also for anything else that she would need to enable her to set up a home.

The flat was in a block of eight on a quiet street, and the one Angela was interested in was on the top floor. The hall was dark and pokey, but the lounge, with its dual-aspect windows, flooded with light. The kitchen had a space for a small table, the bathroom was new, and the bedroom was adequate. At least, Angela thought it had fitted wardrobes and not the overly large Victorian ones that her mother insisted they all have at home. Looking out of the window, she realised that she wasn't far from Christchurch Park and imagined herself and Gary in the summer, a picnic laid out under a shady tree, the drowsiness of food and drink as they whiled away an afternoon. Then in the winter, with the air crisp and cold, they could go for brisk walks around it before hurrying home for hot chocolate and baileys. Angela sighed. None of it would happen.

Gary would moan, 'Why stay in Ipswich? Let's go to the coast.'

Angela tried to use her imagination to see what it would look like with furniture and failed. Her old bedroom had been designed and chosen by her mother. Angela had no idea what her taste was. She did like bright colours; at home, they were boring and muted. Walking around the flat, for the first time since she had thought of leaving home, Angela felt excited at the opportunity of living by herself would bring.

Determined to put aside her hatred of shopping and get the chore over with as soon as possible. Knowing that it was not unusual for her father to act generous before becoming a bit of a miser once the spending started, Angela asked if she could have the money in cash.

Waving her hand to cut off his reply, her mother had snapped out.

'That is not going to happen. As we cannot trust Angela to buy anything sensible, I shall be going with her to supervise her purchases.'

Angela was beyond delighted that her mother had only managed to last one day in her company, even chickening out by sending her sister around to her flat with a cheque so that Angela could continue shopping alone. As soon as she opened her front door, Judy thrust it into her hands while at the same time accusing her of traumatising their mother with her actions. Stomping off, she turned to shout over her shoulder.

'Why do you always have to be so *mean*? Mum was only trying to help you.'

Angela thought that perhaps jumping on and off the beds like a child would do had probably been the wrong way to test if they were suitable. Their mother, she felt, only had herself to blame. For most of the day, her face had worn the look of someone sucking lemons, and whenever Angela suggested something or asked her opinion, she walked away.

'What was the point of her being there?' She had yelled across the store. 'If you are not going to help!'

The last straw had probably been the table. The wood was so smooth and inviting to the touch. Angela had felt the overwhelming urge to lay down on top of it. That soon made her mother stop and take notice of her.

'Get up.' She'd snarled. 'Stop making a show of yourself,' her face puce, her anger barely contained.

Sitting up slowly, Angela patted the table, raised her voice, made heads turn in their direction, and laughed.

'That's rich coming from you, mummy dear. If I remember correctly, over the years, I have seen many tables that have felt the weight of your body lying on them. Legs spread, glass in one hand, bottle in another. A cheery drunken smile on your face and a warm welcome to all brave enough to come anywhere near.'

Silence fell like a blanket to cover the shop. No one moved. Even the tills stayed silent as if in anticipation of what would happen next. All customers and staff had turned to look while pretending they weren't. Some even shamelessly lifted their phones, ready to be the first to take a picture. Angela grinned. Happy no matter what the outcome. Her mother's stillness made her look like a statue, even though she could see her body trembling with suppressed anger. Like waves on a shore, Angela felt it break over her like a physical thing that wanted to hurt, strike and batter. Hatred spilled from her mother's eyes, and only her sense of reputation held her back from attacking her daughter. Angela was sure if her mother had been a superhero, she would be dead from their laser-like gaze.

Pulling her shoulders back and with a dismissive shrug, Wendy turned away from Angela and marched through the store, head held high, blinkers on, ignoring the titters as she passed.

All eyes swung back towards Angela. Hopping off the table, she brushed imaginary crumbs from her clothes and bowed to her audience before leaving with a swing in her step. Angela felt satisfied for once at being brave enough to say what she usually kept locked inside her head. The release made her smile, knowing that Maureen would be pleased with her. Her friend had been urging her for years to break free. Now the genie was well and truly out of the bottle, and as far as Angela was concerned, it would never be going back in.

Returning home after the shopping debacle with her mother, she knew her father would be on her case trying to be conciliatory – not because he cared, only so he could appear to be the big I am in trying to smooth over their fall-out. Angela was determined this time not to play ball. Sure also that when her brother heard, he would want to put in his two pennyworths. The memory of the last time he'd tried – when she needed a black dress for a funeral, could still make her smile. Bullying and swearing had always been Mark's forte, especially where she was concerned.

She remembered barking at him. 'That as he wasn't even *there!* He can have no idea how horrible their mother had been to her,' before asking sweetly, 'how's the new girlfriend bearing up? Does she know what a liar you are? Have you told her there's no chance …?'

Mark hung up while she was still in mid-flow. Unsurprised to hear the words, 'Fucking bitch,' thrown her way before he did so.

The humiliation burned and raged inside Wendy like a fire. Walking out of the store with her head held high had taken all of her courage. Dislike for her youngest child had grown steadily more and more over the years, and she still found it hard at times to deal with it. In the past, she had tried to put her feelings aside and make an effort, if not to love Angela, then at least find something to like about her. Nothing worked. A difficult problem child while growing up, Angela was also one who always wanted her way.

Every time they clashed, Wendy knew that her feelings of dislike grew out of all proportion to what had caused it. Each shouting match that had occurred with Angela still managed to reverberate inside her head, one particular row going on for days...

'Angela, for the last time, you cannot go out in your pyjamas no matter how many tantrums you pull.'

Her answering shouts.

'You can't make me. What would be the point anyway? Everyone will still ignore me even if I were to dress up like your darling Judy.'

Everything always had to be yelled at fall volume. Wendy still shuddered to remember how Angela had refused to shower or change her clothes for months. When they all went out, it made her stand out, like a tramp they had found and decided to bring along with them. Her mood swings, which came out of nowhere toward Mark and Judy, were legendary. With only over a year between them, the pair had always been close. Even as a baby, Angela, sensed this and did all she could to get between them.

Spoiling their family holidays seemed to be Angela's ultimate high. She and Lennie spent most of their time apologising for her wild behaviour. Wendy frowned to remember one memorable event when Angela decided to follow her sister and Paula – a girl Judy had got talking to while swimming. Going to the beach also were several youngsters, fed up with the constraints put on them by their parents, they had organised a party.

Angela, making sure to keep out of sight, hid in the shadows before grabbing the drinks and bottles left by the partygoers. Drunk, she staggered back to the hotel. Not content with singing loudly, she threw the sun loungers into the pool.

Eventually restrained by security, she bellowed and fought to be released, kicking shins and scratching faces. They were woken from their nap by someone banging on the door. When Lennie cautiously opened it, Angela stood outside bound with rope while a sea of angry faces stood behind her. The manager told them to pack up and leave immediately. Angela had once again soured it for them all.

'I haven't done anything!' She swore, blaming others as usual for her bad behaviour.

*

Wendy threw open the front door, her anger barely contained. Heading for the kitchen, she kicked off her shoes before yanking open the fridge door, sighing with pleasure, to see a bottle of Shiraz. A large drink – or several, that's what she needed. Only alcohol had enough power to cast thoughts of Angela into oblivion. Filling her glass to the brim, she downed it in one before pouring another. Her hands shook like someone with palsy as thoughts of throttling Angela filled her mind.

Head pounding like a drum Wendy slugged back her wine as the hatred she felt for Angela went round and round her head making her realise that with her gone, she would finally get a chance to breathe. Ipswich may be a few miles away, but it was still too near for Wendy, and she wished that Angela was moving to the other side of the world, somewhere like Australia or New Zealand.

The phone rang, making her jump.

'Shit.'

The wine poured over the worktop as she missed the glass.

'What?'

'Mum, are you okay? You sound upset.'

She smiled to hear Judy's concern, Wendy, was always happy to tell everyone she met that they were more like best friends than mother and daughter and dismissed Lennie's repeated suggestion that it was not healthy as jealousy. His relationship with Angela and Judy was either full-on or non-existent; Mark was the only one of his three children he had any affection for, and even that was always dependent on him doing whatever his father told him to. Now that Mark was an adult, Lennie wasn't finding him so easy to control, especially as both were quick to take offense, were competitive to the point of stupidity, and were both stubborn in their refusal to apologise first.

'I have had the dubious thrill of shopping with Angela, and I swear one day that child will be the near death of me!'

'Do you want me to come with you next time?'

'There won't ever be one,' growled Wendy. 'You can do me a favour and take a cheque over to her. I don't want to speak to her, let alone see her. I would pay the money into her bank account, but knowing what she's like, she'll swear that I didn't do it to be awkward. All I was trying to do was to help her set up a home. To give her advice on what to buy, instead, she threw it back at me in spades. Stupidly I thought that by her moving out, things between us would improve. Sadly, I think they may get worse.'

After they had spent half an hour catching up on the trivia of life, Wendy ended the call feeling much better. Finding the bottle of Shiraz empty, she pulled an Argentinian Malbec from the rack. Unlike Lennie, Wendy didn't have any aversion to mixing her drinks; red, white, beer, or spirits. As long as it was alcohol, she would gladly drink it and chose to ignore his not-so-subtle hints that she was drinking too much. His penny-pinching was getting worse. He never used to be so bad. In the early days of their marriage, anything she wanted would be hers, all she had to do was say, and nothing would be too much trouble. Then he began to stray. Being pregnant with Angela wasn't a good time for either of them…

For Wendy, another child was the last thing she wanted. Mark and Judy were more than enough to look after. The continuous bouts of nausea throughout her pregnancy didn't help either. Even now, when hearing someone throwing up, the memory of having her head stuck down a toilet with her arms wrapped tightly around the bowl could still make her want to vomit. Each time they went out to The Salthouse, their favourite restaurant, adding to the soundtrack of her retching would be someone banging on the toilet door, yelling.

'Are you okay, love?'

Her so-called morning sickness was no respecter of where or what she was doing. Walking in the park, shopping or relaxing, one moment she was fine, the next she'd be looking down at her clothes splattered in sick, wanting to cry at the injustice of it all. She would look for a quiet spot and try not to move. Unfortunately, someone would always lope over and demand.

'Is everything all right?'

Waving them away, Wendy wanted to be left alone. The complete stillness was the only thing that worked. When going out with Lennie, he'd been sympathetic at first and would stay by her side, wipe her forehead, or hold her hand. Because it occurred so often, boredom set in and embarrassment at her heaving. One day, in particular, would be forever seared into her brain.

'Let me call a cab,' said Lennie. 'Best if you go home and rest.'

When it arrived, he shuffled her towards the open door, she'd tried to wipe the mess off her dress in the toilets, but she could still smell the sick, crumpled, and dishevelled Wendy felt broken.

'Aren't you coming with me?'

She remembered how furtive Lennie had looked, his eyes flickering towards the window. Turning, she caught sight of a pale face staring toward them. Fury bit hard, making her jaw clench.

'You bastard. She's young enough to be your daughter. Look at *me!* Have you no shame?'

Without answering, Lennie bundled her into the cab and barked their address to the driver before slamming the door and stalking off.

Now, with the last of their children leaving home, she couldn't help but wonder where their relationship was going. Kissing and hand-holding, or any sign of affection, was now forced rather than done without thinking. Sex only reared its ugly head when they were both drunk. A get-out clause; each used to abstain from it happening. The last time had been particularly embarrassing. Wendy snorted at the memory. Lennie appeared to have fallen asleep, his weight pressing her down into the mattress.

'Lennie, wake up. Get off me. I can't breathe. Oh, for god's sake, you didn't drink that much. If you're mucking about, I swear I'll ...'

She laughed. Lennie's head had snapped up, and his

face turned puce. He flung himself away from her, stumbled into the bathroom, and slammed the door. Since then, they unconsciously worked hard to put on a front to friends and family. Lennie continued to womanise while Wendy drank.

One day, feeling brave while basking in the sunshine and peace of their garden – and fortified by a couple of glugs of gin, she broached the subject.

'This is nice, the two of us. I know we've had our differences, and things haven't always been easy.' Ignoring Lennie's snort, she continued, 'I've been thinking. What I mean is we each have our demons. I believe they are linked. I will stop drinking if you stop chasing women.'

Remembering his look still made her go cold. Laughing like a loon, he had sniped.

'You are a drunk and will always be a drunk, and as such, you would not be unable to stop even if you wanted to.'

Her rage at his words had threatened to overwhelm her, realising that even if she changed, he never would. Unable to hold her gaze, he'd flinched to see her body stiffen and her fists clench as a wealth of hatred filled her face. His death, her release, flew around her head like a mantra wanting nothing more than to batter him into oblivion.

*

Putting the phone down, Judy sighed in frustration. Angela could be a handful, but then so could their mother. She had a short fuse, and during their childhood, there had been many times when she had looked as if she would like nothing more than to give them all a good whack. Even though their mother's anger was more likely to be aimed at Angela, if either Judy or Mark found themselves on the receiving end, both agreed that it was somewhere they would rather not be. When Judy was younger, seeing her mother's demeanour change when angry or drunk would scare her because, like a deranged person, her mother would patrol the house looking for an argument. Her sister would never disappoint, Judy and Mark would make themselves scarce, while Angela would always stay behind in defiance of their mother's threats. Neither of them had ever been able to figure out what exactly Angela did that drove their parents, especially their mother, so mad, and sometimes just the word hello, between them was enough to start an argument.

With her wedding on the horizon, Judy was worried that the tensions between them would soon spill over into more rows. The wedding day may be theirs, but her mother would want to control everything, including what the guests should wear, and her sister would be at the top of her list. Angela's tramp phase as a teenager meant that her mother didn't trust her to be able to dress appropriately, and Judy's suggestion in a moment of recklessness that Angela may like to be one of her bridesmaids had made her mother snarl, "Never." Followed by an explosion of swear words, leaving her with no doubt it was not an option even to be considered.

Judy had been feeling out of sorts about marrying Paul and had put it down to wedding nerves. Wishing he was a bit more adventuress fell on deaf ears, and his hesitancy when dealing with the most mundane things didn't make sense as his colleagues had likened him to a Rottweiler, taking on all comers. His bosses described Paul's climb of the corporate ladder as meteoritic; Judy was still not convinced that accountancy warranted that degree of excitement, even though sometimes, she enjoyed basking in his reflected glory. Her father was particularly impressed with his progression and liked nothing more than to pit him and Mark against each other. Happy to sprout that if her brother had applied himself more at school and gone on to University, he too could have been high up on the corporate ladder like Paul. Her father ignored the fact that Mark practically ran his friend's small engineering company, as Terry liked to spend his time playing golf and chasing women.

Private Paul was another matter entirely. Even though he meant well, sometimes Judy could see he was confused by how she acted. She had tried several times to explain that it would be good to have their own space. Because although he was not controlling, Judy, at times, felt smothered by his presence. His texts, emails, and phone calls followed her everywhere, and in the main hardly seemed to bother him that she never answered them. Getting angry and yelling, 'please stop, or at least not be in touch so much.' Also seemed to do no good except to make him look at her like a whipped puppy. Judy refused to feel guilty and continued deleting anything received from him and only answering when it suited her to do so.

Hearing a thud, Judy sped into the hall, her face breaking out into a smile as she snatched up what she knew to be another wedding brochure. With a pot of coffee, she settled down to read the magazine from cover to cover. The sneaky voice that had been walking around her brain for the last couple of months broke cover. Judy's enjoyment of the preparations was clouding her judgement. She kept her true feelings hidden not just from Paul but from everyone.

The truth was that getting married had never been high on her agenda. When she had said yes to Paul's proposal, she had quickly realised her mistake, but once her mother knew, there was no chance for her to back out. It was a done deal. Having to live through her parent's turbulent marriage was enough to put most people off wanting one of their own. Most of the time, they managed to hide their animosity toward each other. Sensitive to other people's moods, Judy had often picked up the warning signs earlier than her siblings, removing herself from the situation before the explosion came.

Her mother's dislike of Angela, even as an adult, was one of the things that still bugged Judy. Children she knew could drive their parents mad, and if asked, many would probably love to walk away and leave them to get on with it. Mainly though, most people sucked up the bad behaviour of their children as best they could, their love for them overriding everything. That, unfortunately, did not seem to apply to her mother and Angela. Judy used to rack her brain to find out why her mother should hate Angela so much. Plucking up the courage to ask what her sister had done that was so bad, even now, her chilling answer, "Being born," sent a shiver down Judy's spine.

As to her father, Judy knew he was playing away, seeing him with one of his ladies when she had been lunching in Trongs, the only decent Chinese restaurant for miles. Old enough to be the girl's father, she wondered if he realised how stupid he looked as he fawned over her. She had tried not to stare, sickened by the sight of him, yet fascinated at the same time. The girl had a laugh that could shatter glass. Each time a waiter went past, they waggled their eyebrows at the noise she was making. Judy never mentioned to her father or anyone else that she had seen him. Sure, even if she did, he wouldn't even care that she had; Mark's opinion of him was the only one to matter. Where her mother was all over Judy like a rash, her father was sometimes standoffish and even rude, blowing hot and cold with his affection, a pastime he enjoyed. Judy had gotten used to his smirk when he said something that was outrageously rude to either her or Angela. Their father knew he shouldn't be talking to them like that. His eyes would gleam with anticipation of their reactions, making her blush red and Angela swear. Up yours! Being one of her more moderate offerings, he would laugh in delight. It was at times like those when she didn't like him very much and wished that she had more backbone. Inside her head, she had all the answers and enjoyed thinking of him broken and snivelling for forgiveness at her feet.

'You don't seem close to either Mark or Angela. I would have thought you would be, especially as your parents don't get along,' said Paul, a few weeks into their relationship.

'With just over a year's difference, in ages, between us, my parents always believed we were close and would tell anyone who would listen that we were. As they were too involved in arguing, they ignored any disagreements between Mark and me,' explained Judy. 'Mark, as a teenager, was as moody as Angela, always wanting his way and would sulk at the least resistance to him getting it. As an adult, he still expects adulation.'

She surprised herself by letting Paul know her true feelings about her family.

'I tolerate my brother and try to ignore Angela's behaviour. I love my mother, even though, at times, I dislike her, and I have always been wary of my father.'

*

Moving out of home, Angela had hoped that with space and time away from her family, all the tensions between them would soon improve. So far, that hadn't been the case. None of them had yet been to see her or even phoned to find out how she was coping. Her phone calls to them cut short, telling her they had things to do or places to go. While her visits to them; were often met by long stretches of silence, the only animation they showed was when told that she had better be going. It didn't help matters that each time she opened the front door to her flat, she would find herself pausing, expecting someone to jump out and shout that she was in the wrong one. Each time she came home, she felt she was walking into someone else's space. Even after weeks of living there, the flat still retained a vacant and unlived feel, and nothing she did seemed to help make her feel welcome.

Thinking to try and pep it up a bit more, Angela made a list, trawled through the sales, and bought nothing. Easily distracted by other people's conversations, she joined in their discussions on what would look best, even going so far as to grab items to show them how they would look when put together. Her opinion was listened to, her advice often taken, and their thanks effusive, failing only to make purchases for herself.

Speaking of the problem to one of her work colleagues, Jason suggested she organise a moving-in party and offer to supply food and drink; in return for help transforming her flat into more of a home. Those she invited were too busy, including her best friend Maureen, and so decided the only option was to have a go herself. After all, she thought, how hard can it be? The paint she had chosen was supposed to turn out to be lovely buttery colour. The blurb on the tin promised to fill her home with the golden glow of sunshine. Instead, it looked like a saucepan of scrambled eggs had been splattered all over the walls.

Angela found herself condescendingly advised that the vibrant abstract artwork – for which she had felt coerced into purchasing, would perk up any dull wall; instead, it looked like a dozen people had thrown up all over it. Angela then tried to enliven her grey sofa by buying several cushions, paying over the odds for their plumpness and vibrancy, and now after just a few days, they looked like a load of mismatched lumpen blobs.

A client, Mrs. Robinson, where Angela worked at Hudson and May, heard her moaning about how she could make her flat look more homily and interrupted her monologue to tell her.

'Candles; will enhance the sensory perception of your space and create an ambience.'

Angela was lost at the word sensory and failed to understand what Mrs. Robinson meant. Willing to give anything a go, she plumped for one smelling of wild berries and juniper and was disappointed to smell anything other than hot wax.

2

FEBRUARY

What shall I *wear*? Angela thought for the hundredth time. Everything in her wardrobe now littered the bedroom floor and had been tried on twice. Nothing fitted right. Unable to shift the few pounds of weight she had gained over Christmas, her clothes still felt a bit on the snug side. The new dress, which did at least fit – mainly because it was a size bigger than she usually wore, now hung on the wardrobe door, and each time her eyes fell onto it, she winced. Bought on the spur of the moment, without Maureen's cries of, 'That is so lovely, it suits you,' ringing in her ears. The confidence this had engendered in the changing room, had on returning home, disappeared. Now, its vibrant patterned swirls of colour did nothing to lift her spirits. Instead, it made her feel bilious.

Angela frowned as she caught sight of herself. Stopping to peer into the shop window, not for the first time, she wondered why no matter what she did, she always looked so unkempt. Unlike Judy or her mother, either could throw on any old thing and still look good. Angela's body had a life of its own. Convinced that she still wore a size twelve, she couldn't understand why nothing fit. Changing rooms was anathema to Angela, her mother's words like an echo on repeat.

'Look at the state of you. Cover yourself. You're all … *everywhere.*'

With tears threatening to fall, she would quickly dress, forcing her body back into her old clothes, convinced that she was deformed.

Angela had dismissed the new dress she'd bought in favour of her old reliable suit – mainly because the skirt still had a bit of stretch, and now she regretted the decision. Looking into the shop window and seeing her reflection with her hair scraped tightly back, the thought emerged that she looked rather like a black crow. I should have washed and straightened it. Not for the first time wishing that she had glossy red hair like Judy instead of a halo of unruly fuzz. Perhaps, mum is right, she thought. Knowing as far as her mother was concerned, Angela was a big, fat, unattractive lump. Although they had the same brown hair and hazel eyes, her mother always described Angela's as dull and drab. Not for her, the colourful ribbons that adorned Judy's locks as a child. For Angela, it was only ever black or brown, her mother telling her with such an ugly face she wasn't worth the bother. Angela was sure even now, as an adult, it was why her clothes chosen in a moment of madness were always bright and colourful. Though, the reality of what she wore often made her look as if she were attending a funeral. She leaned her head against the glass and sighed at the injustice of life. It was too late now to go home and change. Her suit would have to do. Would Gary even notice? Lately, when they had been out together, she had seen his eyes begin to wonder.

Once fed up with being ignored, she had deliberately split her wine. Snaking towards him across the table, he'd jumped up, unsettling the bottle, which then sprayed all over the place before dripping onto the floor. Angela had to clamp her mouth shut to stop the giggles she could feel bubbling up.

Opening the heavy restaurant door of Simply the Best – a pretentious name, she thought. Angela hadn't expected to be greeted by such a blaze of colour. Red balloon hearts hung from the ceiling, fairy lights were strung around and over every available surface, and the candles on the tables made the roses in the vases look even redder. It was the diners though, who shone the most. Unlike Angela, all the women had made much more effort to dress up. Their sparkly dresses twinkled every time one of them moved. The men in their snappy suits added to the party atmosphere. The receptionist, unimpressed with what stood before her, barked.

'Do you have a reservation?'

Seeing Gary seated, Angela waved away her offer of showing her to the table and stalked off.

'A bottle of prosecco, please.'

Deliberately scraping her chair as she pulled it out. Gary looked up, spluttering. 'Sorry, Angela. I thought you were a waiter.'

'Well, I'm not,' she retorted, making him blush.

Embarrassment and anger flared through her at not wearing the stupid dress. Gary, as usual, smelt and looked gorgeous. One of the few men who could throw any old thing on and look good. If Angela was being honest, she still didn't understand what he saw in her. Her plain face and lumpy body had been on view the first time they met. She was drunk. The fact that her make-up was sliding off her face or that after throwing up, the smell of her cheap perfume now tinged with sick had not stopped her from thinking that she was beautiful.

Not yet slurring her words or falling over, but at the point where she believed everything that came out of her mouth was witty, exciting, and dangerous. Angela could still remember his laughter when she'd cornered him and demanded.

'Why have you danced with everyone else except me?'

She'd spat out the words slowly one by one as if to an imbecile while at the same time prodding him in the chest.

Angela would usually be content to sit and observe rather than take part in any proceedings, preferring to people-watch. When told about the party, Maureen had nagged her for days, telling her, for once, she should take the opportunity to let go and enjoy herself. Getting so drunk, Angela was sure, wasn't what Maureen had meant. The cocktails on offer had been hard for her to resist with their jaunty umbrellas and slices of fruit.

'I'll have a large one,' she giggled.

Dancing with Gary had been a dream, aware that everyone was watching and thinking them jealous – unaware of being laughed at, Angela snuggled further into his arms as if she always belonged there. At the end of the night, he had shown himself to be a proper gentleman, assuring her that he had her number and would phone the next day before insisting on putting her in a taxi and paying the fare.

Angela crawled along the path on her hands and knees before stumbling up the stairs. She remembered shouting as she tried unsuccessfully to get the key to fit into the lock.

'Bastard fucking thing!' Her neighbour opened his door and closed it quickly. She shouted. 'For fucks *sake*.'

Giggling and snorting at the look on his face, on her fifth attempt, the door finally opened. Slamming it shut, she dashed to the bathroom. Her new friend, the toilet, was all Angela could think of; flopping down the cold floor was a boon to her aching head. Spinning away and back made her feel like she was inside a washing machine, on the highest spin cycle.

While retching into the bowl for the third time, a vision of Gary popped into her head. With a groan, she slid back down onto the floor, convinced that she would never again see him; she let sleep claim her.

Angela brought herself back to the moment. The atmosphere between her and Gary was getting more noticeable, she had seen the furtive looks being sent their way by the other diners. Looking around, she thought, for all the restaurant's myriad of decorations and effort, the meal was not that good, filled mainly with couples who all appeared to be loved up, and chatting made her and Gary an oddity as they muttered their way through the first two courses. Having drunk one bottle of prosecco and now on their second, both looked glassy-eyed and ready for a fight. Angela was aware that things between them had not been right for a while, Maureen always the font of all knowledge, blithely telling her to dump him and find someone else. Angela had laughed.

'It's not that easy. Someone like me wouldn't attract someone of Gary's standard a second time, and I have no intention of going back to the losers; I used to previously always end the night with.'

Maureen snorted in disgust as she reminded Angela that it wasn't that long ago when her opinion of most men was that they were only fit to be used and discarded as soon as possible.

Deciding that she had better do something to rescue the situation before it got any further out of hand, Angela offered an olive branch and plucked up the courage to ask about his mother.

'She's not very well. The fall she had last week has shaken her up. I'm glad you brought it up. Our weekend away, would you mind if we postpone it to the following week or even the week after? Only she keeps asking when I am coming to see her.'

Angela stilled. Here we go again, mummy's calling, and her little boy is jumping. Before she could stop, her thoughts had become words.

'Your mother is a nightmare. She doesn't stop, like a leaky tap; drip, drip, drip. Every little thing that goes wrong – mostly made-up problems, I'm sure. Then, she's on the phone, texting, calling, and generally making a nuisance of herself, appearing only happy once she has caused the maximum disruption.'

Gary's face went white with shock. Angela swigged her wine, not sorry at her outburst, only wishing she had saved it for somewhere more private.

Her thoughts; returned to the disaster of Christmas when he had phoned to say that their plans to spend it together would have to wait until the New Year. Explaining that his mother's sister was now coming over from Australia, and his mother wanted him home to meet her. Thinking he meant both of them, Angela told him that it would not be a problem as they still had time to cancel the hotel booking. Expecting him to be pleased instead, she had gotten only silence back, making her think they had lost the connection. Gary mumbled, annoyed at having to explain.

'I'm sorry Angela, my cousins Olly, and Sam, are also coming over with my aunt, and it will be a bit of a squash for mum to fit us all in. It's not … Perhaps um … could you go to your parents?'

Angela was stunned that he would suggest such a thing was even possible. He knew that if she had a bucket list, then spending Christmas with her family would be at the top of it. He also knew that it was never likely to happen and hadn't since she was a child, and then only because they had to include her. Out of sight and out of mind; was always her family's mantra, especially when she left home. They would enjoy reminding Angela that she was all grown up, an adult, making it seem they were doing her a favour by not expecting her to be with them. However, it didn't apply to her siblings, who were always welcome.

Before she could stop herself, Angela had let rip, telling Gary what she thought of his mother.

'Your mother is a hypochondriac, and her selfish problems are all made up to bring you running.'

He retaliated with equal venom.

'*What?* Because you don't get on well with your own family. Don't take it out on mine.'

Angela heard nothing from him until the New Year. Both stubborn. Only by accident did they bump into each other again. Without mentioning their argument or his mother, they carried on. Now when they were together, and Gary's phone pinged or rang, she ignored it. Angela liked that he found her new attitude harder than her ranting. With no acknowledgment from her, good or bad, regarding his mother's interruptions, she could see that he struggled to know what to say or do. She had to hold back a grin when he apologised over them and got more and more humble each time they happened.

Angela had never felt as if she belonged. When asked questions about her family, she would always answer that she came from a close-knit one. Yet as soon as the words left her mouth, inside her head would reverberate, except you. In many families, the youngest was often the spoilt one. Not in her case. For her parents, her elder brother Mark and sister Judy had been enough. Angela knew this with certainty. After a night of drinking, her mother had revelled in telling her how she was an accident, a mistake. Inured by now to her nastiness towards her, Angela tried hard not to react. Drunk and slurring her words, her mother had taken great delight in explaining.

'I tried drinking a whole bottle of gin. Not that it did any good! It made me even sicker. So desperate was I to be rid of you I even chucked myself down the stairs hoping that it would expel you from my body. Leech like you clung on no matter what I did.'

Angela could only stare in shock as her mother wagged her finger in front of her face while at the same time enunciating each word.

'Like a limpid mine, you hung on inside of me. You ruined my life. *If only ...*'

The rest tailed off as she slid down the wall and passed out.

Hitting her teens, it hadn't taken Angela long to realise that while the adolescent traumas of Judy and Mark; would be tolerated, hers would not. There would be no slamming of doors for her, no backchat. She'd tried once and had gotten a slap for her troubles.

'Get out of my sight. Go to your room before ...'

Words her mother shouted at her on many occasions, any freedom she thought to have crushed. Pushed aside from an early age, Angela had gotten used to being in the background. Even though her reports and exams were much better than her siblings, her homework was deemed unimportant and never praised. Instead, her parents expected her to do household chores as soon as she came home from school. She also learned to cook out of necessity.

Her mother hated cooking. Angela took over the task of preparing their meals. With no thanks for her efforts, her mother was nevertheless quick enough to find fault if Angela dished up something no one liked.

Things hardly got any better when Mark and Judy left school. Neither of them had grades good enough to get into university. Instead, they were encouraged to take a gap year and enjoy themselves before looking for work.

'You can take on their chores.'

Announced at dinner, which, considering as far as Angela could see, her siblings didn't do anything! For once, she found her mother's instruction no hardship to bear.

Mark eventually found work with Terry, a friend of their fathers who ran an engineering company, quickly rising through the ranks, soon making a name for himself for being ruthless. Used to being the centre of attention at home, he took the same attitude to work and expected everyone would be willing to accommodate his whims. Those that did not comply were soon ousted. Made to feel uncomfortable, they either put up with his ways or left. Terry, his boss, was happy to let him have a free hand as long as his actions did nothing to get in the way or interfere with him playing golf.

Judy found love. Paul sold to all as someone going places, his job as an accountant spoken of in hushed tones. It wasn't long before he became a feature in their lives. Angela found him irritating. Tall, with a lecturing tone of voice, he set her teeth on edge each time she heard him whine. Each time Judy moved, his eyes would follow, Angela thinking it more than creepy. Her parents, of course, loved him. Easy to see that her father enjoyed putting Mark's nose out of joint by praising Paul's latest efforts. Mark would retaliate with sarcasm which got nastier by the minute. One day though, Judy had surprised them by reacting to his jibes like a lioness with a cub. That Angela enjoyed.

The champagne had already been flowing when Mark and his latest girlfriend arrived. Offered a drink, Cassie for some reason, blushed.

Straight away, her mother started crowing that Paul was in line for a big promotion earning a scowl from Mark. She then went on to make it worse by saying how much she was looking forward to Paul being her son-in-law and how lucky Judy was to have someone like him to take care of her. Her father sensing

Mark's anger then had to step in and make it worse by clapping him on the back and announcing.

'And unlike my son here. Paul knows how to play golf. What's not to like.'

Her brother's reaction to his words was to pour his drink away, grabbing Cassie's; Mark did the same with hers. Her father's grin slipped when Mark growled back.

'I can play golf. I choose not to. Anyway, what's so great about being an accountant?'

'Don't be like that,' Judy retorted. 'You always have to make it about you. Paul has worked hard to get where he is. Let's face it. You only got your job because Terry is a friend of dad's, and from what I have heard, none there thinks much of you. Stuck up is the least offensive comment; that is banded around about your behaviour.'

Angela watched Judy and Mark's spat with interest. Like all siblings, they had disagreements when growing up. In the main, she felt any animosity was more likely to have been directed toward her. Though their stance today, was the most combative she had ever seen them. While Judy had been talking, Angela could see her brother clenching his fists, a sure sign that Mark wanted to strike out. Occasionally on the receiving end of one of his punches, Angela knew what it felt like to be hit by him. Red spots of colour appeared across Judy's usually pale cheeks, making her look clown-like.

She had seen his hands. Leaning toward him, she spat out a warning and threatened.

'*Do not!* Even think about it.'

Cassie, trying to be the peacemaker, stepped between them only to be barged out of the way by their mother waving her glass around and sloshing its contents.

'We're supposed to be celebrating, not fighting. Lennie, fill up their glasses.' Lifting hers, she toasted, 'to family.'

Lost in her thoughts, Angela became aware of Gary staring at her and smiled.

'You've changed,' he told her. Looking everywhere but at her face.

As the waiter placed down their desserts and refilled their glasses, she waited a moment before answering. Her voice loud, her tone belligerent, made the waiter spill wine onto the tablecloth.

'For better or for worse?' Angela raised her glass in a toast. 'Perhaps, you shouldn't answer that.'

Peering at him over the rim of her glass, Angela was glad that he had no idea what she was thinking. Sure that he wouldn't like it at all, shrugging off her old persona was one of them. Angela was glad to see that Gary, like Maureen, had noticed the change. She was going to own this year, and she wasn't going to hide in the shadows or step back to let others take the lead. Discarded and left alone at Christmas by both Gary and her family. Her thoughts lingered on their treatment of her. Making plans for all of them had been the only thing that had kept her sane, all she had to do now was to find a way to carry them out.

*

Here we are again, thought Wendy, no card and no bloody present. In the early days of their marriage, Lennie had not been able to pass up the opportunity of spoiling her on Valentine's Day. Now he barely mentioned it. She grimaced as she watched him spooning cereal into his mouth as if the world was about to end in five minutes. The morning paper propped up, eliciting grunts and groans as he read the news. With his head bent, she could see where his hair had started to thin, smiling as she thought, he won't like that. Like an old-fashioned dandy, Lennie was very particular about how he looked and had been one of the things that attracted her to him in the first place. Her first sight of him had been in the park, everyone else in shorts and t-shirts while he came striding along suited and booted, not a blonde hair out of place. The waft of his aftershave lingered long after he had disappeared around the corner. She had gone back each day for a week in case it was his route to somewhere, but she never saw him again. Until exiting a café, she held the door open and looked up to see his smiling face peering down at her.

'Thank you,' he uttered with a grin.

Wendy was lost. Staring like a loon, she could only splutter, 'you're welcome.'

After that, it was as if the fates stepped in. Everywhere she went, he either was or soon turned up. It became a running joke, each calling the other out for stalking. Until she saw him pushing a pram, although bereft to think that he was not only married but had a child, it had not put her off from approaching him.

'Hi, have you stolen it, or is it yours?' Wendy asked before grinning. Hoping she sounded friendly rather than nosey or desperate.

Smiling back in return, Lennie pushed the hood down and announced with pride.

'This is my son. Say hello, Mark.' Lifting the child's arm, he made it wave. 'My dad's name is Lennie Stubbs.'

Her smile plastered to her face hoping it was not looking too forced, she replied, 'pleased to meet you both. I'm Wendy Page. He is so cute.' Tickling Mark under the chin, she added, 'how old is he?'

'Nearly sixteen months. The light of my life and the bane of his mother's. Today he will not stop crying, even when fed, watered, changed, and burped. So, to give her a chance to rest.

I decided to take him for a walk.' Looking down at his watch, he tutted, 'I didn't realise the time. I had better go. It will soon be time for his next feed.'

Throwing caution to the wind, Wendy gabbled as she told him. 'I know how she feels. That is why I am here. A bit of time away to recharge is always a good thing. My daughter Judy is staying with my friend at the moment.' Deciding if you do not ask, you don't get, she suggested, 'perhaps next time I will bring her along, we could have a coffee. Let the kids bond.'

That was all it took. Looking back, Wendy realised that although it was the most stressful of times, it was also the best. Finding what made each other tick, laughing to see they had similar tastes, both enjoying visiting museums and art galleries. When Lennie told her that he and his partner Elaine weren't married, she breathed a sigh of relief. Lennie explained that they had talked about it but had not gotten any further and that Elaine was finding motherhood a bit of a strain, and he didn't want to push her into making a decision.

Asking what he did for a living, Lennie told her that he had his own successful business as a financial advisor, and when not out visiting clients, he worked from his office at home, describing himself as a bit of a "One-man band." Impressing her that he managed to do all his filing. As secretary and general dogsbody to her boss, Wendy was sure Colin wouldn't be able to find his way out of a paper bag without clear and concise instructions, preferably with a diagram thrown in for good measure! Let alone be able to find out where the files were.

At first, their time spent together was sporadic, often cancelled when Elaine was having a bad day and Lennie would have to look after Mark. Although it only happened so often, Wendy found it hard to contain her anger at Elaine for spoiling their precious time together. Remembering the first time she had met her still made Wendy cringe…

Waiting in the park on what had become known to the two of them as; their bench. Seeing Lennie, she waved before realising that someone else was with him. Strolling over, he introduced her as a client he was helping with financial advice. Not usually at a loss, Wendy could only stammer a greeting as Elaine's eyes raked her up and down, questions spilling from her mouth about what type of advice Lennie was giving her. Tongue-tied Wendy could only look blank; fortunately, Mark started crying. Wendy glanced at her watch, announcing that she must go as she had an appointment. Marching away, she left them both staring at her retreating back.

Lennie phoned to apologise, telling Wendy he'd had no idea Elaine was in the park until she had appeared in front of him. Explaining that although he still wanted to see her, he thought it best if they had a break for a couple of weeks so he could let things calm down at home. When Mark was born, anxiety had dogged Elaine night and day, turning her from the happy-go-lucky person he had come to know into someone who worried over every little thing. With Mark now unsettled most nights and coupled with these feelings, Elaine was finding it hard to deal with the lack of disturbed sleep this entailed.

It was a whole month before they saw each other again and decided this time to meet a bit further afield. Wendy's breath caught in her throat; as she caught sight of Lennie. His smile allayed all the fears she had been having since she had last seen him. As if his partner had been swept aside and confined to his past. She knew Elaine would be a stumbling block; if their relationship were going to progress any further, then Wendy would have to find a solution, a way to get rid of her.

After months of heady days snatching time together and flirting, the opportunity to spend the night together was too good to miss. Lennie was going away to a conference. He attended every year. Only this time, Wendy would be going with him. To allay any suspicions Elaine might have, she had booked into a different hotel. The first time they had sex cemented Wendy's decision for them to be together. How could she achieve her goal? Ideas and plans popped into her head at the most inconvenient of times. Caught staring into space, her boss snapped at her to get a grip telling her she should be taking notes.

Wendy had returned from staying with friends when she got the phone call that changed their lives. Sounding deranged, she had rushed to Lennie's side. Haggard was the word that sprung to mind as he opened the door. Declaring melodramatically, Elaine had gone, leaving not only him but Mark as well. Coming home from his mother's, he had told her, he had felt as soon as he opened the front door that something was wrong. Usually, the radio would be on as Elaine prepared dinner, and he would always call out, 'Honey, I'm home,' and she would reply, 'My name is not honey.'

He eventually found her note in Mark's cot. Short and to the point, she'd written, I never wanted to be a mother. Please do not bother to look for me. I am sorry. The police said that as he could confirm the handwriting was hers and added to the fact that she was an adult, there was nothing they could do. He soon found coping with a baby while trying to run a business was impossible. His mother was worse than useless. When asked for help, she refused to come and stay, telling him that it was not convenient and that he earned more than enough to employ a nanny.

Feeling sorry for him, Wendy offered to help on her days off by looking after Mark when Lennie had to go and see a client. She dismissed his offer to bring Judy with her, telling him she was happy spending time with her friend Betty.

'Without her there, Mark will have my undivided attention.'

Luckily for her, he accepted Wendy as his mother's replacement. With Elaine now gone, Wendy knew she couldn't any longer put off Lennie meeting with her daughter, especially if they were now to be a family. He had already spoken about how it would be nice for Mark to have a sister. Each time he had told her to bring her to meet them, she had fobbed him off, and even to her every excuse she used was getting thin. When first speaking about Judy, she'd tried to explain that she was a sensitive child, and even though, a baby, she didn't like change. She and Betty had been her only constant, and she was loath for her to get upset. Assuring him that as they were to be a family, then, yes, of course, he must meet her.

When Lennie proposed marriage, she accepted with the proviso that because their children were too young to understand the details of their parentage, Mark and Judy should never find out about their other biological parents. Adding, that in regards to my family, they will not be a problem. I have not seen them in years, and I have no intention of ever doing so. Besides, none of them know that I have been pregnant, let alone that I now have a daughter, and I would prefer to keep it that way.

Even though she had only met his mother a couple of times, Wendy instantly saw how wrapped up in her non-existent problems she was and laughingly assured Lennie that she probably would not even notice that he had swapped Elaine for her. Like her, he avoided the rest of his family. The last time had been ten years ago at some aged aunt's funeral that his mother had insisted he take her to.

Their wedding was a small affair; Wendy wore an off-the-shoulder short white dress, making the most of her bust and trim waist. Her hair had been curled and threaded with flowers. She'd nearly forgotten her bouquet in her eagerness not to be late. Lennie looked every inch a film star and wore a blue suit that perfectly matched his eyes. His blonde hair flopped over his forehead, making him look impossibly young. His smile on seeing her tugged against Wendy's heart.

'I love you,' she mouthed.

Fortunately, Lennie's mother expected, but cancelled at the last minute, pleasing Wendy, who thought that having to put up with Lennie's friend Alan and wife Louisa, putting in an appearance would be more than enough to stomach. Elaine had been gone for over a year, and she and Lennie had not been married, and so did not impede their marriage, yet they were incapable of letting her disappearance go. They were first on her list of people she would prefer neither of them to see again. When they moved, Wendy made sure to destroy the change of address notice they sent before Lennie could see it. When they also moved out of the area and into the house where they now lived. Their new friends and neighbours only knew Mark and Judy as their children.

Looking at him now, she wondered when it all had started to go wrong. And then Angela's name popped into her head. Her birth had changed everything. Before she came along, they had been a happy family of four. Like an intruder, Angela had insinuated herself into their lives, and in return, Wendy heaped the unhappiness she felt onto her daughter. Adamant that everything wrong in her life was Angela's fault; and not of her own making.

*

Thank god that is over with, thought Mark while sipping his coffee. Yesterday morning at footie had been a nightmare. He'd had to listen to his mate's constant ribbing about their Valentine's evening to come. Flowers, champagne, and a slap-up dinner de rigour as demanded by their other halves. Nudges and winks abounded as they ribbed each other about the sex that would be on offer at the end of the night. So far, he had managed to field most of their questions about where he had taken Cassie. Knowing that it would not go down very well if they knew that the only thing they had planned for the evening, besides a takeaway, was a good book for him and a laptop for her. Judy, he understood, had gone back to the same place, Simply the Best, where Paul had proposed. He had overheard her telling his mother last weekend in the restaurant. He had choked on his drink when Angela had chimed in loudly.

'If anyone was interested? She was going out to dinner with Maureen, and no, they weren't gay.'

He had met Angela's latest boyfriend, Gary, by accident, Mark was leaving the Greyhound pub with his mates, and they were entering. Loved up and unaware it was her brother who held the door open. Mark laughed. As they swept through the door, he murmured.

'And a hello to you too, Angela.'

Ducking back out, she had hissed in his face, 'do not say anything to mum and dad.'

'You are not a child. You hardly need their permission.'

'They think I might be gay,' Angela whispered theatrically.

Her words hit him like a blow. He gasped, feeling cold as his face drained of colour, while at the same time, sweat ran down his back. Angela laughed to see his reaction to her words.

Once the door closed on his sister's grinning face, Mark's mouth flooded with all the retorts he'd wished he'd made. Instead, he stood like a fool, wondering what she knew and whether she would say anything out of spite. Although their parents always acted liberal in their views. Mark was not so sure that it was a true reflection of how they were. Listening to them acting up at family get-togethers and with their friends. As their language around race, immigrants, and anyone deemed different; got more objectionable as the event went on. He and his sisters had felt uncomfortable on many occasions.

Drink played a part in bringing out most people's true feelings, and his parents were no different. Once they got started on a theme, nothing could make them stop. Their solutions to these so called problems got more and more outlandish. Many a restaurant had suggested that they either tone it down or leave, leading to money being thrown by his father in recompense as his mother hurled foul mouth abuse toward the staff and customers. All in all, they were often a nightmare to be seen anywhere with. Walking home, he decided to phone Cassie. Before Angela started spreading her poison, he wanted to put their relationship on a more permanent basis.

*

Judy sat on the end of her bed and sighed in desperation. She could find no inclination to go out to dinner or the where with all to find the energy to sit and play nice. Each year, Valentine's Day got more and more commercial, some places starting in January in their eagerness to sell; a special day. Simone at work was a typical case in point. Her husband would send the biggest bunch of red roses he could find. She would then breeze down to the reception desk as if she had no idea they were coming, display them prominently, and wait for the oohs every time someone went past her desk. Today though, Judy had no intention of colluding with the rest of the office. Instead, each time she looked at or passed them, all she felt was the overwhelming urge to snip their big blousy heads off.

Paul, ever the romantic, loved the day, which is why he chose it last year to propose. He had set everything up with the restaurant. The diamond ring sat on top of her chocolate dessert, twinkling in the candlelight as staff and customers looked on. Flustered by all the attention, Judy could only stammer.

'Yes.'

As soon as the word left her mouth, she immediately felt trapped. Calling for champagne, Paul was the most animated she had ever seen him, plans for their future tripping off his tongue in his haste to tell her all about the new life he would provide for her. Never much of a drinker, whether it was nerves or excitement, he downed most of the bottle himself. Reaching across to take her hand, words slurring together, he told her.

'I love you so much, and I know our life together will be perfect. My promotion will guarantee that you can give up your job. I know how much you dislike it. You can be a homemaker instead.'

Too drunk to notice the look on her face, Judy stared in horror. Yes, it was true. She didn't like her job. Her title of Regional Logistics Manager meant only moving stuff around on spreadsheets and dealing with the drivers who continually moaned about taking on the long haul jobs. But, at the same time, she also didn't want to be stuck at home doing nothing. What the hell was Paul thinking? She raged inside. Homemaker sounded like something out of a 1950's B movie!

Before her thoughts could stray again, her phone pinged with a text saying he was on his way. She looked down to see that the dress she had been thinking of wearing now lay crushed between her hands. Flinging it aside, she pulled her pink go-to dress out of the wardrobe. Stepping into it, Judy paused. The last time she had worn the dress had been at her friend Sally's hen party, and remembering the good time they'd all had made her smile. Short and sparkly – Judy was forever pulling at the hem. Even so, it clung to her figure, and whenever she'd worn it, someone would always pay her a compliment, lifting her spirits. Her mother had been telling her since she was a child how beautiful she was, but it didn't help Judy with the feeling of inadequacy she felt when out with her group of friends.

Angela was fat, and Judy was curvy, words she heard her mother use to describe her daughters. Neither description fit them, especially in their teenage years when puberty and puppy fat were the stuff of most girls nightmares, and weight could rise and fall at the drop of a hat. If asked to describe herself, instantly, she thought pale and chubby. Having red hair didn't help, its vibrancy seeming to sap any colour out of her face, mascara, eyeshadow, and blusher her armour. Reaching for the zip, Judy sighed. Slipping her feet into a pair of high heels, she spritzed perfume behind her ears before tipping her head upside down to shake out her hair, managing to do it all while avoiding looking into her mirror. Everyone said that she should be on cloud nine. Judy felt more like stuck in the middle of a storm. She knew that if she looked at the face staring back at her, it would not be a happy one.

Judy and Paul's senses were assaulted by the loud noise from the diners already seated. Bored, the receptionist, barely civil, barked.

'Have you booked?'

Distracted, Paul replied, 'yes, under Ross.'

Judy looked to see what had drawn Paul's attention and groaned. Angela was sitting against the far wall, talking animatedly to a dark-haired man.

The receptionist plucked two menus and indicated that they were to follow. Fortunately, the table she took them to was in the corner, and though they could see Angela, she would be unable to see them. With relief at being hidden, they tried not to let their eyes roam.

'Did you know that she was seeing someone?' Paul whispered.

Judy shook her head. Her sister had always given the impression that she was not interested in either men or women. As the waiter took their wine order, Angela raised her voice. Her interest piqued, Judy glanced over to see the man looking annoyed while her sister looked drunk.

'Forget about them,' said Paul. 'Let's enjoy our meal.'

Grabbing for her hand, she knew what was coming and tried not to frown. Savouring the words, Paul informed her.

'Mrs. Paul Ross to be. Not long now.'

Judy hated it. She would not mind changing her surname. But as for using his name instead of hers. That was never going to happen. Ever since they had gotten engaged, the feeling that he was in a time warp; had been gradually growing. His old-fashioned ideas, cute when they had first met – annoying now, were being given full reign. The problem with them, she was finding, was that they were also some of the same ones that her mother still held. Together they would gang up on her, wearing her down until she gave in. Like the flat, she had wanted them to buy, dismissed out of hand. The house Paul had finally chosen in Kesgrave, and for which her mother had stamped her approval, was their choice, not hers.

She also felt that sometimes all they saw in her was a type of broodmare. She winced to remember trying to explain how she felt.

'Will you both stop going on about children? I don't want any. Well, not straightaway, or at least not for a few years.'

Her words went down like a lead balloon.

'Children are a big commitment. I want to be sure of us.'

Unaware that her mother even wanted grandchildren, the explosion of anger from her she had only in the past seen directed towards Angela. In reality, with the doubts that assailed her daily, she should either call the wedding off; or stop the preparations. The continual toing and froing in her head made it ache. Paul, she knew, had no such doubts. Every day he told her how he couldn't wait to get married, his texts, phone calls, and even emails peppered with his happiness. Judy assured herself daily. She did love him, the mantra quickly falling apart when thoughts intruded. Demanding, was that enough?

3

MARCH

As Angela sat in her car, her gaze fell onto the flowers she had bought from an expensive shop in the high street. Pink roses, and white carnations, her mother's favourites. To complement them, she had been encouraged by the assistant to add a small bottle of pink champagne and a box of white chocolates. A last-minute decision Angela hoped she would not come to regret.

Someone had gone to the effort of putting bunting up all around the garden. At any other time, it would have been a cheery sight. Today, it was easy for Angela to see that her mother had been drinking more than usual. As they air kissed, the wash of alcohol coming from her breath smelt fetid.

At Angela's grimace of distaste, Wendy pointed her finger, admonishing. 'It is not your place to police what I do.'

Before she could retort, Judy bounced over, practically hidden behind the bouquet she held, looking as if she had bought out the entire florist's shop. Much to Angela's amazement, instead of her mother's usual gushing thanks at anything her sister did, she waved them away, snapping.

'Much too big. I am not dead yet.'

Judy's face crumbled. Unsure what to do, she turned to Angela. Unable to suppress a smile, she also walked away. Thinking a little taste of what she usually got wouldn't hurt her sister.

Angela was disgusted to see that by the time they were ready to leave, her mother and Judy were again the best of friends. Linking their arms, heads together as they shared a joke. She, of course, was left behind, expected, as usual, to follow them like a dog. As they climbed into Judy's car, not for the first time, Angela thought that her mother's laughter sounded forced while Judy's rang hollow. The men had left earlier to go to the pub and had, as they entered, finally finished their game of darts. Cassie sitting down as they arrived, decided for reasons of her own to stand up and clap on seeing them. Wendy curtsied, Judy blushed, and Angela rolled her eyes in disgust.

Assuming that Mark would make his usual long-winded fuss over the wine – having been to France a few times, he believed that he was now an expert. Deeming that Merlot was the only red worth drinking. Not a big drinker, Judy decided to get her request in first for a white wine spritzer with lots of ice. Mark and her father would always sneer at her choice, one of the few things they could find to agree on together. Nudging Paul, she asked what he was going to have to drink. His faraway look prompted the unkind thought that, for all his brains, he was as empty-headed as Mark often quoted.

Heads down, they all studied the menu; Angela never understood why, as everyone always ordered the same as they usually did. Since she was a child, the Maybush had been her family's go-to place to eat in Waldringfield. As children, they had liked to play down by the waterside. Some of her happiest memories were of summer days spent along the shore. They would eat their fill; then be sent outside while their parent's sat drinking. Those days though were long gone. Now they often forgot to invite her. Angela would often pop down on the weekend to find them together, she the outsider, making their faces fall on seeing her. Today had been an exception. She had overheard her mother telling Judy. Both unaware of her standing near them while shopping in Woodbridge, Angela decided to surprise them. They both jumped when she leaned forward and said.

'What time? Shall I come to the house first? Or meet you in the pub?'

Their faces had been a picture.

'I'll come to the house, leave my car. Then we can go together. What a treat.'

The waiter placed their drinks on the table and, raising their glasses, clinked them together. Angela looked over at her father and thought, please do not make a speech. As if hearing her words, he pushed back his chair, loomed over the table, and bellowed at them to raise their glasses in a toast to his beautiful wife.

'Sit down, Lennie,' snapped Wendy. Notorious for only liking a fuss if she was the one to make it.

Cassie clapped before putting her two pennyworths in, twittering like a child as she extolled the many virtues of dear Wendy. Ignoring her monologue, Judy looked around for a waiter.

'I think this calls for champagne,' said Lennie, looking at Wendy for agreement.

Judy found it too dry. Ignoring her father's sigh of annoyance as she asked the waiter for another spritzer and a glass of Shiraz.

Angela pointed at Paul, 'I will have the same as him,' she commanded. Earning a grimace from Mark. In response, she pulled a face and poked her tongue out at him.

'So childish.'

'I'll have whatever you pour,' shouted Wendy as she headed for the loo.

Judy thought, once again her mother had mixed her drinks. Unable to walk in a straight line, she bumped into every table she passed her merry shouts of 'sorry' ringing around the room.

Angela was unsurprised to see her family talking over, around, but not to her. Fed up with being ignored while waiting for the staff to clear away the starters and bring the mains out, she decided it was time to have some fun.

As the excluding conversations continued, she reached for the pepper and deliberately knocked over Cassie's drink, splashing her white linen dress with the ruby-red Merlot that Mark loved so much. Startled, Cassie jumped and caught the edge of the tablecloth, sending the other glasses tumbling. A waiter rushed over, and the other diners tittered. If looks could kill, both of Angela's parents would now stand accused of her murder.

Her brother leaned across the table, 'bitch.'

His expletive, Angela felt unusually restrained for Mark. Perhaps, she thought, it was because of all the faces now turned towards their table. The fact that Cassie was blubbing like a demanding baby; didn't help. Angela, as the only one holding her glass, drained its contents. Wiping her mouth with the back of her hand, she announced mockingly, 'delicious.'

At Cassie's shrieks, Mark began gesturing wildly for the staff to clear up the mess, nearly upending the plates of food they carried, only the quick reactions of the waitress avoiding another catastrophe. No one spoke. The mood soured as Judy and Paul, their voices raised, argued about leaving early.

'Please stay, don't go,' implored Wendy. Before snapping at Cassie, 'why did you have to make so much fuss? Angela didn't do it on purpose. It was an accident.' Ignoring Cassie's shocked face and Mark's dark look, she continued, 'let's enjoy ourselves without any arguments. Other families seem capable of managing it. Surely for once, we can.'

They all stared at her as if she had gone mad.

Her mother, Angela thought, never stood up for her, and it was so out of character that she couldn't help but wonder if she had an ulterior motive. For the life of her, Angela was unable to think; about what on earth it could be. She could see by the looks the others were giving her that they must wonder the same thing. If her mother thought by her words that it would make Angela apologise to Cassie, then she was very much mistaken.

The waiter arrived with their desserts breaking the tension around the table as they all remembered their manners and said thank you.

Angela once again felt ostracized, her mother throwing her looks of annoyance each time she tried to interrupt anyone by inserting her views into their conversations. Deciding a frontal attack was the only thing to do, she raised her voice above theirs to regale them with tales about the houses that the estate agents where she worked had on their books. Mark quickly jumped in to remind everyone that she was employed to work in their back room and therefore did not get to sell any houses, and smugly turned the conversation back onto himself. Angela wanted to punch him. She zoned out...

Angela liked her job in administration. She loved reading the old forgotten files, the documents yellow with age, often smelling a bit mouldy. Many a happy lunch hour; had been spent amongst them. It was among these treasures that she had found the forgotten house. Pushed right to the back as if someone had been trying to hide it, the box squashed and battered, the name Byford House written in faded black marker pen had caught her eye. Pulling off the tape, she peered inside to find only a scrunched-up piece of paper. A key fell out with an old-fashioned luggage label attached, with the name Gibson and Yoxford written in red ink and held no other clues as to its owner. The name on the box brought back a memory.

She had heard of this house and seen photos of it in the papers and on the news. Someone had been killed there and buried. Only found when new owners were having an old barn demolished. After that, it changed hands a few times, some buying it for its notoriety, some for its seclusion. Nobody could ever settle there, and it had lain vacant before finally being sold. Angela only knew this from watching a programme about unsolved murders.

Checking Hudson & May's online records, Angela was surprised when she could not find any listing for the house on the site. Because she wasn't keen to ask anyone outright about the box, Angela decided to wait for the Thursday team meeting – which no one enjoyed, bored and wanting to return to work. Her colleagues would be less inclined to quiz her about her interest in the house.

Angela, would usually sit at the back of the room and play with her phone. Today though, much to everyone's surprise, she asked what should be done with the old files when she had finished cross-checking them with the system. Angela's task was to sort out the chaos the last administrator had caused. Both to their online systems and filing room. The lost data, coupled with Jackie's insane filing system, had caused numerous problems and headaches. The situation was made worse by her boss, who was old-fashioned in his ideas. Mr. Cooper had no trust in the new computer system that had been installed and still insisted on keeping a copy of everything. Because of this, the filing room had become stuffed floor to ceiling with new and old files mixed. With the lack of office space, the consensus was to get rid of them. Most of the information in them was now redundant and needed destruction. In this pile of boxes is where she had found the box pushed to the back and the only one that Jackie had put a note on reminding herself to shred the contents.

Mr. Cooper's smile looked more like a grimace when he told her to make sure before she did so that nothing of importance; was shredded by mistake. Her question.

'What if I find any keys?' was dismissed with a sneer by Gale.

'Keys are always kept in the safe. Not in the filing room.'

Ignoring her and knowing it would start her other colleagues twittering, Angela asked.

'Is the space left going to be another office?'

With thoughts of possibly having one of their own, none of them would be looking into what she was doing. They would be more concerned with who should have first dibs on the space.

For once, her colleague's shouts of good night and see you tomorrow held an affectionate ring to them.

Angela knew without them saying a word that they would expect her in bright and early each morning, the shredder pushed to full throttle, eager to see the room cleared as soon as possible. All day one after the other, she had seen them badgering Mr. Cooper, wanting to state their case time and again as to why they needed an office to themselves. Steve, one of the two senior sales assistants, who Angela had quickly nicknamed Piggy. Due to the daily cakes and sausage rolls that he shoved into his mouth while managing at the same time to splatter crumbs all over his desk and drip icing onto his tie had no chance.

Overhearing his disparaging comments about Piggy on the phone, she knew that Mr. Cooper did not like him and could never understand why he kept him on and didn't get rid of him. Perhaps it was because, for all his shabby appearance, he did make a lot of sales. Without being blessed with good looks or a toned body, his one ace was his gift of the gab. Punters liked his attitude. Gale, on the other hand, was an outright bitch. Her snappy fingers, waved in Angela's direction, if not acted upon quick enough for her liking, were often followed by a snide remark. Not in the least tech-savvy, Gale's laptop was often dumped onto Angela's desk with the instruction, sort it out. As if it was her fault; it wasn't working.

Hudson & May also employed three junior assistants. Dave, Sharon, and Jason. They acted like satellite stars as they followed Steve and Gale around, hanging on their every word as if they were the font of all knowledge. Dave, Angela knew, thought of himself as a lady's man, his aftershave testament to him having no idea that it made him smell like a walking cat's piss. Sharon thought she would try the same attitude towards Angela as Gale put out, but this changed after several trips to the toilet, accusing her of putting something in her coffee. Angela denied all knowledge. Affronted, she told her that perhaps she should take her accusation to Mr. Cooper. Sharon declined. Jason was the only one of the bunch that Angela liked. He was all arms and legs, gangly, like a puppet on a string, unable to keep still even when Gale shouted at him across the office to stop fidgeting. She often found herself chuckling when Dave, the font of all knowledge where women were concerned, tried to give Jason detailed tips on how to break his dry spell as he saw his lack of a girlfriend. Blind to the fact that Jason was gay and happy in his skin.

They had bonded over the kettle, Angela making her coffee, Jason tasked with getting one for both Dave and Gale.

They had realised that their opinions of them both were the same when Sharon scuttled in to get a glass of water. Frowning at both of them as if they were up to no good, she slammed shut the cupboard door before turning the tap on full and showering them all in water. Angela and Jason hooted with laughter. Sharon fled her face as red as a beetroot, her white shirt turning see-through.

Angela had left work with the key to the house feeling weighty in her pocket, the violent history attached to it thrilling her. Over the next few weeks, while she cleared the room, Angela was determined to search every file it contained for any other reference to Byford or Gibson.

Bringing her thoughts back to the moment, Angela was unsurprised once again to find that the conversations still flowed around her. If aliens had zapped her from her seat, she was sure that none of them would have taken any notice, well, not until the bill arrived. A standing joke within their family, and they all knew what to expect. Handed the bill, her father would scrutinise it for accuracy, and each item ordered was apportioned to the correct person. Totted up and the tip added, payment from each expected. Much to his embarrassment, her father occasionally liked to bring up Paul's reaction the first time he had asked him to settle not only his share of the bill. But Judy's as well.

When asked out to dinner by her parents, Paul thought the invitation meant that they would be paying. He'd accidentally left his wallet at home. He had assumed, wrongly it wouldn't be a problem. Her father had not seen it that way and demanded that he go home and fetch it. Paul's suggestion that Judy pay and he reimburse was met with a stony face and a pointing finger. Instead, they waited, her father shooing away the staff who wanted the bill settled and the table freed up. He ordered another round of drinks, telling them Paul would pay when he returned. Never again had he forgotten his wallet. His bill for himself and Judy toted up first, her father demanding prompt payment.

With that thought in mind, Angela surreptitiously picked up her bag and jacket, announcing to anyone who cared to listen.

'If the waiter comes, tell him I would like another large glass of Shiraz.' Before pushing back her chair and heading towards the toilet.

Angela took a quick look over her shoulder, unable to see any of her family, which meant they could not see her. She pulled the door open, calling a cab as she walked quickly away. Before Angela had gotten outside, her phone pinged with a text to say the taxi was on its way. Shutting the car door, Angela wondered how long it would take them all to realise that she was not coming back. Would any of them bother to go and see if she was okay? What would her father do? Pay her share, or make them split the bill between them all? Angela chuckled at the thought of how livid he would be when she did not return, sure that his anger would explode and they would all feel the fallout. With a satisfied sigh at a job well done. She turned off her phone.

'Good day?' the cabbie asked.

'The best.'

*

Wendy slugged back her drink and stared at her husband across the table. And not, for the first time, wondered. What? It would be like if he were dead. She fancied the life of a merry widow. She would travel and have affairs with younger men, perhaps a little bit of nip and tuck first to make her more attractive. She was sure that with all the money she would have available to spend with Lennie's death, the men would soon come flocking to her side.

His little speech did nothing for her self-esteem. The start of their relationship had been romantic. That was before Elaine left when the stolen time they grabbed had made them both happy. Time and again, fed up with his moaning about the subject, Wendy had lost her temper and snapped.

'Never forget, it was her choice to walk away from you and Mark. Nobody would want you to be unhappy. Your trouble is that you still do not like the thought that Elaine wanted to leave you.'

For all the empathy he spouted, Wendy thought, Lennie was still a dinosaur where women were concerned.

Earlier, she'd snapped at Judy before realising it wasn't Angela speaking to her. Seeing Angela smirk, the urge to smack her daughter's face rose. To make matters worse, when they entered the Maybush's restaurant, Mark's imbecile girlfriend stood up and clapped. What a mismatched couple they are, she'd thought. She liked Mark, but unlike Lennie, she could see him for what he was. As for Cassie, well, dim didn't do her justice. Lennie, of course, thought her *divine!* Wendy was well aware that even though she was his son's girlfriend, given half a chance, he would be chasing after her.

The first time they met Cassie, he had spent half an hour waxing lyrical about her bust and was mesmerised by how someone so small could maintain her balance with such large breasts. Wendy was hard-pressed to understand why he thought she would be interested and not mad at his thought processes. Reminding him Cassie was his son's girlfriend made no difference. As Lennie had gotten older, any woman was fair game in his eyes.

She had seen Angela deliberately knock over Cassie's drink and had surprised them all by defending her. Though, having to listen to her whittling about her job, she wished she had told her to leave. Even though Mark owed his employment to another friend of Lennie's, it hadn't taken him long to slap Angela down and draw the conversation back to himself. Making her think, and not for the first time, how insufferable he was.

Glancing at Judy, Wendy couldn't stop the thought emerging that she was looking a bit strained lately and could only put it down to worry over her forthcoming wedding. Wendy could hardly wait and revelled in the thought of being named the mother of the bride. The outfit she would wear had already been planned since Judy and Paul had first met. Her daughter may have been unsure of them as a couple. But Wendy knew men. She could tell that Paul was determined to marry Judy no matter what.

Ideally, she would have wanted Judy living nearby in Woodbridge, a plot of land had become vacant, and she had tried to manoeuvre Paul into buying it but instead, he had found a house in Kesgrave. Showing it to them with pride, Judy had been silent, but for her, it was a dream house and all she could have wanted her daughter to have. As much as she liked Paul, Wendy often daydreamed that it was Angela getting married and would imagine her announcing that they would be living on the other side of the world, the imagery would extend with Mark quickly following. Sure that if she and Lennie could have some space to themselves, everything would come right between them.

Then the waiter placed the bill in front of Lennie, and her thoughts changed to what a skinflint he was. What she found hard to understand was the wedding would cost an arm and a leg, yet, he had not once questioned the invoices. Hand him a restaurant bill, and he would change, becoming miserly and furtive. Whipping out his pad and pen, taking great delight in writing down each item consumed, he made sure they all paid their share. Many a row they had about it once they got home, dismissing her complaints as nonsense. Once demanding he tell her why he did it, and in the process made such a show of himself by doing so, he announced with glee.

'Because I like seeing them squirm.'

Filling her glass, she downed it in one, wishing she could drown her unhappiness in much the same way.

*

Judy tuned out, letting the play of the same old conversations wash over her. Her thoughts of the large bunch of roses and carnations Paul had insisted that she buy for her mother. Lately, he always had to go over the top, lavishing her with presents that would arrive on the doorstep, followed by a phone call or text.

'Do you like them?' he would ask. 'Please say if you don't, and I will get you something else.'

If she didn't answer, the same message would appear until he finally gave up. It was all getting a bit too much. Judy knew that some men in a relationship liked to take over. Paul wasn't like that, but he could be smothering and reminded her of a puppy looking for approval for his good deeds. Judy would not have been surprised if he knelt to be patted on the head and told what a good boy he was.

She knew she was being a bitch. But the thoughts kept on coming. The nearer to the wedding they got, the more she felt the need to back away. She could stop it. Tell him no, that she did not want to marry him. But she wasn't brave enough. Her mother would have a fit. Not because of all the arrangements that were underway or the cost. But because she liked Paul and thought of him as a good catch. More importantly, though, he would never take Judy away from Suffolk, something her mother would not condone.

For Judy, her mother's need to put her in a box called marriage made her hackles rise. Even with the evidence of her rocky marriage for all to see, when they were together, she would often announce.

'I cannot wait to see you walk down the aisle. "Mother of the Bride" has a nice ring to it. Don't you think? As for Angela, only a lunatic would contemplate marrying her.' Going on to tell her, 'no man will be able to resist you. You will have to fight them off!'

In anyone else, this may have given them an inflated sense of themselves, whereas, for Judy, it made her feel trapped. Her mother's expectations for her had always been at the forefront of any previous relationships. Meeting Paul, she knew, had solidified them for her. He was the one Judy was to marry, and as far as her mother was concerned, nothing would be allowed to get in the way of that happening.

Judy was brought out of her reverie by her father snapping his fingers as he called for the bill. Taking out his pad and pen, he flourished them with relish. Angela stood up. Poised to write, her father swore as she called out to the waiter before heading to the loo.

Her father stared with annoyance as her mother and brother joined her in demanding another drink. While everyone chatted, he fumed to he kept waiting.

Angela hadn't returned to the table.

'Judy, find out what's happened to your sister.'

'Why don't you go?' she snapped at her father.

Pushing back her chair, Judy thought that Angela had the right idea. Neither she nor Paul minded paying their share, but they hated how her father went about it. Crowing when each of them paid up while wearing the same smug look on his face as Mark had earlier when attacking Angela. Like a hunting dog, pen and paper at the ready as he totted up a separate bill for each couple. For once, Judy shared Angela's anger at his attitude.

'Angela has gone,' she announced. Surprising herself and everyone else by adding, 'and so are we.' Grabbing her bag and coat, she signalled to Paul to join her.

Her father's steely gaze raking the back of her neck only served to spur her on as they marched towards the exit.

4

APRIL

Once again, Gary had let her down. This time though, Angela let her anger bubble to the surface.

'If we don't go, then we may as well be over. I won't allow you to keep messing me about in this way. I won't let you. It isn't fair!' she snarled, wanting to cry in frustration.

Slamming down the phone, Angela shouted.

'Fuck, bloody *fuck*.'

Her mind filled with hate at the injustice of it all, asking herself again.

'Why am I the one always being let down.'

She had stupidly thought that when she met Gary, he would be different, yet he was acting as her family did toward her. Idiot that she was when he'd first mentioned the possibility of going to the Lake District, Angela had assumed she would be the one going with him. Instead, Gary planned to go away with his brother.

'It's not my fault that you jumped the gun,' he'd yelled. 'It was only ever a suggestion.'

Moaning to Maureen had gotten her no sympathy, reminding Angela that she had never liked Gary and had called him shifty on more than one occasion. Her question.

'Is it his brother he was going away with?'

Beat like a drum inside Angela's brain. Gary could never pass up looking at an attractive woman. She didn't mind that so much it was the second and third looks that she objected to. Not happy with her shape, Angela always felt that he was comparing her with them and that she would be the one to be found wanting. Only once in her life had she ever been told that she was beautiful. Which, even Angela knew, didn't count as the bloke who had said it was drunk.

Angela never thought of herself as obese. She knew though she carried a bit of weight as various parts of her wobbled in different directions as she walked. Like many women, Angela thought and talked about going on a diet and always failed. When she heard a woman talking about the benefits of the exercises she had been doing and how as a result, she had toned her arms and hips, Angela thought it could help her to fight against her wobbly bits. Deciding to try the gym near where she worked, Angela booked a taster session. Hoping, like the lady on the bus, it may help her to tone up.

The experience was something Angela told herself sternly that she must never be foolish enough to think of doing again. With only thick baggy shorts to her name and suggestions from Jason at work ringing in her ears. She went in search of something stretchy. The heat inside the changing room made Angela feel like she was standing inside an oven.

Shimmying out of her trousers was like trying to slough off the skin from a sausage, the fabric clinging to her legs like a second skin. Then came the fun of trying to pull the leggings up and over her legs and bottom. The cubicle was way too small for such a manoeuvre. Angela was sure she heard her body groaning at being so squashed. Pulling the equally tight top over her head and wriggling it down her body, she turned to look in the mirror and saw an overstuffed teddy bear staring back at her. Angela cried out as the curtain was yanked open, and the assistant's face loomed towards her.

'Sorry, I thought something was wrong. Only you've been in there nearly an hour.'

'And it will probably take me another one to get this lot off!' Angela raged, shooing her out.

*

As she opened the door, Angela's eyes swept the gym to see that all the beautiful people had come out to play with their lithe bodies, form-fitting clothes, and no bulges. Even their sweat managed to smell sweet. Catching sight of her bedraggled state in the mirrored wall behind the receptionist's counter made Angela feel even more self-conscious. She had been in such a rush to get to the class on time; she had forgotten her umbrella. The rain had plastered her hair flat to her scalp, water from it now sliding down her face taking most of her mascara with it. Her clothes were so wet Angela wasn't sure if she would even be able to take them off. The receptionist tutted as she spied the puddle she was leaving on the floor. Loudly pointing the way to the woman's changing rooms as if not sure what sex Angela was. She tried a cheery smile and got a grimace back in return. Leaving her wet footprints on the pristine floor, Angela entered what she would later describe to Jason as a. 'Living hell.'

Stumbling, when her eyes snapped shut at the appearance before her of various naked women of all shapes and sizes.

Unconcerned, they dried themselves while at the same time talking to other equally naked women.

'Surely!' Angela exclaimed in panic. 'There must be some private cubicles.'

She knew there was no way that she would be attempting to undress, let alone wrestle into and out of her gym gear in front of any of them. Ignoring the big red sign above the toilets, advising; that they were not a changing room, Angela wrestled her gym bag inside and locked the door. After a lot of wriggling, swearing, and hitting of elbows, she emerged and shuffled towards the lockers. Aware that her misery was not yet over, next, she had to tackle the actual gym, mumbling as she opened the door.

'How bad can it be? It was only a taster after all and not a full-on session.'

Then Angela saw the instructor, a tall, well-built man in his forties, looking like a reject from the army, staring at her and the rest of the group with a look of pure disdain.

'At least the showers are private,' railed Angela, throwing herself inside and locking the door.

Her anger and embarrassment fought each other to be the top dog. Call me "Jimmy," not "Jim," started okay, explaining what he wanted the group to do. His frustration only set in when he soon realised that most of them could not or would not act on his instructions. The majority of them were more than a bit overweight, plain lazy, or both.

Angela did try, but the bike was too much. She wanted to feel like she was cycling down a country lane with the wind in her hair. Jimmy however, wanted her to ride as if she was angling for a place in the Tour de France. And as for the treadmill, Angela was sure if Petra, dressed all in pink, and looking like a blancmange, hadn't fallen off while trying to battle an impossible up-hill climb, he would have had them all running a marathon. His relief when their time was up was palpable. The enrolment forms he had been holding when introducing himself; were now nowhere to be seen. A quick bye, a backwards wave, and off he went, scuttling back to all the beautiful people, leaving the unfortunate ones to their fate.

With Gary off enjoying himself and still feeling fraught from the gym, Angela thought she would pop over to see her parents and take them both an Easter egg as a peace offering. Walking up the path to their house, she could immediately hear shouting. Creeping towards the back gate, remembering that the latch squeaked, she was glad to see that it was open. Pushing it wider, Angela had to suppress a giggle at the sight of her mother spraying her father while screeching at the top of her voice.

'I have had enough! Do you hear? Enough!'

Grabbing the hose, they wrestled each other for ownership, Wendy tripped, and Lennie knocked her down.

'Bloody mad cow. *Mad!* That's what you are!'

Angela snorted so loudly they both turned.

United in their dislike, they jeered at her and demanded.

'What are you doing here?'

'Charming. I'm sure,' Angela replied sarcastically. 'Look, I have brought you a present.' She lifted the Easter eggs she had managed to find in the garage. 'If you've both finished acting like children, is there any chance of a cup of coffee?'

The silence lengthened as they posed statue-like, her father still holding the hose, her mother on the ground, water cascading around them as if raining. The spell was broken by Judy and Paul as they came twittering into the garden. Unlike Angela's greeting, her parents immediately welcomed them both.

'Shall I put the kettle on?' trilled her mother.

Grabbing hold of Judy, they both disappeared indoors. Angela glanced at Paul. For some reason, he was always nervous when around her. His eyes would flicker across her face before skittering away, and for her part, unless he spoke directly to her, she rarely engaged him in any conversation. Left alone, Angela decided to pounce.

'Paul,' she cooed sweetly. 'How are the plans going? I bet Judy spends all her time swooning over wedding magazines and jeweller's shops. With a fully paid honeymoon, you must both be very excited. How about the house renovation? Is it going well? I am surprised you can fit it all in. What with your high-powered job as an accountant? How do you find the time? Or have you got the builders in?'

To say he looked stunned at her verbal attack would be an understatement. Her father, dry now after a change of clothes, gave Angela a dirty look.

'Why are you so interested all of a sudden?' asked her mother, banging the tray down and making the cups rattle. 'And do not be getting any ideas about being a bridesmaid that honour is going to someone who will do the job nicely. No one wants to see you shuffling along, least of all Judy. It would be best if you sat at the back of the church, and if any children play up, you can take them straight outside.'

That told me, thought Angela. Picking up her coffee, she sipped and stared at each in turn, trying to look amused rather than angry. Angela had always found it strange that Judy, who always carried more weight than her. Yet she was the one always referred to as fat. Her mother, a yo-yo dieter, had often found herself on the hefty side. The term; Nellie, the Elephant, was brought to mind. The drink also didn't help her in the fight to stay slim. Taller than both she and Judy, Angela would admit that her mother carried off any excess better than they did. Sensing trouble, her father and Paul moved away. Like most men, they found it hard to be near women when spite reared its ugly head.

'While we are on the subject, do not forget about this Saturday. We are going shopping for your outfit. No more cancellations.'

Since the wedding; was first mentioned, Angela felt her mother had gotten more obsessed with what she would wear and how she would look, insisting that she vet any outfit for her approval before Angela bought it. For some reason fixated on her wearing peach, which Angela hated with a passion. She had managed to avoid the drama on three separate occasions, but she could see by the glint in her mother's eye that she would not be getting out of it again. Happy to have made her point, her mother turned her attention back onto Judy. Deliberate or not, she knew that talk of hair, nails, and massages would usually bore Angela to tears. Not this time. Much to her chagrin, Angela joined in. Oohing over Judy's choice of possible hair do's, voicing her opinion on the various nail colours offered. Angela asked for the details of what type of massage Judy was having, making her blush when she laughed suggestively. 'Have you ever felt ... anything?'

'How can you be so vile,' her mother spluttered. 'It's a salon for women. And that includes those who work there. Lennie,' she screeched. As if he were on the other side of the street. 'What time are we eating?' Without waiting for his answer, she turned to Angela, 'you should be going. I'm sure you must have things to do.'

Angela would have left. Not because of her mother's words but because being with her was always hard work. Then Mark and Cassie appeared. While he clutched a monster-sized Easter egg, she hid behind a large bunch of flowers. Catching sight of Angela, their smiles slipped from their faces.

*

Lennie thought, for god's sake, why does Wendy have to hang onto Judy as if she were a life preserver? Even with a husband in the offing, you would think her bloody mother would back off. Wendy may not be drunk, but with her make-up smudged and dress creased as if she had slept in it, she looked as if she were. He wished he was brave enough to walk away. Lennie knew he couldn't, and neither would Wendy, held together by their secrets, life on hold.

And here she comes. Lennie wondered – not for the first time, how Angela could be so ungainly, walking as if on a rolling ship. When she was born, he'd often seen a look of disgust cross Wendy's face whenever she had to feed or change her. Lennie let her get on with it. He had no interest by then in either of them. As Angela had gotten older, his dislike for her had lessened. Sometimes he even felt sorry for the treatment meted out to her by Wendy. However, Lennie wasn't brave enough to intervene and would prefer to choose not to see. Judy was a different matter entirely. The first time he had laid eyes on her as a baby, he had fallen for her charms. Her sunny disposition and the smile she gave every time she saw him made him hug her tighter. He would lift and pretend to drop her, making her whoop with laughter.

'Lennie, you'll hurt her,' Wendy would shout. Arms, out ready to catch her.

Seeing Judy and Mark playing together had always brought a smile to his face until Angela was born and broke up their happy family unit. For him, everything began to fall apart from that moment.

'Dad, are you in there?'

Seeing his son always gave Lennie a thrill. Tall and good-looking, he could have been an actor. His one regret in their relationship was their need to compete. It had started when Mark was young as a bit of a joke, getting out of hand as he reached his teenage years. Now an adult, it was ingrained in him to try and go one better than Lennie. He knew that it was partly his fault. He had wanted to foster a feeling of arrogance in Mark that would drive him to succeed. The trouble is he had done his job too well. As Mark's confidence in his abilities grew, so did his reputation for being a hard-line boss.

Lennie noticed that since dating Cassie, Mark appeared calmer; more laid back in his outlook. The first time he had brought her to one of their garden get-togethers, Lennie knew that he had made an idiot of himself, the memory not one of his finest as Mark had introduced her...

'This is Cassie,' said Mark. While drawing forwards, a pale-looking girl with curly auburn hair. Cassie smiled and held out her hand.

'Hi. Your garden looks lovely. I especially like the fairy lights.'

Before he could say anything, Wendy let out a screech of laughter, making Cassie wince. It was then that Lennie took a better look at her and, without thinking, said out loud.

'Blimey, what a pair!'

Gazing at Cassie's chest in awe, Lennie glanced at Mark. She blushed, and Mark swore.

'Dad, for fuck's *sake!* Can you give it rest?'

Brought out of his reverie by Mark's hand on his shoulder, Lennie smiled.

'Sorry, Mark, I was away with the fairies.'

'Have you heard from Terry? Only I have been trying to contact him since yesterday. We have a big contract in the next couple of days, and I need to discuss the figures with him.'

Chuckling, Lennie told him, 'you've got no chance. He's gotten himself a new woman. Sure that this is the one. Silly bugger! How? Can such an intelligent man be ruled so much by what's in his pants? He is already talking about her being wife number three. He must be mad.'

Loud shrieks cut through their conversation. Glancing over to Wendy, Lennie wasn't surprised to see her dancing about the garden, drink in one hand while singing out of tune at the top of her voice. Thank god they lived on the outskirts of Woodbridge and had no neighbours near them. Not for the first time, he wished he could trade her in for a new model. Affairs were all well and good, but they were tiring, having to be at the top of his game all the time. These days he liked the chase, but after the catch, boredom would soon set in as the initial thrill went, and he would feel empty again. Pulling himself back, he smiled at Mark.

'How is Cassie? All's well between you both?'

'Everything's fine, dad. What about you? You seem a bit down. I see mum is being her usual self.'

As Mark's words left his mouth, Wendy grabbed his hands, pulling him into a dance and cackling like a witch as she spun around him. Lennie watched as once more she made a fool of herself. Like a thunderbolt, it hit Lennie that his life could have been so much better if he hadn't been so quick to tie himself to Wendy.

5

MAY

The thought of another trawl around the wedding dress shops gave Judy a headache. In their last merry-go-round, her mother had found fault with everything she had tried on, and by the end of the day, she had begun to understand how Angela must feel.

Judy felt like a condemned prisoner on the way to the scaffold. As she walked behind her mother, her usual excited chatter was exaggerated much more by the vodka she had no doubt already been drinking. Her father found by accident that it wasn't water in the glass his wife constantly carried with her. Feeling thirsty, he grabbed it, downing its contents only to cough as if he were bringing his insides up through his throat. Her mother's manic laughter had brought Mark rushing in from the garden to see what all the noise was. Since then, whenever she left a glass of liquid anywhere, they all steered clear of it.

'You drive, Judy. You're much better at parking than me, and with it being the market day, the town will be busy. Manoeuvring into those tight spaces that the council insists on making us use. Make's my blood *boil!* Why is it that while cars get bigger, parking spaces get smaller?'

Judy held back a retort, knowing that it would do no good to answer. Her mother had a set of rules regarding behaviour. The problem was that they shifted depending on how much she was or had been drinking. Though her mood today, for all her complaining, appeared buoyant, so perhaps shopping with her might not be such a trauma.

Even though her mother had no intention of parking the car, she nevertheless wanted to instruct Judy on how to do it.

Staring through the windscreen, she shouted, 'go over there.'

Judy grimaced as a pedestrian shuffled in front of the car and got an earful.

'Get out of the bloody *way.*'

She suppressed a smile at the two-finger salute her mother had gotten in return. Unfortunately, rather than acting as a deterrent, it elicited a further ear-splitting bout of profanities, ending with one of her favourites.

'Fucking moron!'

Here we go, Judy thought. The possibility of a calm and enjoyable hunt for a wedding dress would now turn into her mother ranting through it. This Judy knew from experience could be anything from her mild refrain.

What a waste of space. Or. If she got overly angry. People like that should be strung up. To her more extreme. If I had a gun. I'd shoot the bastards.

Hoping to defuse the situation, Judy linked arms and

pulled her mother along like a recalcitrant toddler, chirpily telling her. 'Isn't this nice? Perhaps we can grab some lunch afterwards. Make a day of it. What do you think?'

Having aborted their search in the most popular shops in the high street, Judy made a beeline for the older part of town situated on St Peters street. Her mother detested the owner of Billies Emporium with a passion. Their strong personalities had clashed on several occasions. Judy's left-field thinking was that by taking her mother somewhere she didn't like, she would be so annoyed and less inclined to notice what Judy was trying on.

The owner Billie was in, Judy had checked, explaining all about their fruitless search and telling her that she would appreciate her attention. Apologising first that, unfortunately, her mother would be coming with her. Billie had roared with laughter before informing Judy that she liked a challenge and that she could handle Wendy with one hand tied behind her back.

Opening the door made the bell tinkle. Drawing Billie, her face wreathed in smiles from the back room. With a curt nod in Wendy's direction, she pulled Judy into a hug.

'Let's see what we can find for you, shall we?'

Judy was happy to be left alone. Her mother was dozing, having drunk most of the bottle of prosecco supplied by Billie. Now and again, she would wave a hand, Judy unsure if it was in agreement or dislike of what she was wearing smiled in response.

Finally! She had found the one. The dress was like a silken puddle pooled around her feet, and the off-the-shoulder bodice fit her like a glove, the sequins catching the light as she turned this way and that. Stepping out of the changing room, she was surprised to see Angela hovering by the door.

'Nice one, it suits you. Give us a twirl.'

While her voice wasn't loud, like a switch, Wendy instantly reacted. Her head snapped up. Seeing Angela, the bane of her life, standing next to Judy, the bright lights of the shop made their differences in looks even more evident. Even though Angela had the same colour eyes and hair as Wendy, she never admitted to anyone that they looked the same. Betty had once drawn the comparison, and Wendy had soon put her right.

'How can you think she is anything like me? Washed-out and boring spring to mind when I look at Angela. I am neither.'

Fortunately, Mark was the image of his father, tall and blonde, looking more Nordic than English. Judy, the anomaly, with her red hair and freckles, resembled none of them.

In one part of her brain, she knew it was illogical to blame Angela for ruining her life, but someone had to take responsibility for the direction it had gone in since she was born. They had been a family of four until she came along to spoil it all. Wendy hated being pregnant, and the memories of being so still made her shudder...

Unhappy to see herself in the mirror, looking and feeling like a lumbering beached whale. Wendy's once hourglass figure ballooned out so much, that when standing up, she couldn't even see her toes. Her breasts had grown so huge that they spread sideways, morphing into lumps under her arms. Her back and legs ached so much as the weight of her belly pulled her forwards, and she tried to pull back against it. Who needs the gym? She'd often thought. Worn out and irritable, it hadn't taken long before she and Lennie had started nit-picking at each other over everything. As their arguments gathered pace, she would end up shouting.

'I'll be glad when it is born.'

Lennie had been away playing golf when her waters broke. Bringing the baby home and laying her down, Wendy remembered staring with indifference as she cried and flailed her tiny fists, demanding attention. Only brought out of her dark thoughts by the return of Judy and Mark home from school and eager to see their sister and find out her name.

Angela. She had said, and to this day, Wendy had no idea where it had come from as both she and Lennie avoided any discussions about what name to choose.

They didn't talk anymore, locked inside their anger at each other, he for her getting pregnant and Wendy for being pregnant.

'I assumed wrongly. I realise now. That Judy and Mark were the only children; we would ever need,' snarled Lennie.

Wendy ignored his jibes.

As she got bigger, they both skirted around the issue of the forthcoming birth, making the distance between them grow. Things they both let slide now took on much more relevance and importance. Even with the knowledge; that the way she was acting was pushing them even further apart. Wendy was unable to stop herself from complaining about every little thing.

Even with the birth of Angela causing issues within their marriage, Wendy firmly believed their life together only started to go majorly wrong after attending a golfing dinner dance. Full of his cronies, she was not going to go at first. After their last round of arguments, she wanted to punish him by making him go alone. Bumping into Margery soon changed her mind.

'Have you met the new manager at the golf club yet? It's all my David can talk about. She has legs up to her armpits and breasts that could give a page-three girl a run for her money. Added to which she has the face of a Madonna.'

Wendy, aware how Margery's David liked to chase women – and also knowing he had no chance of ever catching one – laughed. Her face soon changed to a scowl when Margery, with particular glee, informed her.

'David has also implied that Pippa had taken a shine to Lennie.'

A few days later, Wendy broached the subject, his red face and caginess soon changing her mind about going. Making a special effort, Wendy thought she had brushed up well until she saw Pippa. David had not exaggerated. Though what made it worse was that she came across as someone nice. The women that had spoken to her all said the same thing making it clear that what they objected to was seeing their men follow her with their eyes each time she walked past them. Wendy was amused to see Lennie blushing as Pippa approached their group. The women moved closer to their men while they tried to step away and into Pippa's orbit.

As the night wore on, she realised that she had not seen Lennie for a while. Asking his friends if they knew where he was; only elicited raised eyebrows and a bellow of laughter, which only made her think the worst.

Staggering away from the bar, she had miscalculated her condition as tipsy rather than drunk. Everything spun as she held onto the wall. Climbing the stairs had been difficult. Her legs didn't want to obey her, wanting to give way instead. Halfway up the stairs, an arm snaked around her shoulders, the voice gentle but firm telling her.

'Let me help you. Come and lay down. You'll feel better.'

Wendy still flinched when remembering how he had stretched out beside her. She had felt suffocated.

'Lennie's a fool and a bastard,' he'd told her while pushing her clothes aside.

Peter's large body enclosed hers blocking out the light and making her feel entombed. Having gotten what he wanted, he left without a backwards glance. Straightening her clothes, she put on her game face and went for another drink.

For a while, life settled down, and Angela appeared to

be an easy baby until she was three months old, and then it all changed. Angela's crying caused so many disturbed nights Lennie began sleeping in the spare room, and Wendy's resentment at Angela and him grew each day; Angela for keeping Wendy awake, and Lennie for distancing himself from any help with her care.

After one particularly fraught night, all Wendy wanted was to enjoy a cup of coffee in peace and asked Judy and Mark to look after Angela for ten minutes.

'Why should we,' Mark exclaimed. 'Between Angela's crying and your continual slamming of doors and swearing at the top of your voice, where are the fucking *nappies*? No one has had any sleep.'

Before she could think, she had slapped his face, Judy cried out in shock, and Mark stormed out.

As a toddler, Angela was even more of a nightmare and never fully slept, and once she was awake, she would constantly shout. Too small to reach the door handle, she would bang on it with whatever was at hand, calling their names until someone gave in and went to get her.

When the day came to take her to school, Wendy remembered the sigh of relief she had felt.

Angela wouldn't attend the nursery, Wendy would arrive home, and they were on the phone telling her to return, Angela wailing in the background that she wanted her mother. Deaf to her daughter's cries to slow down, Wendy marched her home, slamming shut the bedroom door before pouring herself a large drink.

Now she and Lennie were further apart than they had ever been, Wendy often wondered if she even liked him anymore. Her love for him was complicated, eroded by her drinking; and his many affairs. Made worse when he was feeling down; and had a sporadic desire to talk about Mark's mother, Elaine.

'Who cares?' She kept on telling him each time he brought the subject up. 'Mark can't miss what he doesn't know. How would you explain to Mark your reasons for not saying anything about her disappearance until now.'

She blamed the programmes on telly that Lennie had taken to watching on catch-up. A show about family members who appear after spending years in the wilderness. Everyone would hug, kiss, and throw promises to keep in touch like confetti for the cameras. However, Wendy was confident that once they stopped rolling and things settled down, some, if not all, of those involved would soon come to regret opening their particular can of worms. Where her family was concerned, she had always believed that the further away they were, the better. And she had no intention of any of them being looked for or found.

*

'Are you here to try on bridesmaid's dresses?' Billie asked. Sarcasm dripped off her tongue. She knew it wasn't true Judy had told her earlier that Angela was not allowed to be one.

Pulling herself upright, Wendy swayed drunkenly, quickly catching hold of the chair to steady herself, she slurred, 'not that it is any of your business, but Angela is never going to be a bridesmaid. She is too …'

'Now Wendy. That's not very nice. You should be proud of your girls. Lovely they are,' said Billie, patronisingly, to wind Wendy up.

Incensed, Wendy sneered, 'you're nothing but; an interfering old woman, and your shop is crap. Or should I say Emporium? What sort of nonsense is that? Pretentious, that's what you are.'

Angela, ignoring her mother's assessment of her lack of refinement, instead watched her sister's face as she closed the dressing room curtain. Not for the first time since Judy announced her engagement had the thought, all is not well, popped into her head. She would love to ask what the problem was but knew she would only get knocked back. Angela had always been unsure if Judy hated her as much as their mother did. Wary, Angela felt, was more Judy's stance. She often caught her sending furtive looks her way as if assessing whether or not; Angela was going to explode.

'Thanks for your help, Billie. I've left the dress hanging up.'

'So you have chosen? Funny how I don't appear to be getting any say in it. Though I expect I will have to foot the bill!' Diving into her bag, Wendy rooted around to find her credit card.

Billie crowed with enjoyment, 'you can keep your money, Wendy. Lennie has already made plans to settle the bill. All I have to do is send him the invoice. Such a lovely man. So pleasant. So caring, only wanting the best for his daughter.'

Wendy's heart rate went into overdrive. How dare he humiliate me, especially in front of her! As for wanting the best for his daughter. *Huh!* Smarmy git. He only wants to make himself look good.

Angela smirked at her mother's embarrassment while Judy walked away, both aware that a storm was about to break as Wendy launched herself in front of Billie, thrusting her head forwards, fists clenched.

'Who do you think you are? Interfering old cow. Keep your nose out of our fucking business.'

Billie. Much to Angela's amusement looked her mother up and down, leaned forwards, making sure to enunciate each word, and said, 'get out before I throw you out. You are a disgrace. I feel sorry for Lennie being married to a harridan like you, and as for your children, you should be ashamed of yourself with how you act towards them.'

'Mum!' Judy shouted before Wendy could retaliate. 'That is enough. I am going. Either come with me now, or you can get the bus home. Thanks, Billie. The bridesmaids will be in next week to pick out their dresses. Unfortunately, I cannot come with them for their first fitting. However, they both know which colours I'd like them to choose.'

With a murderess look on her face, Wendy pushed passed, Angela. Yanked open the door and sped off, leaving Judy standing alone. Her rage focused only on a large drink.

*

Sitting in her mother's kitchen, it took all of Angela's self-control to keep a smile plastered onto her face. Again she was being regaled with the details of Judy's forthcoming wedding.

'I'm so pleased,' exclaimed her mother. 'That Paul has accepted our offer of not only paying for the wedding but also paying for your honeymoon. Spain will be lovely! He took a bit of cajoling. I told him. Nothing is too good for my Judy.'

Listening to her mother's gloating made Angela mourn her single state. Convinced if Gary were to propose marriage, her parents would then focus their good intentions on her for once. She was sick of hearing them talk about how Judy would soon be able to be a stay-at-home wife. A lady that lunches if she so wished. How Paul's rise up the corporate ladder; would enable their house to be renovated to the highest standard.

Just two days to go, and Angela would be glad when it was all over. Worrying over what Angela might wear, her mother was driving her mad. Usually, the thought of spending hours shopping was always more of a nightmare; than a joy to her. Angela decided to put aside her dislike of doing it to find something that would make her stand out from everyone else.

After her disastrous gym experience, she looked to see if there was an aerobics class she could join. Finding a pamphlet at the library, she had furtively put it into her bag. The title, Lose Fat Get Fit, seemingly with people like her in mind. The exercises were gentler than the gym, probably because the people doing them were even fatter, making her feel svelte next to them. The dancing was fun. Not a natural mover, even so, she found that once the music started blaring out, she, like the rest of the class, had to move. Not only did Angela's weight go down, but toning up her body meant she dropped a dress size.

Angela threw caution to the wind, and with her newfound confidence and suggestions from her classmates noted, she went shopping with a smile and found the perfect dress in a little shop tucked on a side street not far from where she lived.

Angela had always liked that her bust was on the ample side. Fortunately, when losing weight, it stayed the same. The cherry red silky dress clung to it like a second skin, and even though it fitted a bit snug around the waist, it flared nicely over her hips. To compliment the dress, Angela asked for a pair of high heels in a similar colour, more used to flat shoes, she wobbled as she put them on. Not wanting to squash her hair by wearing a hat, the assistant suggested a fascinator. Eyeing the black feathers with alarm, Angela allowed it to be placed on her head. The word chicken immediately sprung to mind. Looking at her appearance in the mirror, Angela decided that the whole ensemble would have even more impact with a bit of hair and makeup pampering. Plucking a small black clutch bag from the shelf, she turned this way and that, for once liking what she saw.

*

'**S**top fussing, mum!' cried Judy. For what felt like the hundredth time. Swigging another glass of champagne, her mother looked fit to burst. The pale lilac suit she was wearing did nothing for her, making the red blotchiness of her face stand out in contrast. The skirt was stretched taut across her belly, the zip in danger of breaking, while the tightness of the jacket made her arms look like sausages forced into their skins. When shown with pride what she intended to wear, Judy had tried diplomatically to suggest that perhaps her mother needed a bigger size.

The chilly look she had gotten while being told with utter conviction, 'I'm a size ten, always have, and always will be.'

Judy held her tongue, her mother's tone leaving her in no doubt of her anger.

Hearing the ping of her phone, Judy swore under her breath. Paul had sent five texts, telling her how much he loved her and that he could hardly wait to see her at the church. She had not replied. Judy wanted to marry him one minute, and the next didn't. She also didn't understand why she was worried. Paul was a good man. Kind and gentle. With her best interests at heart. Many of her friends were envious of the catch they thought she had managed to bag. Being good-looking and having prospects had not hurt either.

Judy had never been motivated by money and had seen the change in Paul since his last promotion. He now earnt, in her estimation, silly money and had gone from someone who was always careful to someone who liked to splash it around. The builder had assured him that the house renovations; would be completed by the time they were back from their honeymoon. He'd offered them a bonus if they finished in record time. Judy got given carte blanch to furnish it however she wished, and her mother had been ecstatic. She loved shopping and had already written out lists of things she thought they would need, taking over as usual and trying to organise Judy into the box she liked to keep her in.

Glancing over to her mother, seeing her slugging back champagne like there was no tomorrow, Judy wondered, not for the first time. Why had; she come to dislike her so much? Her mother often said to outsiders and her cronies, Judy and I are more like sisters.

For Judy, it was not so. She had to work hard to paper over the cracks she found in their relationship and to give it the appearance of love. Guilt played a big part in how she felt. Not standing up against the treatment of Angela weighed heavy on her mind.

Her relationship with her father was either full-on or non-existent. His love for Mark was never in doubt. Unfortunately, the sense of competition between them; made for uncomfortable viewing. Mark had youth on his side while her father had experience, and both thought that each was the better man for it.

Today, she knew, would be a case in point. Her father giving her away would be front and centre of the festivities, Mark as her brother pushed to the back. Something would happen. Somehow her brother would make sure that he was the one that people remembered. The rivalry between him and their father would, she was sure, rear its ugly head. The fact that it was supposed to be her and Paul's day would be immaterial to Mark. Being one up on their father was more important to achieve.

'Beautiful,' said her father as he entered the room. Frowning at her mother, he asked, 'have you been drinking? Or is that a silly question?'

'Lennie, Lennie, Lennie,' Wendy slurred in an imitation of a drunk. 'Unlike you, I can hold my liquor.' Bending down, she kissed Judy's cheek and hiccupped, 'don't trip my lovely. Keep hold of your father's arm. Those stairs are lethal.'

Winking at them, she downed her drink and sashayed out of the room.

The car journey was excruciating as she listened to her father harp about her mother's behaviour. Judy zoned out. Over the last few hours, she had been preened and plucked to within an inch of her life. Her hair, which she usually wore in a ponytail, now sat on top of her head like a hat. The complicated style that her mother had seen in a celebrity magazine Judy felt did nothing to enhance her, making her instead look like a relic from a bygone age.

Her mother, once again, had taken no notice of her feelings, brushing them aside as not worthy of thought. Judy stroked her dress which at least she had chosen. Billie made sure the bridesmaid's dresses, chosen by Sasha and Kim, stayed the same. Judy had worried that her mother would try to cancel the order, choosing something for them that she deemed more appropriate. Her thoughts kept flying to the words, do you take this man? Telling herself, willing herself to say yes. Her mouth dry and her brain fuzzy, Judy was not sure that she could.

*

For once, being forgotten worked to Angela's advantage. She had ordered a taxi to take her to the church, sure that with her new look, she could coerce someone into giving her a lift to the reception. Determined that her entrance would have the maximum effect, at the same time making sure that her mother would not be in any position to say anything or able to stop her.

While waiting, Angela sent her mother a picture of herself dressed in the pale blue suit which had been approved by her a week ago. The photo showed Angela's hair swept back into a classic chignon which her mother also insisted she had done.

Maureen had taken the picture the night before, giggling like teenagers at the thought of her mother's face when she saw what Angela was really wearing. Their loud laughter was let loose by the two bottles of prosecco they had drunk between them on an empty stomach.

Now, sitting in the taxi, Angela watched with amusement the arrival of the guests to the church, everyone air-kissing each other, compliments flying all over the place. Her mother honing in on some of the women brave enough to have added a splash of colour. Angela couldn't hear her words, only see her expression, enough to know that she was annoyed. Personally, the pastel colours they were all wearing, Angela felt, made them look washed out, like something from an old sepia photograph.

'How much longer?' asked the driver. Impatient to be off. 'Only we've been here nearly a quarter of an hour.'

Looking at her watch, Angela smiled and paid the fare making sure to give the driver a decent tip. Quietly closing the door before crossing the road, she checked that everyone outside had entered the church, hoping that with Judy's car due any minute, everyone would want to be inside waiting. Angela hurried across the road and followed a path leading to the back of the church. Pushing the door inwards, the noise from excited voices rose to greet her.

Entering the church, Angela let its coolness wrap around her and stood behind a pillar as she waited for the arrival of her sister. Her heart boomed inside her chest as Judy came into view, her father beaming with pride as she held onto his arm. Angela stepped out, and now that she had everyone's attention, she paused to savour the moment. Her disturbance was enough to make her mum gasp and her father glare. Loudly apologising to those who would have to move for her to sit down, Angela made her way along the pew.

Angela's mouth twitched to see her father's red face and bulging eyes as his temper rose at the sight of her. As a child, that look would frighten her and send her running in fear of the explosion to come. Today, her courage prevailed; as she straightened her dress and sat down, knowing her mother would want retribution for her disobedience.

She had told her to sit at the back and blend in. How, it was Judy's day, not hers. It would never cross their minds; if they were to stop excluding her, perhaps stunts like this would never happen in the first place. Bring it on, she said to herself, ignoring the disgruntled murmuring from the congregation at her entrance.

Wendy seethed with anger, her temper barely held in check as she tried to focus on the ceremony. She'd nearly jumped up, only Betty's firm hand on her arm holding her back.

'Don't react. That's what Angela wants. Trouble is her middle name. Relax and enjoy the moment. Look how beautiful Judy is; ignore Angela. You usually do.'

Lennie, as usual, wasn't helping, his muttering getting on her nerves which were already stretched paper thin.

'*Leave it*,' she hissed. 'I will deal with it.'

As everyone filed out, Wendy grabbed Angela's arm. Wrenching it away, Angela ignored her mother's angry words to follow her out of the church. Instead, she linked arms with the nearest man and marched out. She made sure to swish her dress as she did so. Relinquishing the man to his wife, Angela waited for the fun to begin.

'What happened to the blue suit we chose?' Wendy cried, trying to keep a smile on her face; and not let her anger flare. 'You're making a real show of yourself. Go home and change.'

The scowl soon disappeared after hearing the photographer call out her name.

'Coming,' she trilled. Before turning her back on Geoff and barking at Angela, 'stay out of the pictures.'

Watching her scuttle off, Angela held back a retort and paused to take in the scene. She had to admit that her sister did look lovely. Though still convinced that something was wrong. Judy's smile wasn't reaching her eyes. Paul hovered as usual, like a fly that wouldn't go away as he fluttered around Judy, his arm clamped tight around her waist as if proclaiming to all that she was now his.

Standing back and letting them all get into their positions, Angela suppressed a smile. She had no intention of being left out of the pictures. After all, what would have been the point of making this much effort?

Wendy made another grab for her wayward daughter, determined to make her go home and change. Shrugging her mother off, Angela walked away. Wendy's ire rose like a flame inside her. The need to smack the smirk off her daughter's face was so overwhelming it was making her body shake with anger. With more pictures taken, she had no time to deal with her as Lennie pulled her against him as the photographer was preparing to say cheese.

Once everyone was in place for another group shot, Angela casually strolled away as if she were leaving before nipping around the back of them. Using her elbows, she manoeuvred forwards to get between the bridesmaids as the flash went off. Wendy's eyes widened on seeing Angela's dress. It stood out like blood against their paler lemon ones, and her smile was even more noticeable against their looks of horror.

Wendy needed a drink. The chatter around her was like a barrage. Some were laughing at her daughter's antics, others saying how lovely she looked, wishing they had worn something brighter.

Angela was letting the dust settle. She had no intention

of going anywhere. A few days ago, she contacted the photographer Geoff to request a picture of her and Judy. Explaining that although estranged from her parents, she and her sister were close, and they wanted one together. Angela waited inside the church doors. As everyone began to break away into smaller groups, Geoff drew Judy aside to stand her in front of the porch. As his assistant bent down to fuss with her train, he signalled to Angela to come forwards.

Moving quickly, she clamped her hand tight to Judy's arm and whispered, 'smile.'

Judy jumped like a startled rabbit, and Geoff and a few stragglers began snapping away. Within seconds they were surrounded, angry faces all turned towards Angela. To hear them, she thought, you'd think she had killed someone. She smiled with the knowledge; that if she waited long enough, they would turn on each other. Hearing her name called, she looked up to see Gary striding up the path, a determined look on his face. Another grumpy one, she thought to enter the fray. He had expected to come with her. When she told him she wanted to go to the church by herself and that he could come later to the reception, he'd lost his temper and shouted at her.

'I'm supposed to be your boyfriend. Don't you see it as ironic that you continually moan about your family excluding you, yet, that is what you do to me?'

Then he accused her of being a hypocrite and making him feel worthless. Bored by his ranting, when he drew breath for another onslaught, she had mused to herself. Yadda, yadda, yadda, and tuned out.

'Did you bring your car?' she yelled over the noise everyone else was making. As she had thought, it hadn't taken much before her parents were at each other's throats.

'Let's go.'

Not waiting for his response Angela walked off. Mark tried to stop her. Slapping her arm, pushing his face up against hers with his anger barely contained, he demanded.

'What do you think you're playing at?'

'Leave her alone,' Gary spluttered, squaring up to him. While Cassie, as usual, waited beside Mark like a whipped puppy.

Angela smirked at the thought and leaned forwards before screaming, '*boo.*'

'Are you mad?' hissed Mark. Cassie let out a wail.

Angela stared at her brother, 'possibly.'

Before she could say anything else, Gary dragged her towards his car. Silence, Angela knew, would now be his weapon of choice. This time though, she was happy to sit with only her thoughts for company. Their relationship; was complicated by the fact that Gary didn't want one, but Angela did. The last time she had brought up the idea of them being together on a more permanent basis. He'd looked terrified, telling her.

'I like my own space. I don't like your family. Every time you come back from seeing them, you take your anger at their behaviour out on me. Besides, being with them is not enjoyable. Your brother Mark is up himself. I detest; how your father talks down to me, and your mother's mood swings scare me. Judy, the only sane one, but having caught her vacant expression a few times, I have my doubts about her as well, and as for Paul, he's plain creepy the way his eyes follow her every movement. The thought of being more involved with any of them does not have any appeal to me what's so ever.'

Nothing she said could change his mind, refusing on most occasions to come with her to see them or even entertain being in the same restaurant as they were. If there was any chance of their relationship progressing, Angela felt that Gary would want her to walk away. Let her family get on with their lives. Repeatedly telling her that even as an outsider, he could tell they didn't want anything to do with her.

'It's time to walk away from them and make a fresh start,' Gary had advised.

Angela heard his words but knew she would always crawl back, wanting their attention. Their love. When things got bad, she made a real effort to avoid contact. But, like a nagging tooth or a spot you had to pick, she couldn't stay away for long, no matter what they did.

*

Seeing her daughter leave, Wendy could only hope that after making a spectacle of herself, Angela would stay away from the reception. As their car turned onto the hotel's drive, Lennie swore. Looking over to where he was pointing, she could see Angela and Gary making their way toward the venue. Flinging open the car door, intent on stopping them, before she could, other cars started to pull up, everyone spilling out excited at the party to come. Surrounded, they could do nothing but follow them inside. Ignoring the offer of a drink by the waiter's handing them out in the doorway, Wendy pushed past and made a beeline for her daughter.

'To be clear, Angela, if you do anything more to spoil this day for Judy. I shall make sure that you pay dearly for it.' Turning to Gary, she barked, 'keep her in line if you know what's good for you.'

Without waiting for a reply, confident her message had got through. Wendy walked away, composing her face as she did so. Remembering her position as mother of the bride, she smiled, waving her hand to those she passed as if a queen on parade. Taking her seat, Wendy breathed a sigh of relief and clicked her fingers to attract a passing waiter. And not content with a drink from his tray, she took the bottle.

Only after the speeches ended did Judy find herself starting to relax. Through them, Paul had looked at her in the dopey way he had adopted lately, which made him seem more like a needy puppy than ever. Trying not to let her irritation show, Judy gazed around the marquee. As their eyes met, Angela raised her glass in a toast while her partner Gary looked fed up and bored.

'It won't last. I'd bet money on it. Gary is much too good for her!' Her mother said to Judy with relish.

Her mother's face had taken on a drunkard's sheen, her eyes unfocused and flitting from one person to another as if desperately looking for something. Meanwhile, her father and brother had their usual verbal competition, both wanting to get their point across by getting louder and louder. Cassie hovered like a spare part beside Mark, trying various ways to change the subject, but both ignored her. Sensing Judy watching her, Cassie tried once more to intervene. Flouncing away, she pulled out a chair, unable to stop a sigh as she slumped down onto it.

'Why are they always like this? They are getting nastier by the minute.'

'They have always been the same,' explained Judy. 'Their competitiveness is so ingrained between them that I think it is hard for them to stop. Best to stay out of it and let their disagreement run its course.'

As the night wore on and the drink flowed, Wendy finally relaxed. Lennie had done his speech as she had asked and kept it short. Everyone commented on how Judy and Paul made the perfect couple. All evening she had enjoyed basking in the glory of being the mother of the bride, loving the feeling of people she knew and those she'd barely met, telling her how fortunate Wendy was to have such a beautiful daughter and handsome son-in-law. Angela and Gary had obeyed her instructions and kept mainly to themselves, worried earlier when she had seen Angela talking to Judy. Wendy had gotten up to interrupt, only to be side-lined by Mark complaining that the room booked for him and Cassie; was cramped and in the attic. Whining like a spoilt child that she does something about it.

'For *fuck sake*, Mark, get a grip. After all, it's only for one night. You're hardly slumming it.'

Leaving him fuming at her words, Wendy went in search of Lennie. Sure he was up to his old tricks, she scoured the room, looking for him. His cronies had not seen him – or at least if they had, they weren't telling her – all they offered her was a smirk. Checking out the women, she tried to figure out who was missing. As far as she could tell, no one was. That meant it must be a member of staff. The busty one, she thought. The waitress, who had been displaying her charms while serving dinner.

Fuelled with anger Wendy climbed the hotel's stairs. With each step, the pressure inside her head built, wanting release. Flinging open the door to their room, she expected to find them inside and floundered at the sight of the empty bed. Further along, the corridor, a door opened. Wendy stepped outside to see Lennie pressed against the wall with the busty waitress attached to him like an alien as she smothered him in kisses. Nausea rose in Wendy's throat. Her gasp made Lennie catch sight of her. As he peeled the waitress away, Wendy pounced. Slapping her hard across the face, she shoved her onto the floor. Wendy heard Lennie's shouts like a roaring in her ears. Turning towards him, she pushed him against the wall and brought her knee up hard into his balls.

'*Bastard*,' she screamed into his ear as he slumped, moaning in agony.

Marching away, her pride in tatters, Wendy made for the bar. Her thoughts focused on drowning her sorrows. She knew it wouldn't make them go away. But it did at least stop her memories from surfacing. Lately, when sober, she had found herself getting maudlin and drifting into the past. Somewhere she would prefer not to visit. Feeling sorry had never been high on Wendy's agenda. She could never understand those that wallowed in feelings of guilt. After all, what purpose did it serve? Nothing would alter the outcome. And in her opinion. Sorry was a catchall word used to make those who wronged feel better. It had nothing to do with them feeling guilty over what they may have done. She knew she certainly didn't.

6

JUNE

All week, a litany of "Happy bloody families" had been thumping over and over inside Lennie's head, making him sigh at the thought of another father's day to get through. His children would arrive, and the sniping would begin, then Wendy would get drunk and start an argument while their friends would try to ignore the show they all made of themselves. Everyone Lennie knew assumed that he liked to be the life and soul of the party – it might have been true once, but that was before his life had taken a downward spiral, and unhappiness dogged his days. When at his lowest ebb, he liked to blame Wendy, but if being honest with himself – something he avoided, the guilt he held was all his…

Lennie's father was more absent than at home, left in his mother's care, which meant that he shouldered the full force of her complaints and hypochondria. Determined to change his life and make something of himself, he erected a mental barrier to separate himself from them. His mind was quick, and he liked numbers, so he set his sights on a career in finance and convinced his mother that hiring him a personal tutor would give him the edge he needed to succeed at university, reiterating to her.

'If I do well, it will enable me to get a worthwhile career, which means our life will be even better.'

Lennie also wanted to escape from his father. Whenever he returned home, the rows would begin, and his demands for money, if not quickly gratified, would turn violent. Passing his exams with flying colours allowed him to pick which university to attend. Telling his mother that he was moving to Suffolk had set her wailing.

'What about me? I'll be left all alone. Why not London? Then you can still live at home.'

Lennie had listened to her in horror because the last thing he wanted was to live with his mother while carving out a career. But he realised that leaving her in London wasn't an option. With all the ills she believed she suffered, Lennie knew from experience that it wouldn't be long before she began to make a nuisance of herself. The lesser of the two evils was in having her living nearby so that he could at least control any visits she proposed making. Deciding to make it a condition that she didn't tell any of her friends where she was moving to, meaning his father wouldn't be able to find them. Not that the man was interested in either of them, but he did like money – the only reason he came home, and the last thing Lennie wanted was for his father to turn up and ruin his new life.

With that in mind, he suggested that when he left to take up his studies at Suffolk University, she also moved, assuring her that he would find her a flat in Ipswich.

'Won't we be living together?' she had asked.

'No, mum, it is best if you have your own space, make a new life without the worry of dad turning up unannounced.'

Realising that by doing so, she could leave her husband and his violence behind, she jumped at the chance.

Starting his own financial services business had been exciting and scary in equal measures, and he quickly realised that his client's word of mouth was everything. Working hard to garner their trust, it hadn't taken long for the success he'd craved to materialise and enable him to have everything he thought he deserved. As an act of defiance against his old life, he changed his style and threw out all his clothes, bespoke suits, shirts, and handmade shoes to become his new armour. Lennie had often heard the phrase – good-looking, applied to him, and so playing to his strengths, he always made the extra effort to look and smell good and never left the house without first checking that everything about him was first-rate.

His mother informed him in one of her more observant moments as she watched him preen in front of a mirror.

'Well turned out.'

Lennie used it all as an act to draw the punters in, finding out early in his career that his clothes appeared to have as much importance to his clients as his competence did and that nobody would trust their finances to someone who did not look or act the part.

When he'd met Elaine, she had been like a breath of fresh air. Dee, another of his clients and Elaine's friend, had recommended him to her. Expecting their meeting would take place in his office, his suggestion that they meet instead for lunch had thrown her. They'd both laughed when she said.

'I thought Dee had gotten mixed up and set me up with a date instead.'

It didn't take long before they started seeing each other, with Elaine arranging meetings on the pretext of advice needed, quickly dropping the pretence in favour of having a good time. After a particularly long and languid afternoon spent in bed, she surprised Lennie by suggesting he move in with her.

'Please say you will? My parent's house is too big for one person. The probate on their wills has finished, and as a result, I have inherited lots of money sitting in various banks, saving schemes, and properties, and I could do with your help to sort it all out.'

Untangling everything was like a puzzle, something Lennie enjoyed. Disinterested, Elaine was unaware of what her portfolio contained. Confident he could sort it out, she gave him access to everything. Asking for her signature, she would quickly scribble her name, brushing him aside with a smile when he told her to read through the documents first, dismissing his explanations of why he needed her to sign with the words.

'I trust you.'

While she saw a mountain of paperwork, he saw an opportunity. Her disinterest was a boon and made any thoughts of him dealing honestly with her inheritance redundant. Waiting for the transfers to go through made him sweat with fear as he worried that his deceit would become known. His temper, short at the best of times, broke free with everyone, making Elaine think that the pressure of dealing with it all was getting to him.

'Why don't we get someone to help you?' she suggested.

Sweat coated his back, and it took all of his self-control to stay calm as his heart raced at her words.

'Honestly, I'm fine, just a bit run down. Everything is nearly sorted, why don't we go over everything at the weekend? I can explain what I have been doing.'

Fortunately, Elaine never mentioned the subject again, and their life settled down.

When she told him, Lennie thought that all of his dreams had come at once, and he could remember the day as if it was yesterday. He had been working in his home office on a particularly knotty problem. The rain and wind had been battering his windows, giving him a headache. Elaine arrived home, and Lennie, distracted, was less than welcoming before realising she was soaking wet and in a panic. Peeling off her coat and sitting down, she refused his offer of brandy and asked instead for a glass of water. Gulping it down, her hands shook.

Patting the seat beside her, she mumbled, 'sit down, Lennie. I have something I need to tell you, and I do … I know … if …'

Elaine's words tailed off as she sobbed into her hands. Wrapping his arms around her shoulders, Lennie pulled her close, fearful of what she was trying to say.

Elaine whispered into his neck, 'I'm so sorry … I'm pregnant.'

These were words Lennie had never thought to hear in conjunction with himself. Stunned, he sprang up, his thoughts all over the place, his heart racing.

Interpreting his movement as anger, Elaine muttered, 'I had no idea it had happened. If I'd have known, I wouldn't have …' as more tears ran down her face, she wailed, 'I'm sorry.'

Gathering her back into his arms, Lennie kissed them away, 'my darling, please don't say that I am so happy, a son of my own it's the best news you could have given me.'

'You don't understand. It's … not … I don't think that it …'

Lennie talked over her explanation, dismissing her worries with a smile.

'I know it could be a girl, but I am convinced; it will be a boy, and I would bet on it being so. You've made me so happy. Now stop crying. We have to celebrate. Oh no! You can't drink. Well, we will have to make a toast with water instead.' Filling a couple of glasses, he passed one to Elaine, announcing. 'To our son.'

He had religiously foiled all attempts by Elaine to get him to engage in any serious talks about the timing of her pregnancy. Or the possibility of the baby being a girl. Turning any conversation onto the fact that he had always wanted a son, and therefore he would have a son. When Mark was born, he was over the moon, couldn't get enough of him, and would tell everyone he met in the hospital what a miracle he was.

Unfortunately, cracks soon started to show in their relationship, Lennie had wanted to get married before the birth, but Elaine was adamant that she wanted to wait until she got rid of her baby bump. Nothing he said could convince her, then, he overheard her crooning to Mark.

'You're all mine, my own little man.'

Feeling paranoid, Lennie made her jump and Mark yell.

'*What* do you mean?' he'd snarled.

Elaine raged back, 'nothing, it was only baby talk.'

He couldn't get the words out of his head, making Lennie think that by not being married to her, somehow, his relationship with Mark could be at risk.

After his outburst, things with Elaine gradually deteriorated, and he would listen carefully, especially when she cuddled Mark, questioning everything she said for any hidden meanings. They started to row. Elaine began to pull away from him, and then when the baby blues hit, she would ignore Mark's cries. Leaving him wailing as she stared into space, Lennie would lose his temper and shout at her.

'Can't you hear him crying? Are you going mad?'

The loudness of his voice only served to make Mark cry louder as Elaine shrugged before walking away, leaving Lennie to deal with his unhappiness. Life became difficult for all of them as they became stuck in a cycle with Mark at the centre.

Catching him at a particularly low ebb, Lennie judged Wendy's come hither look for what it was. Always happy to flirt, he soon found that he was more involved with her than he wanted. She'd entwined herself around him like ivy. Everywhere he went, she seemed to be.

Then, one day during one of their many spats over her treatment of Mark, Elaine had flung at him that she did not now want to get married. Incensed, Lennie's face changed, his fists clenching as he let his anger show.

'What do you mean? What about Mark? We have to get married for his sake. Otherwise, he will be called a bastard. Besides, I thought you loved me.'

'Let's see how things go. We're already a couple, parents, and getting married will not change that,' she answered contritely.

For him, her words changed everything, searing into his brain and the love he had felt for her began to die.

*

Angela tried hard to hold her smile in place as her father once more made a fool of himself. A minefield as to what present to buy him, she had opted for the safety of a new shirt.

'Lovely,' he cried sarcastically.

The shirt fell to the ground when his friend Terry gave him a bottle of whiskey. Cavorting, like a loon, he soon had several glasses lined up and filled to the brim, demanding that everyone come and try.

Accepting no refusals, her father thrust a glass at Angela, announcing, 'It's father's day, so my rules apply. Stop being a party pooper.'

Everybody began to chant like they were involved in some drinking game and her parents were the loudest as they screeched at her to drink up.

Watching people was one of Angela's favourite things to do. Today though, after being made to drink the whiskey, she had retreated inside to get some water. Standing at the sink, she watched her father waving a spatula around to make his point as he half-heartedly turned over whatever was cooking on the barbeque. Her mother hovered, wanting to step in and take over; cooking, in general, she hated. Give her a barbeque, and she guarded it with her life, the only type of cooking she enjoyed and wanted to do. As they stood side by side, their body language made it easy to see how tense they still were, meaning that the screaming fight they had engaged in last night was still ongoing.

In the next village, dropping off some papers to a client, Angela had only gone around on the off chance, not something she usually did or was encouraged to do. Visiting always felt more like an appointment she had to make, with a timeslot that she mustn't go over.

As Angela opened the front door, she could hear her mother shouting.

'Who is she this time?'

Her parents were so wrapped up in their argument they were unaware that Angela had entered the house and was creeping along the hall to the dining room. Hiding beside the serving hatch, Angela was glad to see it wasn't closed and had to stifle a giggle as she listened.

Her mother was pacing back and forwards, coming in and out of her eye line. Her father appeared cowed, diminished as she ranted.

'You're a *bastard*. I've had enough, and if you don't stop messing around with other women. I will leave you.'

Even Angela knew that, with those words, her mother had lost the argument. He may leave her, but she would never leave him. That fact she felt was immutable...

She had tried once. Angela remembered her mother standing in the hallway, with Judy and Mark hovering behind her, their suitcases packed, and a determined look on her face. She, of course, hadn't been asked to join them. Instead, she had crouched on the stairs waiting to find out her fate as her father blocked their way out of the front door. The silence stretched. Her mother plucked at her bag, refusing to look her father in the eye. Judy and Mark were getting bored. Like Angela, they did not understand what game either of their parents was playing, especially when he pointed at Angela. Words forever etched in her memory.

'You can take her, but you are not taking Judy or Mark. They both stay here.'

Before her mother could reply or move, her father grabbed and pushed them into the living room. The three of them stood like statues in the hallway. Angela started to cry, earning her a dark look from both of them.

'You have got to stop. It's not fair. Each time it happens. I feel so humiliated,' her mother wailed and began to cry.

Her father had laughed, a burst of real belly laughter, and made himself cough.

'*Me*, that's a good one, especially as you are the one drinking, and you are also the one who always manages to lose control.'

Angela tried to remember what had happened next. She knew that she woke up in the night having wet the bed. But she also knew that no one would come to help her, her tears of self- pity only she had brushed away.

Returning, her thoughts back to the moment and the garden. Angela grabbed a bottle and moved a chair into the shade. As she sat down, a voice she recognised and didn't much like boomed out.

'Lennie, Wendy.'

Peter, an old friend of her parent's, clutched a bottle in one hand and his wife Betty's in the other as they lumbered down the steps together. Overweight, red-faced, and obnoxious, the type Angela hated, the sort who only spoke to your breasts and, if given half the chance, would also have their hands on them. He and his wife didn't like Angela; they had a history…

At another one of her parent's garden parties, bored with listening to them sing out of tune to songs Angela did not even recognise, she went inside to make herself something to eat. Busy making her sandwich with the whoops and shouts from outside getting noisier, she was unaware of Peter coming up behind her. Angela found herself pushed against the kitchen counter by an unattractive lump of blubber blocking her exit. Twice she asked him to move.

'I am pretty sure you don't mean that,' he leered. At the same time, winking his left eye suggestively.

His beery breath was the ultimate insult as it wafted over Angela's face, incensed, she punched him and made sure to put as much power into it as she could; his head snapped back, his body shifted, and her knee shot out. As he bent over and shrieked in pain, she grabbed a chopping board and brought it down hard onto the back of his head, feeling the floor shake as he fell.

Still enraged, she went in search of his wife Betty, not difficult to spot, the dress she wore a stretchy material which not only managed to empathise her many rolls of fat but made her look as if they were about to explode out of it. Unlike her husband, Betty always tried to ignore Angela; grabbing her by the arm, Angela twisted and pinched it hard – something Betty had done to her when younger, making her yelp before snarling into her ear.

'I think your disgusting husband may need your help, as I have nobbled the pervert.' Angela grinned like a loon as Betty's eyes went wide in panic; with a sneer, she told her, 'wobble along, fatty.'

Smiling at the memory, she could see that Peter had not changed as he pulled her mother into a hug, and his hand began snaking across her backside. Unlike Angela had done, her mother slapped his arm playfully, laughed, and wriggled away. Angela stared at him and, as if feeling its weight, Peter turned.

She raised her glass, at the same time mouthing the word, 'pervert.'

His face flamed red, embarrassment or rage Angela, could not have cared less as long as he kept well away from her.

Next to arrive was her brother Mark, his insipid girlfriend Cassie trailing behind like some stray he had picked up on the way. Angela had laughed when her father had pronounced on an earlier occasion that she was very ethereal looking with her pale skin and long curly hair. Vacant is how Angela would describe her and her hair. In her book, frizzy does not mean curly. She thought Mark only probably liked Cassie because she was mostly silent, reminding Angela of those nodding dogs in the back of a car and made looking thick into an art form. Whenever he spoke, she would gaze awestruck as if his words were those of a messiah coming back to earth to save the world.

*

Mark, for once, did not want to go to another of his parent's numerous gatherings, even if it was in aid of father's day. The scene, he was sure, was already set for a row. His parents seemed unable to spend more than a minute in each other's company before tearing into each other, and he was getting fed up listening to it. Since meeting Cassie, his life had changed, and although he still hid his true self in the shadows from family and friends, the relief at not having to at least lie to himself anymore was a release. Mark had also changed how he acted toward the people he worked and dealt with; used to him shouting or losing his temper over the smallest of things, when he began giving out compliments instead, they all looked startled, as if someone had jumped out at them shouting, joking!'

He could hear Cassie yelling.

'Mark, hurry up.'

Why? She was so keen to go he was finding it hard to fathom. Angela was likely to be rude; his mother always smirked whenever she tried to make any conversation, and the less said about his father's behaviour towards her, the better. Judy was the only one that at least tried to make any effort, but if he were honest though, Mark felt at times that she only did so to wind his mother up.

Because of the unwritten rule at any gathering, whether at his parent's or anyone else's, the expectation was that Judy would stay by his mother's side. Marriage to Paul, Mark felt, would not change anything, and their mother would still expect to come first where Judy was concerned. In regards to his brother-in-law, he found him intensely irritating and could see clashes between them happening. He, another one who wanted Judy's constant attention, his eyes, like a puppy, followed her every move, and as Mark watched him track her, he couldn't help the thought that she must find it stifling, if not a tad creepy. Then there was his father, who could be very childish by either trying to get one up on him or crowing about how brilliant Paul was. Mark knew that he should keep calm and not react where Paul was concerned, but he had a short fuse and found it hard not to fall into the traps his father set for him.

'Have you got the present,' asked Cassie for the third time. While flicking a brush through her hair, making her curls bounce.

'Mark!' she exclaimed when he didn't answer, 'come on, it won't be that bad, your father will probably get drunk, and your mother assuredly will; with a little bit of luck, they will both be so out of it we can all enjoy the party,' she pronounced hopefully.

Mark could only laugh at her optimism while thinking how lucky he was to have found a partner who was on his side and who could understand him better than he did himself. If he had one wish, it would be that she would cease going on about his family history. Their last conversation about it had ended in a row with him shouting.

'Just because you live and breathe your ancestry doesn't mean I feel the same way about mine. My parents are more than enough to deal with, and the thought of finding any more like them terrifies me.'

*

Last to arrive were the golden couple, as Angela had recently dubbed them. Judy hesitated, and Paul stood at the top of the steps as if listening to applause only he could hear. Angela smirked.

Unlike her parent's greeting, 'oh, it's only you.' When she arrived, they had gotten a much more effusive one.

Still tanned from their latest holiday together brought back her disappointment at not being asked to go with them. Angela could barely contain her anger, and it flared at the injustice of the treatment her family insisted on doling out to her. Her mother had taken great delight in phoning her to say that they would miss her birthday as they had a last-minute opportunity to join some friends in the south of France.

'I'm sure you understand, you are not a child, and besides, I'd have thought that perhaps Gary or Maureen may ...' Into the silence, unable to help herself from making it worse, she gabbled, 'isn't it great that Paul has managed to get time off so that he and Judy, can come as well.'

'*Fuck you*, mother,' she yelled as she slammed down the phone.

Again Angela had been clearly shown that no matter what she did or how she acted, her family would always leave her outside their family group. Her head pounded to hear her mother's thoughtless words, and like a caged animal wanting to be released, the vengeful thoughts which had been bubbling up since the start of the year pulsed like a beacon inside her head.

Fortifying herself by filling her glass from the bottle of red that she had purloined for herself earlier, Angela ambled over to the edges of the group to hear her mother gush with excitement at Judy.

'Oh my, don't you look wonderful, such a lovely colour, is it a designer dress?'

Her father joined in, his compliments though aimed at Paul. Shaking his hand as if he were a visiting dignitary. Much to Angela's amusement, she saw a flash of jealousy wash over her brother's face. Seeing the six of them all standing close together, Angela realised, and not for the first time, what she had thought of as a close bond running between them was not true, and the air between them was taut with tension. Angela thought this interesting, as usually any animosity flying around would be directed toward her, and realised, looking at them now, that not everything was as rosy between her family as they tried to make everyone believe. Deciding that she would enter the fray, Angela stood beside her mother, trying not to react when she flinched away.

*

Another get-together to endure, Judy thought as she sipped her drink each invite she received made her question why her parents arranged them. Rows would emerge out of nowhere, fights break out, and as the evening wore on, old grievances and sleights, still festering, were re-examined to apportion blame. Tears would flow, and the party would quickly degenerate as the atmosphere changed.

Father's Day was always a case in point; it would start okay, but it wouldn't take long for Mark to start competing with their father over the tiniest thing. Sarcasm would rear its ugly head, and her brother would switch from saying, dad, to Lennie. Her father would retaliate by calling her brother Mucky Mark, which he hated. Then there was how her mother acted toward Angela. Her tolerance level for her sister's presence; appeared to be measured by how much alcohol she had drunk. And in her case, her mother always had to fuss over what type of clothes Judy was wearing. Her head pounded, and she wanted nothing more than to leave. As if sensing Judy's thoughts, her mother clamped her arm through hers, like a vice holding her firmly in its grip, never to let go.

'Isn't this nice,' Angela cooed sweetly. 'All the family together for once.'

Her father's gaze snapped towards her, wincing at her tone of voice as she glared at them and drawled.

'Did you all have a lovely time? Was the weather hot? And what about your meals? I bet they were delicious, and I'm sure with mum there, the drink hardly stopped flowing.'

'Do not start,' snarled Judy. We heard that Gary couldn't come. Mum thought it might make you feel like the odd one out.'

Angela let the silence lengthen before adding calmly, 'aren't I always and where you got the idea about Gary …' she glanced at her mother, who for once had the good grace to look away.

Turning back to Judy, Angela demanded. 'Explain to me why you find it so difficult to have a life of your own. You cleave to mum and dad as if afraid to let them out of your sight and jump to every demand they make. How are you going to get on now that you are married? I'm sure Paul will not want to join you in always being at their beck and call.'

Under her onslaught, Judy crumbled, their father rushing to gather her into his arms.

'Ignore, Angela, she's just being a bitch,' he crooned as if Judy were a baby who needs comforting after a nightmare.

Paul hovered, obviously unsure of his place within the family, indecisive as to whether to pull Judy away from her father or attack Angela. Turning, he chose to ignore them and shouted his annoyance at Angela.

'Why do you always have to be so nasty? Selfish, that's what you are, and I suggest you take a long hard look at your behaviour.'

Angela could barely stop laughing as he pointed and wagged his finger like a headmaster telling off a pupil. Her mother acted like a deranged maniac as she clapped and danced around them.

Her brother may not like her, but he disliked Paul more. Angela smiled as Mark jumped into the argument, their voices getting louder as each tried to get their point across. Their parent's ongoing row once again burst forth, to be shaken, stirred, and made public. Screaming at each other as blame flew about like bunting in the wind, Angela stepped away.

Calm now, Judy watched Angela leave. Left surrounded by their warring family, wishing she was brave enough to follow. Unsurprised to see, as usual, the friends of her parents were carrying on eating and drinking, ignoring the show they were all making of themselves. None of them had any idea of how she felt about her relationship with her parents and Paul, and if they did, Judy was sure they would be shocked. She may appear to be the dutiful daughter and wife on the outside, but her inner self didn't feel the same. And if anyone bothered to ask, Judy would have said one word; trapped.

When she gave in her notice at work, Paul assumed that Judy would now stay home and ignored her when she added that she would be looking for something else to do.

'I am so glad you have packed it in. Now we can start a family. I can't wait.'

His longing for a baby sent Judy into a rage, but it was like talking to a child. Explaining to him that nobody gets a nursery ready before being pregnant; fell on deaf ears as he nodded, appeared to listen, and then carried on as if Judy had never spoken. Another bone of contention between them was the part-time job she had taken in their local garden centre. The eccentricity of people and their plants was the only thing keeping her sane. Paul was not impressed, making it plain that he thought it was beneath her and would cluck each time she left in the morning and sigh when she came home. The more he fought, the more entrenched Judy became. Seeing it as a point of honour, believing that if she gave in to him, it would be like giving up a piece of herself, admittedly, she didn't like the cold, wet days, but even they were preferable to sitting at home with nothing to do. His insistence that she didn't need to go out to work was at the heart of their many disagreements and made her want to scream.

'What would I do all day?' she'd asked, 'I have nothing to do, and because of my mother's continual interference, this house is more like a show home. Look at it. Beige walls, heavy furniture, she even ordered us the same kitchen as hers. I didn't want it. And like a couple of giggling teenagers, you both ignored my suggestions and even went so far as to cancel orders I had made. How do you think it makes me feel? This house is not my home. It's an extension of my mother's and just another box to keep me in.'

*

When home, Angela phoned Maureen, 'you should have seen how quickly they fell apart.'

Although impressed, her friend once again repeated that Angela should step up her campaign, telling her.

'Rows are all well and good, but what do they achieve apart from giving you a momentary sense of victory? If you are serious about causing them real trouble, then you have to be more effective in how you go about achieving it, especially if you want to damage them in the same way you believe they have you.'

When Maureen previously spoke like this, Angela had always sheared away from doing anything tangible, and the only real material damage she had done so far was to her father's prized BMW. Maureen had convinced her that it was a golden opportunity too good to miss, egging her on to scratch and gouge it with a key. Her father had been even more upset to find out from the police that his car was the only one targeted, sending her mother into panic mode, telling anyone who would listen that someone was out to get them. Damaging the car had been fun, but it wasn't enough to sate her hunger for more. The thoughts of revenge, which Angela had entertained at the beginning of the year, kept nudging her to do something about them. The real question she had to ask herself was, how far was she prepared to go in slaking her thirst to see her family suffer?

7

JULY

As Gary handed Angela a cocktail, she could see her smile reflected in his mirrored sunglasses. Since the Easter fiasco, things between them had been tense, and this holiday was supposed to rectify the situation.

'Cheers,' they both said together.

Gary's phone pinged, alerting him that he had another message. Each time he picked it up, his face creased in a frown.

'Problems?' asked Angela. Thinking here we go again. His bloody nightmare of a mother!

'What? No. Someone from work. You know what it is like when you take on newbies, always wanting you to hold their hands.'

'Why are they bothering you? You're not even the one in charge. George is. Why are they not bothering him instead?' she snapped. Annoyance made her tone sarcastic.

Any time they went anywhere, Angela thought. It was bad enough that Gary's mother had to make contact as if out of his orbit, she could not function properly. The last thing Angela needed was for someone else to jump on the bandwagon and start making a nuisance of themselves. This holiday was supposed to be Gary's way of making amends, assuring her it would be all about her and what she wanted to do. Angela was to say, and he would do his best to make it happen. So far, that had not turned out so well.

Bored with lounging around the pool, Angela suggested they hire a car.

'Take a picnic, and find a secluded beach. What do you think? It will be fun.'

In his infinite wisdom, Gary decided it would be much more fun to hire a couple of pushbikes instead. Hot, sweaty, and bad-tempered, they arrived at the beach to find everyone else had had the same idea. Determined to enjoy their picnic, unfortunately, the wine had warmed in the heat, the cheese had melted, and the bread had gone hard. The next day Gary decided that they must visit the old town. Thwarted, once again, halfway there, the bus broke down, and they all had to walk back.

Tonight was supposed to make up for the last couple of days. The restaurant Gary had booked was supposed to be famous for its ambience, customer service, and fine dining. However, the continual messages throughout the day had put them both on edge.

Gary downed another glass of Shiraz, now on their second bottle, and most of it drunk by him. He was well on his way to being legless. Angela, for once, was stone-cold sober. Something was up. She had no idea what. The pinging of his phone had followed them to the restaurant. Whoever this newbie was, they had been relentless. When Angela had tried to speak to Gary about what was going on, he had dismissed her enquiry, telling her, it is nothing, forget it, before surprising her by turning his phone off, something she had never seen him do before.

In the morning, Gary, still grey-faced and sick from his hangover, didn't want to venture outside and decided to lounge in bed. Annoyed at his decision, Angela got dressed, enjoyed a leisurely breakfast, and decided to take a boat trip. Filled with middle age couples, she again felt the odd one out. Surprised to find today, as if by mutual consent, she was not left alone for longer than five minutes before someone would sit next to her and regale her with their life story. Angela usually would have been bored stiff. Instead, she had surprised herself by how much she had enjoyed listening to their stories, feeling that being on holiday had loosened her up. Finding herself able to laugh and ask questions, she even enjoyed the gentle ribbing she had gotten for leaving her boyfriend alone. The only time Angela felt some of her old feelings taking hold was when Marge and Dan, a couple, who had taken a particular interest in her, showed her the pictures of their family. Children and grandchildren all piled in together. Them in the middle, their love for each other practically jumping from the page.

When Angela returned to the hotel room, Gary was nowhere around. She found him by the pool. The curvy blonde he was trying to impress was the first to spot her looming over them. Angela walked away. Waving at the barman, she ordered a large gin and tonic. Breathless from his encounter, Gary sidled up, snapping his fingers for the same.

'Did you have a good day,' he asked. Trying to sound nonchalant instead, it came out sounding peevish.

'Not as good as you appear to have had,' replied Angela flippantly. She glared at Gary, who at least had the presence of mind to look shamefaced.

'We got talking,' he stammered. 'Small world. Vicky lives in Ipswich,' he added. As if Angela had asked.

'In case you are interested, I have had a lovely day. Shame you were not up to coming with me,' she snapped. 'Especially as this holiday was supposed to be about spending time together.'

Miss curvy blonde from their holiday had been on the same flight as them when they returned home. Angela had a sneaking suspicion they had been meeting each other behind her back. After she read through their texts and emails, her worst fears were confirmed. She had always known Gary's password from the first time she had been to his flat. The yellow post-it note sat proudly on his desk. When she had mentioned that he should not leave it lying around, he had confessed that he usually used the same password for everything. GAZ6666, thought Angela, was hardly a difficult one to remember. Seeing that he had another post-it note tucked inside his wallet, she concluded that for him, it was.

Logging into his account, Angela found his inbox flooded with emails. Vicky's flowery prose in many of them told Gary how she hadn't been able to stop thinking about him, how nice he was, and especially how she fancied the pants off him! Those she skimmed over.

Even though for Angela, Gary's looks were what her ideal man would look like, she still found it hard to imagine anyone else thinking the same and was convinced, for Vicky, it had more to do with his money than his personality or looks. She knew that for some women, the whiff of a full wallet was enough to bring them running.

Angela had only found out where Vicky worked by accident, her usual hair salon was having a refit, and in need of a quick haircut, she phoned a new one that had recently opened. A creature of habit, right up until the time of the appointment, she thought of cancelling. Hesitating at the door and glancing inside, Angela was shocked to see Vicky talking on the phone. Stumped as to what to do, sure she would recognise her, Angela backed away and into a woman she vaguely knew.

'Are you going in?'

'Sorry, I'm a bit… Sorry, I can't,' Angela blathered.

'Whatever's the matter? You look as if you've seen a ghost.'

Recognising her voice, Angela finally remembered her name. She pointed.

'See her, find out what you can. I will be over there.' Before Sheila could answer, Angela walked away and crossed the road.

Hair swinging as she walked, Sheila pushed open the door. Ordering her coffee, she asked Angela if she wanted a fresh one. Trying to hold back her eagerness to know what Sheila had found out, Angela complimented her on her haircut, how it suited Sheila much better than how she usually wore it.

'Vicky is recently divorced and is the manager, not the owner,' explained Sheila. 'She lives in the flat above the salon. She took over three months ago when the boss Lynda became ill and couldn't work anymore. Meena, my stylist, doesn't like Vicky. Up herself and a bit of a man-eater was the impression she gave me. I asked if she was seeing someone, and Meena described your Gary. He came in to see Vicky a couple of weeks ago, she made out that he was a rep, but Meena didn't buy it. Saying all the reps she had ever had dealings with were not wearing such expensive suits and certainly never took anyone out to lunch.'

Angela had suspected as much even before finding their emails. It still hurt to have her suspicions confirmed. She was interested to know what Gary was going to do now because, as far as their friends knew, they were still very much a couple. Angela decided that she needed a plan.

Even without Vicky on the scene, he was losing interest. The problems she had with her family were not helping. Angela knew he would never tell her outright. Gary wasn't brave enough and with the expectation that she would be annoyed. She knew that he would try to do it on the sly. Somewhere he felt safe with others around, hoping that Angela wouldn't make a scene.

She had changed, and Gary, like her family, had not even noticed. The pub crawl, which they did every year with his friends in aid of charity, was at the end of the week. Their names were on the list. Angela was sure that would be when he would do it. Surrounded by his mates, and as most of them were his, including the women, he would feel emboldened to act. Except, Angela was not going to let him. Instead, she would let him think she was going and that she had no idea what he may intend to do.

Avoiding speaking to him in case it made him change his plans, Angela left it to the last minute. Phoning the landline of the Crown, she asked the landlady, Hazel, to tell Gary that Angela was ill and that she would be staying with her friend Maureen. Going on to say that Gary was to have a good time and wasn't to worry, and she would ring him tomorrow when she was feeling better. Hazel, unsure why she should be deemed the messenger in the age of mobile phones, nevertheless agreed to pass on the message.

The spare key Angela had found early in their relationship, which Gary had no idea that she had, she now put to good use. Turning her phone onto vibrate, she made her way up to his flat.

Listening for any doors opening or the sound of footsteps approaching, she waited before opening his front door. She paused. She knew there was no one home, yet if caught, she had no explanation for being there. Pull yourself together, Angela muttered. Before locking and bolting the door.

Gary's hall, she'd always thought, looked like something straight out of a fancy magazine shoot, with its black and white tiled floor and hand-made cabinet sitting underneath the mandatory ornate mirror. An enormous display of flowers rested on top of its polished surface. The vase was the first to go.

'Whoops,' she cried as she pushed it onto the floor. The cabinet was the next recipient of gouging from Gary's very own key. What a lovely pattern. She thought. Liking the swirls that she had created. The first door she knew led to his bedroom. Angela sniffed, and Vicky's cheap perfume hung like a foul stink over everything. Backing out, she opened the door to his lounge and stood in shock. Photos of the two of them were everywhere. Angela's face was nowhere on show. She yanked open the cupboards. They had taken loads of pictures of them together.

Frantically, Angela searched for any evidence that would show; that she was still important to him. She found nothing. Anger made her blood boil. Even though she craved commitment and wanted nothing more than a long-term relationship, she also knew that she couldn't envision it happening with Gary. If honest with herself, she liked being his girlfriend. But she didn't love him. Also sure that he felt the same way about her. What she hadn't expected or wanted was to be confronted so starkly with his betrayal. She needed a drink.

Slugging back the white wine she had found stacked in his overlarge fridge freezer, she walked into his dining room and again felt bereft. The whole back wall was one enormous collage of large pictures. It was easy to see that Vicky was trying too hard. Her smile was bright, but her eyes were predatory, and in some of them, Gary looked scared. Good, thought Angela. He should be. He didn't know it yet. But his life was about to take a turn for the worse.

Contemplating, what she was going to do, she poured herself another glass of wine. Washing up the glass she had used, Angela nearly put it back inside the cupboard. Instead, she swept the whole lot onto the floor, jumping as fragments of glass flew everywhere. Pulling open the doors to the fridge-freezer, Angela took out all the food and mashed it into his pristine island. Doing the same with the cupboards, she tossed tins and bottles against the wall. Some broke, and others bounced against it. Next was the wine. Both she and Gary liked red and was surprised to see six bottles of white waiting on ice while two more unopened boxes sat in the pantry. Madame's preference Angela was sure. Removing the bottles from the fridge, Angela emptied them over his sofa, leaving them where they fell. She found a cricket bat to use on the ones in the boxes and left them smashed and leaking over the floor.

The collage was still bugging her, the urge to slash and tear it down making her hands shake. Instead, Angela used a knife to carefully remove the pins laying each picture down on the table until the wall was empty, then she put the pins back. She stared, asking herself, are you mad? Ripping out the drawing pins, Angela then shredded the pictures with her hands and scattered the pieces like confetti all over the room. She used the cricket bat to strike the photos from shelves in the living room, the glass tinkling as they smashed. Angela stomped on them like a child in a tantrum, crushing them into the carpet. Removing the cushions from the sofas – still smelling of her rival even with the addition of the wine she had poured over them, she used a pair of scissors, hacking into them in a frenzy before moving into the bedroom.

The bed dominated the room. Angela tried not to think about the pair of them in it and got on with destroying the bed linen. Madame's stink once again wafted as the sheets came off. Prising off the lid of the small tin of red paint she had brought, she flicked the contents over the walls, thinking very arty as she poured the rest over the duvet and mattress.

Adrenaline rushing through her veins, Angela next turned her attention to the walk-in wardrobe. Seeing all the shirts she had bought for Gary, still hanging and still used by him, nearly made her falter. However, it did not stop her from using scissors to cut off all the sleeves and hack at their necks before pulling them from the hangers and flinging them onto the bed. Steeling herself, she yanked the dresses off their hangers, piling them onto the growing mound of clothes. Next came the shoes and bags. Glad to be wearing gloves, Angela tipped underwear out of their boxes. Lace and silk, all with madam's distinctive smell. The scissors flashed the pile of rags in front of her growing. The sparkly dresses of Gary's new darling Angela took particular pleasure in destroying. Sequins flew as they catapulted around the room. Exhausted, she suddenly came over a bit faint. Holding onto the door, she groaned as nausea hit. Knowing that she mustn't be sick, she slid down the wall. Her heart was hammering, her stomach rolling. She had to go before she – clamping her hand across her mouth, Angela mustered all her strength to stand up. Unlocking the door, remembering to be quiet, she gagged her way down the stairs. Outside she gulped at the fresh air like a hungry fish earning her a wary look from a passer-by.

Angela phoned Gary in the morning to tell him she was feeling better. He had ignored her sorry for letting him down and instead ranted at her about what had happened. Angela had to work hard to feign any sympathy as she listened to him near to tears tell her how someone had gone through his flat like a whirlwind.

'My clothes have been cut up and are now in tatters, the rest, destroyed beyond repair. The whole flat paint splattered. Who would do this kind of thing?' He had shouted in despair.

'Has anything been stolen?'

For a moment, Gary went silent, forgetting that she was supposed to be sympathetic. She snapped.

'Well?'

'Nothing, just destruction.'

Explaining to her that if he had gone straight home, he might have caught them. After the pub crawl, and in no fit state, he and a couple of others had stayed the night in his friend's house. In the morning, John dropped the others off, taking Gary back to his flat to pick up his gym kit. On opening his front door, the sight that met them was like something out of a nightmare.

'Glass from the shattered hall mirror lay all over the floor. My cabinet was scratched. The bathroom was also destroyed and sprayed with red paint, as was the kitchen. The cupboards and shelves are all broken. Everything now lay in a broken heap in the middle of the floor. The bedroom looked like a red tornado had passed, spraying paint over everything. Even the curtains; had been wrenched off of their poles. The police had canvassed his neighbours, telling him he was unlucky for it to have happened when most of them were either out for the night or on holiday and those left too far away to hear anything.'

Making sure to appear sympathetic, she told him she would come round and help him clean up. On entering the flat, the shock she felt at its destruction was visceral. Now in the light of day, she felt aghast that she alone had done this. Gary was distraught, his home destroyed.

'I feel violated and scared that someone could hate me so much. I can't go back. I will get a cleaning company in to sort the mess out. The flat can go on the market.'

Telling Maureen what had happened – not her part in it – she didn't seem surprised. Reminding Angela that she had never trusted Gary, and had always been convinced, that the circles he moved in were a bit dodgy.

'After cheating on you, he deserves everything he gets.'

Angela could only agree, still shocked at the level of violence that she had used, unsure if the replays she had in her head were a good thing or her brain's way of making her feel guilty about what she had done.

*

Tossing and turning all night, Mark struggled to get his mother's words out of his head. It was the look on her face that had made the words stick. Once again, she had been the life and soul of the party and had drunk too much. Usually, he ignored anything she said when under the influence of drink, and if anyone had asked, without hesitation, he would have said that he loved his mother, but if given time to reflect on the question, he would not be so sure. As far as he could remember, only Judy's importance was a feature in her life, and he still found it hard to understand why his mother acted so differently toward her.

Surprisingly, although he'd never felt jealous of their bond, he used to wish that sometimes some of the love given to Judy would also come to him. Cuddles and kisses for her were long and drawn out. Angela's were non-existent, while for him, it was a peck on the cheek and a swift hug before being pushed away to enable her to pick up a drink. His childhood memories were of the smell of alcohol on her breath and sarcasm on her tongue.

Easy to see, as pointed out by Angela, which of his parents had given him his sarcastic manner. His mother's dislike for his sister had always nagged at him. Yes, when younger, she had been a perfect brat, her actions at times embarrassing. Even so, he couldn't see how her behaviour had been any different from how he and Judy used to act. He also didn't understand why Angela's behaviour, in particular, would make their mother hate her. Mothers and daughters, Mark knew, like fathers and sons, could have a fraught relationship. The one he had with his father often left him cold.

Mark wondered, and not for the first time, why they both felt the need to be so competitive, especially with each other. As a child, it had not been as bad. Like his mother, he found loving his father not an easy thing to do. Instructions on what Mark should or shouldn't do barked as if Mark were a soldier in the army. His parents had two sides to how they acted in public to those who didn't know them, they appeared united, but in the confines of the family unit, they were often at war with each other. The dispute was always the same, her drinking versus his womanising.

When still at school, Mark had been presented in his teens on coming home to find his father making love to another woman. Sent home from school when not feeling well, he had let himself into the house. Standing in the hall, Mark paused. The air felt charged, like when a storm was coming and about to break. Even though he'd never had sex, he knew enough to understand that the noises he heard left him in no doubt that that was what was happening. His mother was away with her girlfriends, supposedly going to a spa. He'd overheard her on the phone cackling with her friend Iris, making sure that the sanctuary retreat they were going to would have a bar that sold alcohol; and not juice.

Mark crept up the stairs while avoiding the second one from the top. The noise had gotten louder. The door of his parent's bedroom was ajar. Peering around the opening, his hand flew to his mouth to stifle a gasp. The memory of what he'd seen would always stay with him. Rooted to the spot, he heard his father saying he would bring up some more champagne. Mark scrambled down the stairs, opened the front door, and banged it shut. Flinging himself onto the bottom stair, hands holding his head, nausea rose into his throat.

'What are you doing home?'

Flinching as his father touched his shoulder, Mark groaned, 'I don't feel very well.'

Pulling him up, his father led him into the lounge.

'Lay down. I will get you some water. Best stay down here. I'll bring you a bucket.'

As soon as his father closed the door, Mark leaped up. All he could make out was whispering as his father let out whoever he had been upstairs with out of the house. Hearing the front door close, Mark lay back down and clutched a pillow to his stomach. Knowing his father was looking at him, he kept his eyes closed.

After that, whenever his mother went away, he would race home from school to see if his father had been entertaining. The tell-tale sign was the empty bottles of expensive champagne left in the recycling bin. Whenever they went out anywhere, he also began watching his father. It soon became clear to Mark; that just like his father's best friend Peter, he also thought that any woman they met was fair game. Their comments and innuendos would make him feel ashamed to be in their company.

'Don't saddle yourself with a girlfriend. Play the field. Get some notches under your belt,' words they both spouted, their nudges and winks soon wearing thin.

Many of his friends had the same view. Girls were seen only as something to chase, catch and discard. They would hang out hidden from view behind some old abandoned garages. Swigging cans of lager and smoking, they would regale each other with their conquests by rating the girls they had slept with from one to ten. Mark tried hard to join in, but his experience with girls was minimal. He liked them, but he had no fancy for them. He knew that he hid it well. No one yet had guessed where his true proclivities lay. His father would never understand, and if his mother knew, she would find a way to use the knowledge against him.

Since working for Terry and running his business, Mark knew he had gained confidence. Always a good actor. No one knew how much he suffered from self-doubt. Sometimes he went over the top – usually, when he was anxious, his only recourse was to make someone else suffer. Stuck with his persona of being a bastard, he had gone too far down the path of playing the hard-nosed boss to pull back. Until he met Cassie, unlike his other girlfriends, instead of annoying him by whittling on about a load of nonsense, she hung onto his every word, endearing her to him and making him feel good about himself.

Although his family had accepted her, he wished that Angela would stop taking the piss and his father stop focusing on the size of her breasts.

Even though they had not discussed the subject, Mark had convinced himself that Cassie knew he was gay. The first time they had sex, it was all he could do not to throw up afterwards. Fortunately, Cassie went straight to sleep while Mark crept out and slept on the couch. Waking up in the morning, he'd found it hard to look her in the face. Cassie ignored his sour expression and chatted away as she ate her breakfast while cheerily regaling him with what she had planned for her day. Putting on her coat, she kissed his cheek.

Patting his shoulder, she'd whispered. 'Let's not do that again.'

The front door closed, and he'd sat in stunned silence, not moving from the table for a good hour. Cassie knew. He kept on saying to himself. While at the same time worrying about who she was going to tell. He jumped as the phone rang. Cassie's voice held no malice when she'd told him.

'We're okay, Mark. Please do not worry. I like being with you.'

It had been a year since the – episode, as they both liked to call it. Known only to themselves, to the outside world, they were a couple in love. Their friends were hoping that any day now that they would announce their engagement. The relief Mark felt at having someone he could talk to was life-changing. Cassie's reasons for their arrangement he had not yet explored, plus if he were honest, he didn't want to find out what they were just in case his reaction made her change her mind about their situation.

Now he needed her more than ever. The ancestry site that she was so in love with and which bored Mark silly was showing him things that he would rather not know. While he wanted to confront his parents, Cassie wanted him to wait, convinced that there may be more to find.

He'd railed at her. 'This is my story, life, and past.

Only then had she played her ace card.

'If you do not do it my way. I will walk. I want to get Angela on our side before talking to Judy. She needs to see what we have found. Hopefully, by showing her the evidence, it will also convince her to take a DNA test then I can compare her findings with yours.'

The look in her eye made him realise something other than helping him was driving Cassie in her search for the truth. What it was, he had no idea, convinced though, that whatever it was, it had something to do with his sister Judy.

*

'**M**um, dad, are you both feeling alright? Why are you looking so surprised at the question,' Angela asked, as they both pulled a face. 'Usually, I find out from someone else that you are having a get-together. I can't think why, but for some reason, you often forget about inviting me.'

'Sarcastic as always, and you wonder why we don't! For your information, it is Cassie's birthday, and she wanted you here. I cannot think why,' her mother snapped back. 'I certainly don't.'

The arrival of her brother and his girlfriend stopped Angela from replying, and she watched with interest as Cassie neatly avoided a kiss from her father and a hug from her mother. Mark stalked off to grab a beer. Judging by Cassie's red face, thought Angela, they'd argued. Next to arrive were Judy and Paul. As soon as her mother heard their voices coming through the house, she abandoned all pretence of listening to what Cassie was saying, leaving her mid-sentence to greet them instead.

Sinking into one of the new highly padded chairs, Angela gazed around. Since she last been in the garden, her parents had been shopping. Not only had the inside of the house had a recent and expensive makeover but so had the patio. Three large grey rattan sofa's also now dominated the space, topped off by white umbrellas large enough to block out the sun. It had turned what was a nightmare of a sun trap into a shady nook, while a space-age-looking barbeque had replaced the old vintage one.

Angela often wondered how her father felt about her mother continually spending money. Over the years, the inside of the house had seen many transformations; Angela thought they all looked the same. Beige, beige, and beige. Anything vibrant was tutted over and discarded. Her mother forever saying, 'You cannot buy good taste.'

Where she got her ideas of it from, Angela had no idea. In her mother's opinion, the older the furniture was or looked, the better. Never mind comfort; that was the last thing on her agenda. Only in the garden was her taste toned down, the only place where her father had any influence on what happened. When questioned, she would yell.

'It's my money, and I'll do want I want with it.'

The subject; of where her money had come from was never openly discussed, and if someone asked, her mother would decline to answer. What the big secret was Angela had never been able to find out. None of them had ever met a member of her family to ask if they knew. When Angela was at school, the other kids would talk about their grandparents, aunts, and cousins, always the odd one she found herself with nothing to add. It was the same on her father's side. She knew that his mother died when she was a baby, as Mark and Judy had spoken to her about someone who was always ill. His father, or other members of his family, were never mentioned.

Mark flung himself down beside her.

'How's it going?'

Angela stared, trying to remember the last time her brother had spoken to her without shouting. His shaking hand as he held his beer bottle made her wary of answering.

'Well?'

'I'm fine, thanks. How about you? Only I couldn't help but notice that you and Cassie ...'

Not allowing her to finish, Mark jumped in and growled.

'She's into all that ancestry shit. You know, tracing long-lost relatives who no one knows. Each time she finds another cousin, even several times removed, she bleats on and on about them. She is driving me mad with it.' Glancing at their parents, he added, 'Cassie has found something out. Something weird. I need to ask mum and dad. Would you ask them for me?'

'Why me?'

'Because they are used to you stirring the pot and wouldn't find any odd questions strange. Whereas if I were to ask, they would.'

Cassie sat down next to Angela, her face like thunder as she leaned toward Mark. 'I told you …'

Before she could say anything else, Wendy's shrill cry cut through her words.

'I bloody hate you, Lennie. Bastard, that's what you are, a lying bastard.'

Judy quickly moved away from her parents; sinking into a chair, she blocked out the sounds of their arguing getting louder and more personal.

'Happy Birthday, Cassie,' she said.

Paul joined her, raising his glass and nodding at the antics of Wendy and Lennie.

Angela's interest had been piqued by what on earth Cassie could have found out, especially if it was something that would upset her parents by asking them. But at the same time, she knew that she couldn't always trust her brother. She had been caught out before by his tricks and lies. Intrigued at what it could be, she watched the drama in front of them unfold, sure that it would follow its usual path of shouting, swearing, blaming, and eventual reconciliation.

Glancing across at Judy, even though her sister appeared happy on the outside, Angela could tell that she was far from being so. When worried as a child, Judy would often pinch the skin of her hands. Looking at them now, Angela could see how red they were, a sure sign that things weren't all rosy in her world. What she had to worry about, though, Angela found hard to imagine. She would give her right arm for the life of luxury and indulgence Judy lived thanks to Paul's career. The thought flickered. If it meant being married to him, then perhaps not.

'Why not ask Judy? She is mother's favourite.'

'Ask her what,' jumped in Paul before Judy could answer.

'I can speak for myself.'

Cassie shook her head and stood up. 'Forget it. I'm sure it's me being silly. Can we go, Mark? It hasn't been the birthday party I imagined.'

For once, hearing the goodbyes stopped their parents from arguing in their tracks. Wendy insisted they stay and brushed away Cassie's concerns as a difference of opinion. Besides, she told her; we have a cake. Let me fetch it. Calling Judy to come and help bring the plates. Instructing Mark to open the champagne while ignoring the glowering looks from Lennie.

With the cutting of the cake, the uncomfortable atmosphere started to fade. As the drink flowed and everyone got more animated, for once it was all sweetness and light. Angela was amazed at how her mother could turn on the charm like a tap. Her father, for once, being the grumpy one, refused the champagne and stuck to wine. Now on his second bottle, sitting on the grass with his back against a tree, he muttered to himself contentedly. Mark had tried to get him to come and join them, shaken off by the words.

'Fucking piss off,' to echo around the garden.

For once in her life, Angela felt a part of her family. The night was filled with the sound of their jokes and light-hearted teasing, bringing smiles to everyone's faces, and making time fly. Angela wished with all her heart that it could always be this way. When her mother spoke directly to her rather than as she usually did with her eyes focused over her shoulder made Angela's night. She tried not to make too much of it, knowing that her mother could be fickle where her emotions were concerned. After all, tomorrow was another day. Even so, it had given her a warm glow all evening of what things could be like, given half a chance.

Cassie and Mark were the first to leave. Receiving a hug from Cassie, Angela kept her face from reacting as she whispered into her ear.

'Can you phone me tomorrow?'

Angela patted Cassie's back in affirmation as Mark winked at her. Deciding to leave while the going was good, Angela was surprised to hear Judy and Paul insist they would give her a lift home. As Judy hugged her mother, Angela, tempted to do the same but not wanting to spoil the evening, bottled out at the last moment. Content with a bye Angela from her and a drunken wave from her father, she felt as light as a feather as she closed the door.

8

AUGUST

Sitting in the car going home, Cassie could hardly wait until tomorrow came. Her need to get Angela on their side was the key she felt to everything. Wishing Mark had listened to her and had not approached his sister at the party. Telling him what she wanted to do, he'd laughed in her face. Cassie had been adamant that she wanted to speak to Angela alone and explain what she had found before asking for her help.

'Angela,' he had crowed. 'You want to ask her to help? Why? She will make the situation worse. Besides, she cannot seem to have a conversation with mum and dad without arguing. What makes you believe that by her asking them, they will give us the information we need? Why would they tell her anything? You must be crazy if you think that they would.'

Cassie's view of Mark's family was different from his. As an outsider and with the knowledge she had recently gained about them all, it was obvious that they were both damaged and flawed. Getting together with Mark had not been part of her plan until she saw him out with his family. Fortunately, they moved in the same circles, and it had not been difficult to turn up to the same places where he was. It had also not taken her long to see through his brash exterior or his uppity way of talking to everyone to see that what lay hiding underneath was a frightened man. Easy also to see that his public persona meant everything to him and that he worked hard to project confidence to everyone he met.

They had finally gotten together after both attending a party. The house belonging to Anne, one of her friends, had been full of noisy drunken partygoers. Cassie, her head pounding and with her stomach flipping, wanting a breath of fresh air, had staggered outside and found a bench. Laying down, she fell asleep. Waking with a stiff neck, she heard voices, and saw two men holding hands emerge from behind the walled garden. Keeping perfectly still, Cassie stifled a gasp as they came into view, surprised to see Mark with Anne's brother. She knew that Stephen was gay, but not Mark. Every time Cassie had seen him partying, he had been either chasing women or chased by them. Waiting until she was sure that they had left, Cassie made her way indoors.

Most of the partygoers had by now gone, only the hardcore left. The music turned down to a more muted level while a few stragglers in the middle of the floor still swayed to the beat. Bottles and glasses littered every surface while the air smelt fetid. Making her way to the kitchen, Cassie craved a cold glass of water. Pushing open the door, she managed to stop a gasp from escaping. Mark was kissing a girl who had wrapped herself around him like a snake.

After that, whenever she saw him out, she would watch him like a hawk. She could not decide by the way he acted if he was gay or swung both ways. Thinking that it didn't matter as either would suit her purpose. Making a note of the type of woman he appeared to take an interest in, Cassie began to model herself on their looks and ways. That was the easy part. Pretending to be gormless was much harder work than she thought it would be. Her natural feistiness wanted to burst forth, especially when listening to his mother or father begin ranting. Instead, she had to bite her lip and look vacant. Mark liked her to look up to him and make him feel that everything he said was brilliant. She had slipped a couple of times, the last time surprising him when sarcasm coated her words, and she'd laughed in disdain. The only time he had raised his hand to her. Something in her face and stance had made him pause. Looking embarrassed, he'd yelled.

'Fucking bitch.'

Before walking out and slamming the front door hard enough to make the glass rattle.

Cassie had been helping her mother research their family ancestry for years and was amazed at what information she could find. She often felt like a detective tracking down long-lost family members bringing theirs and her history to life. Secrets and lies that had lain hidden for years, centuries in some cases, pulled into the light she and her mother had found even more exciting. Taking a DNA test was the next step, bringing into her life all sorts of people that she had never even known existed.

She could see Mark was bored senseless by her quest, his eyes glazing over every time she regaled him with any new findings. Meeting with his family, she could see why. His father was an out-and-out letch. Cassie had met men like him before and made sure to sidestep his offer to hug. Angela was just weird, her eyes often flicking toward her mother and back to her father as if she was watching a tennis match. Words popping out of her mouth, her barbs intent to wind them up.

Thinking of Wendy, Cassie clenched her fists. Believing her the cause of everything wrong, she could almost feel her hands reaching for her neck. She hated her potty mouth, her drunken rages, and how she fawned over Judy while excluding Angela. Listening to her again being horrible to Mark, for once Cassie was grateful. When drunk, sometimes his mother would point her finger at him and cackle with laughter. Mark usually ignored her when she did. This time though, she had gone further. Once home, as usual, he picked over the evening. Going back to what his mother had said, time and again, trying to make sense of her words had given Cassie a headache.

The next day gave her the perfect opportunity to put her plan into action, Mark, still moaning about his mother when she'd mentioned the words, family history, hadn't told her to shut up. Before he could change his mind again, she started taking notes. It hadn't taken them long to realise that Mark had no idea about either of his parent's family histories. Uploading the details of what he did know onto the ancestry site, compared with the amount of information she had on her tree, made his look even more pathetic.

Asking him to find his birth certificate, Cassie already knew he wouldn't find one. She had already checked when searching through his paperwork one rainy day when he had gone off in a huff over something. Rather than ask his parents for it and alert them to his interest, she showed him how easy it was to order one.

'It will tell us all sorts,' said Cassie. Barely able to contain her excitement, she suggested. 'Perhaps we should also order your parent's wedding certificate. Your grandfather's at least will be noted on it, which will give us a jumping-off point to start our search. Plus, sometimes even those who sign as witnesses can be a useful mine of information.' Seeing that Mark was in a receptive mood, she added. 'If you take a DNA test as I did, it would enable us to widen our search considerably more. Anyone related to you who has also taken the test will show up on the site. What do you think?'

Surprised and happy that he had embraced all her suggestions, her thoughts filled with the investigations to come, her reverie broken when Mark announced.

'I can't wait to tell Judy. I wonder if she has any memories of any visits to or from our relations.'

Cassie bit back a retort. She felt as things progressed, and they would because she was going to make sure they did. Then all of them might need each other's help. Judy was her primary target, and she would prefer to leave her until last before anything was said to her, and besides, she wanted Angela on board first.

'I would rather not bother her yet. She and your mother are very close. If something is wrong, I'd rather wait until we have definite proof.'

*

Angela had been pondering on what on earth Cassie needed to tell her. Mark had not said any more, and with the evening not deteriorating into what usually happened at their family gatherings – for once being a pleasant experience, she had not wanted to upset anything. Intrigued to know why her brother needed her help, she dialled their number.

Opening the door to the café, Cassie waved to Angela, miming a drink. Her answering nod brought a smile to her face. Since Angela's phone call, she had been on tenterhooks at meeting her. She had decided not to say anything to Mark until after they had spoken. The information she'd found was much more explosive than she had expected. Placing down the drinks, Cassie pulled out a chair. She felt lost for words. Once said, there would be no going back. All their lives would be changed, and not necessarily for the better.

'Thank you for coming. I know we haven't spoken much.'

Angela snorted, 'that is such an understatement. If I hadn't seen you speaking to the rest of my family, I would have thought you were dumb.'

Cassie grinned. 'Come on! Let's face it, Angela. You and your family have always thought I'm a half-wit. I have often seen the way you look at me and the way you smirk when I talk. It may surprise you that it has never bothered me because I feel sorry for you. Your mother makes a good show of hating you. Your father isn't far behind. Where Judy and Mark stand concerning you, I'll admit I am not sure. But I am sure that last night was a fluke. The next time we all meet, I have no doubt you will be at each other's throats again.'

They both stared at each other as the noise of the café washed over them. Cassie, her hands in her lap, crossed her fingers that she had not taken her tirade too far while Angela seethed at what she knew to be true.

'Now that we have got that out of the way. Tell me why you and Mark want my help.'

Reaching across, Cassie patted Angela's hand. 'Thank you. Your parents invited us for dinner. You were not, and Judy and Paul had a prior engagement. If they had been able to come, the evening might have turned out differently. As usual, your mother got drunk, and your father argued with Mark. In between doing his usual leering after my breasts. I played dumb.' To take the sting out of her words, Cassie smiled.

'Lennie went inside to get more wine. I said something, and Mark snapped at me. Wendy pointed her glass and told him.

'If you were mine, I would have drowned you at birth.'

Before either of us could say anything, Lennie came out and tripped down the patio stairs dropping one of the bottles he was carrying. Wendy jumped up, staggered, and fell. It was like something out of a carry-on movie. I went to help her up, and she pushed me away, making me trip. Mark was the only one who hadn't moved.

'You know what your mother is like, Mark – like other people, doesn't listen properly to what she says and will often vaguely nod at her. This time though, her words paralysed him. Only Lennie, banging the bottles he had managed not to break onto the table, seemingly bringing him around.

'By now, both of your parents were swearing at each other. Mark grabbed my arm and practically marched me out without saying a word. Pushing me into the car, I expected him to start ranting. The silence was unnerving. Since then, he has not let go of what she said. Even knowing that she was drunk and probably would not even remember, he wanted you to ask her what she meant by saying it.'

'*Blimey*, is that all? I've had much worse. Even if I agreed to ask her, and if she could recall saying it – remember, she was drunk and probably wouldn't know why she said it. All I would get is a mouth full of abuse. Mark knows full well. Once drunk, especially if she and dad are arguing, anyone caught in the crossfire is fair game. Why should this play on his mind more than anything else she has flung at us over the years.'

Opening her handbag, Cassie took an envelope out and pushed two pieces of paper toward Angela.

'This is a copy of Mark's birth certificate. When you've read it, look at your parent's wedding certificate. I will be very interested in what you make of them. While you are doing that, I will get us some more coffee.'

Standing up, Cassie felt light-headed. What if she had got it all wrong? Basing her assumptions on an old photograph and her mother's vague memories may not be enough. If still alive to answer questions, it would be different. After cancer took her last year, Cassie had felt cast adrift. The shared secret left her anxious and worried that she would be unable to fore-fill her promise to her mother and find out what had happened. Now that she had made a start, doubts assailed her.

Placing the tray onto the table, Cassie sat down and waited, Angela's frown testament that she was failing to understand what she was reading. If this is a surprise, thought Cassie, wait until she sees Mark's DNA results. Angela looked up, her gaze as vacant as she usually accused Cassie of being, before snapping out.

'Explain.'

'I got my love of researching my family history from my mother. We both enjoyed the thrill of finding out secrets long tucked away in the mists of time. After what Wendy said to Mark, he and I decided to look into your family tree. As you probably already know, we had very little information about it. You or Judy may know more. I was surprised when Mark told me that he didn't have a copy of his birth certificate and had never seen it, and not wanting to ask Wendy or Lennie about it, I ordered one online. At the same time, I managed to convince him to take a DNA test, explaining that it would make tracing the other family members easier. Can I ask? Have you never found it strange that even though you are all adults, your parents not only still pay for each of your passports but also deal with all the associated paperwork?'

Cassie's words reminded Angela of something her friend had said. Maureen, a holiday in Greece looming, had been in a state after forgetting to renew her passport and wished that she had parents like Angela who kept everything up to date for her.

'It isn't just passports they look after,' she remembered replying. 'Anything legal has always been overseen by them. Something none of them to her knowledge had ever questioned.'

'Mark says he's never felt the need to ask them about it. Not having to pay or deal with getting it sorted, he saw it as a boon. Now he is wondering why.'

'I haven't given it much thought either,' said Angela. 'You surely have spent enough time with our parents to realise that they both like being in control. It is something they have always done. I think it must come from having money. Though, I have never had any idea how they make any of it because, regarding dad's business, this appears to be either part-time or non-existent. And in mum's case, apart from doing charity work – only undertaken when she wants to make an impression, I believe she has never worked a day since they were married.'

'Mark's birth certificate, as you can see, has father unknown written in the box, which begs the question, is Lennie his father? But more importantly, his mother is Elaine Gibson, not Wendy Page. Yet, they both claim to be Mark's parents. Using his father's name on their wedding certificate, I can trace what may be distant cousins relating to Lennie. I cannot find anything to do with Wendy's father. Although, that may not necessarily mean anything.

'Researching family history is often a side-ways shuffle to get to the truth. The wrong spelling is often the culprit, or people out and out lie. That is why I find it all so fascinating. Apart from when they are needed, certificates are often put away and forgotten. Yet the wealth of information or not, which they contain, can break a family history apart. Hidden for a reason, people do not want their secrets brought into the light. Truth and legality play a big part in what people would rather be kept hidden. In Mark's case, it seems we have both questions which need answering.'

'We should go for a walk,' suggested Angela. 'My brain is aching. It seems so farfetched, like some low-budget soap opera on the telly.'

Cassie found it hard to contain her excitement, pleased that Angela appeared to be listening and not dismissing her findings. What to do about them had consumed her and Mark for days. He wanted to storm straight over to his parents and demand an answer. Unbeknownst to him, Cassie had her agenda in place for his family and did not want him to do anything to spoil it for her. Taking the time to explain that to find answers, they would need much more background information. To deflect him away, she had rattled off some quick-fired questions that needed answering.

'Why did Elaine leave, and more importantly, why did she leave you behind with Lennie if he is not your father? And if he is. Why isn't he named on the certificate as such? Plus, what about Angela and Judy? Surely, Cassie had told him they needed to know first. What if the same applies to them? What else could Wendy and Lennie be hiding?'

Still wanting to come with her, Cassie had insisted that she speak to Angela alone. She had seen by his actions at the party how distrustful Angela had looked at him. More used to him winding her up or being sarcastic, he would probably make Angela think that this was another of his games. The outcome was not something she wanted to put in jeopardy by Mark to satisfy his need to get one over on his sister. He had changed. But not always where she was concerned. Taking his cue from his parents, his treatment of Angela often made Cassie want to punch him.

'Did you say Elaine's surname was Gibson?' asked Angela, pulling Cassie down onto a bench. Looking shifty, she told her, 'I am sure I have seen that name written down somewhere.'

Chewing her lip, Angela was in two minds, whether to say anything further. The certificates were genuine. The explanation of the facts sounded genuine. But still – they were a couple. Her dilemma was whether it was possible to trust Cassie when she had always found it hard to trust Mark.

Sensing her confusion, Cassie stated, 'we are on the same side. I and everyone else have seen how your parents treat you, and yes, I know that Mark sometimes follows suit. I cannot break a trust, but he also has his demons. I am on the outside, and your family is painful to watch. Mark and your father compete on everything. Once the drink is involved, they both get louder and more laddish. Judy is unhappy. Your mother's constant attention gets on her nerves, and since she has gotten married, she's getting worse. I have watched her face tighten when she approaches. Wendy is oblivious. Her belief in their closeness is a wonder of self-blindness. Paul alternates between acting like a damp squib or a puppy. And you, Angela? Well, you have murder in your heart. Do you realise how your hatred of Wendy leaks out? Not only does your face change, but so does your whole demeanour. In full battle mode, you are too angry to notice or care. But I have. You scare her. You scare me.'

Cassie's words hit home. Since the New Year, her anger at her family's treatment of her had grown. Sometimes she could almost feel her mother's neck between her hands while revelling in her pleas to stop. Looking at Cassie now, she applauded her honesty. Perhaps she had found a way for her to kill her mother without getting blood on her hands. Deciding to jump, after all, what did she have to lose?

'What about the DNA results? Do they show any connection between dad and Mark?'

'None,' Cassie replied bluntly. 'I have diligently looked through everything possible that I could find. They are not related. I'd bet money on it. Tracing Elaine's ancestry and crossmatching it with the people who have cropped up in Mark's DNA bubble, they must be related. So far, only distant cousins have emerged. It doesn't look as if he has any brothers or sisters, although, to be fair, we may only know for sure if they had also taken a test. This news has been a bombshell for Mark. However, he is unaware that I have also been looking to see if I can find out what happened to his mother. If I can find her, then that would go a long way to helping him. Am I wrong in thinking you have no idea what I do for a living?'

Angela raised her eyebrows and shrugged. Before grinning, 'I can't say I care.'

Cassie chuckled. 'That's what I thought. Well, I work in what has a catch-all term by outsiders of IT. I will not bore you with what I do. Let me say that it involves lots of graphs, spreadsheets, and algorithms. Not to sound arrogant, but my knowledge of computers is extensive. I am not going to admit to hacking. But at the same time, I cannot say that I honestly haven't been tempted to do so, if you get my drift.'

Angela laughed. The more she talked, the more she was getting to like her. Why Cassie was going out with Mark, Angela found hard to fathom. Being gormless was an act, so was it the same for the looks of adoration she constantly threw Mark's way. She mentioned demons, and there was only one that Angela was sure of that he would not want to make public. Breaking into her thoughts, Cassie told her.

'Elaine is nowhere to be found. She cannot be dead, or at least she doesn't have a death certificate that I can find. It also looks like she has never been married, not even to Lennie. Her online presence is nil. She also doesn't appear on any of the systems I have checked, legal or otherwise. A year and a half after Mark was born, all traces of her disappeared. That is not to say she couldn't have changed her name. What does make it even more suspect is that in the run-up to her leaving, a large property not too far from here, called Byford House, was also transferred over to Lennie. You work in one of the business premises that were also transferred over to him, Hudson and May. Lennie only kept ownership of the other properties for a few months. From what I could find out, everything except the house signed over to him by Elaine was sold.'

Angela was more than stunned. She certainly never knew any of this. Does her mother or Judy? When she got the job, no one mentioned that it used to be owned by her father.

'I found a box with the name Byford House written on it. My job is to sort through all the old paperwork accumulated over the years, input anything relevant into the system and shred the rest. A key stuck to some paperwork inside it that had the name Gibson written on it. The box was flattened and shoved right to the back. I might never have found it if I hadn't been clearing out the room. I checked the system and the rest of the files, but there is no mention of the property anywhere.

'Although my boss has worked there for years, I thought it best not to ask him outright about what I had found. I said I had been reading a book about houses that had bodies found hidden inside the grounds, and it mentioned Yoxford and a place called Byford House, and did he know anything about it? He knew more than I wanted to know. I couldn't shut him up. Talk about a specialist subject!

'Apparently, Hudson & May had dealt with the house, but not until years later. It had been on their books as a rental property. He said that those who moved into it never stayed there very long. When ownership of the property changed, the new one took it off the rental market, and their interest in it ceased. That may have been when dad took it over. If that is so, why couldn't I find any reference to the house being rented or sold? Also, how did the key get into a box inside the filing room? Someone must have put it there, and the question is, did they hide it deliberately or by mistake?'

'Surely that must mean the house has something to do with either of them or both,' Cassie crowed. 'It is way too much of a coincidence.'

While Angela was speaking, like a physical presence in the room, she could feel Cassie's excitement building as she put two and two together and made five. The house intrigued her, and Angela wanted more time to check it out, something she had wanted to do since she had found the key. If anyone was living there, she could say that she had found a key and then offer to give it to them. And if no one did live there? Well, I will use the key to see what's what. Elaine's name on the tag may be a coincidence. After all, they sometimes happen.

'Before we say anything to Mark, perhaps I should also take a test.'

As Cassie punched the air, Angela knew she had hit the right mark to stall her in her tracks.

*

Angela didn't know why she had taken the key to the house. Once home, she had pushed it into a drawer and forgotten about it. With Cassie's revelations ringing in her ears, she was eager to understand why no one knew anything about it. Also, why was the box hidden away?

Sitting in the sunshine on her balcony, Angela spread out the paperwork that Cassie had printed off for her. Taking a sip of her coffee, she picked up the one with the most writing on it. Written in legal jargon, Angela had no chance of ever understanding it. However, she did recognise her father's signature at the bottom of it. The property was his, that part she did understand. Elaine Gibson's signature, clear and bold, sat next to his, meaning that she must have signed it over willingly. The question why? She could understand Elaine wanting to leave her father – who wouldn't? Angela understood that someone could leave their child – after all, her mother would gladly have walked away from her, but signing over what appears to be a substantial property, she found more puzzling and hardly made any sense. What was even more worrying, Cassie had been unable to find anything about Elaine. It was as if she had disappeared from the face of the earth. Her mind kept on slewing to possibilities that Angela would rather not contemplate. Cassie said Elaine's family had money, and although when she left, somehow Lennie appeared to have acquired a lot of property that was once hers, she would still have been a wealthy woman.

Checking for the umpteenth time that she had everything she needed, Angela tapped the details into her sat-nav. As she turned the key, a text message flashed on her phone, Cassie's name highlighted. Ignoring her request to make contact, she pulled out onto the road.

Two hours later, she had finally arrived, she had missed the turn-off to Yoxford four times, and each time it happened had to drive further down the road to find a passing place where she could turn around. The road leading to the house was more like a dirt track, the sign ivy-covered and barely readable. Bumping along, Angela hoped that her suspension could take the strain, and going by the state of the rutted track, her expectations of the house were low. Rounding a bend, she stopped the car and got out.

'Bloody hell, I did not see that coming.'

Angela felt that the large bay windows were reminiscent of eyes staring out, waiting to see who was arriving, making a shiver run down her back. Honey-coloured bricks glowed in the evening sunlight. The door was black, the brass on it dull, staring, daring her to enter. Angela banged on the door. She found the silence unnerving. Now dark, she was also getting spooked.

Taking a gamble that no one lived inside, and before unpacking the car, she decided she had better try the key. Shaking her shoulders, telling herself to get a grip, she turned the handle. The door opened with a squeak. Holding her breath, Angela paused, before stepping into the hall, her ears straining to hear any sound. Silence. The only thing to greet her.

Exploring upstairs, she found six bedrooms with ensuites. The stale air inside them was cold, and all were shabby. The beds, unmade, their mattress dimpling in the middle, looked forlorn. The heavy and solid Victorian furniture reminded Angela of her parent's house. She'd always hated it. Set against her mother's choice of a neutral background made it seem even more imposing. Here though, with expensive wallpaper on the part panelled walls and the floor covered with floral carpets, it worked. The kitchen had cupboards handmade in oak, once again the same as in her parent's house. Here though, the marble worktops looked unused. Next to this was a formal dining room, fully panelled, gave it the feeling of being inside a cave. The fireplace was enormous, and beside it was a door leading into a library. Angela had never seen so many books on display in a house before. She wondered if they were for show or had actually been read.

A long half-panelled lounge swept across the back of the house. Another fireplace, looking even older than the one in the dining room, had three sofas surrounding it as if waiting for guests to arrive. Wooden doors opened into a conservatory, giving a view of the gardens. Arranged in a semi-circle, wicker chairs and tables looked towards them.

The house felt huge. Angela was overwhelmed that her father possibly owned all this and had never spoken of it. Sure that even her mother cannot have known, the house they lived in was not small inside or out; they had at least four acres surrounding it. Neighbours had never been a problem, but it was nowhere near as grand as this, and if her mother had known about it, there's no way she would not have forced him to move. As she walked through its rooms, it was easy to see that no one had lived inside the house for years. Thick dust lay over everything. Opening the windows and a good clean would see it right while the mustiness, accumulated over time, would soon dissipate. Angela sighed with longing.

'What I wouldn't give to live here.'

Opening the back door was another revelation. The patio was endless, and the sunken seating area she found particularly fascinating. Even though overgrown, Angela could easily see the design of the formal gardens. Grabbing her torch, she headed towards the outbuildings. Forgetting she might need keys, peering in the windows, all she could see was a spacious office and storage.

Back inside the house, Angela was surprised and pleased to find that the utilities were still on. Which begged the question, why? She had brought plenty of candles, blankets, and bottled water, expecting that she would have to rough it. Instead, she was sitting at a lovely old wooden farmhouse-style table, eating from a Wedgwood bowl with a radio playing in the background – but she had begun to find the house even spookier as it had gotten darker. Now though, warmed by something to eat, Angela began to relax. Unsure still if she was brave enough to sleep in one of the beds, she decided instead to go through every drawer and cupboard she could find. Angela found nothing, leaving her no choice but to tackle the attic and see if she could find anything relevant hidden within its confines.

Unlike the one at her parent's house, this one had stairs leading up to it, with a door at the top. Fortunately, the key hung on a hook. Another creaky door led her to a clean space, with shelves, cupboards, and wooden chests filling every available space. Angela groaned. The attic looked so tidy, just as if the army had been in to sort it out. In films and books, information would always be found in a dusty corner and usually without much effort used. Without knowing what she was looking for, she could disappear inside and never be seen by anyone again. Shutting the door in defeat, she decided that perhaps a glass of wine would get her brain cells working.

Glancing at her phone, which she had left in the kitchen, she saw that she had missed calls and messages from Maureen and Cassie. Ignoring Cassie's, she rang Maureen in a panic only to get her answering machine.

'Fuck! Sorry. It's me. Angela. I should have cancelled. I forgot, please don't be angry, only I am up to my ears in – Well. Busy. Send my love to Toby, and I hope you both have a great time. Once again, sorry.'

Oh dear, thought Angela, she is not going to be happy. Maureen and Toby had been going out together for what felt like forever, both adamant that they did not want to get married, let alone engaged. Then out of the blue, he proposed, and she accepted, their engagement party booked. In normal circumstances, Angela would have been first in line to go, but with all that was going on, she had forgotten. Maureen would relent in time, but for a while, any communication between them would be non-existent. And as Maureen was adept at weeding out any information, Angela wanted to understand the situation she found herself in before discussing anything about it with her. Another problem was how to stall Cassie. Angela was sure she wasn't telling the truth and wanted to know what she was hiding.

It was pointless to continue her search of the attic or house without more help, deciding that when they left to go away at the end of the week, she would search her parent's house. Angela was determined to be the one to find their hidden secrets.

*

Running, Mark had found early on in his life, was a way to clear his head. As his feet pounded the pavement, his body became looser, and his mind slowly began to relax. Cassie's revelations had been hard for him to fathom. She had to physically restrain him from storming around to his parent's house and confronting them there and then. Tossing and turning made sleep impossible. The question, if not them? Then who? Buzzed around his head like bees inside a hive each time he had lain down. Today she was meeting Angela, he had wanted to go with her, but she had been adamant it would not be a good idea.

'The facts need explaining without emotion,' she told him. 'Which you cannot do.'

Though, if honest, what he was finding hard to understand was Cassie's insistence that they get Angela on his side first; before involving Judy. She'd also intimated that she had other information that she wanted to run past his sister before telling him. No matter how much he shouted and cajoled, she would not budge, something was going on, and for the first time in their relationship, he didn't trust her.

'I'll follow you then,' he'd retorted. 'After all, you cannot stop me.'

She had left without saying goodbye, venting her anger by slamming the front door.

Stopping to have some water, his chest heaving, he suddenly had the overwhelming urge to cry. Flopping down onto a bench, glad he was sweaty, hoping no one passing would notice the tears running down his face. His body felt pushed aside, and with only a husk left in its place. With the identity he had known all his life now removed, Mark's feelings of being lost and alone rose to the surface. Stretching out, he closed his eyes, calming down as his feelings settled.

Mark tried to remember if, at any time in his life, he had felt or heard anything that would indicate he did not belong – that those he thought of as his parents; were not. Surely he thought, he would have felt something over the years. But, no matter how much Mark racked his brains, nothing came to mind. His father loved him, of that he was sure. Even when they rowed, any bad feeling between them didn't last long before either would call the other. Arguments were never mentioned by either of them and neither apologised, both carrying on as if nothing had happened.

If honest, he'd never been sure of his mother's love for him. Even though she had always looked after him when ill, fed, clothed, and hugged him when needed, there had always been a slight distance between them, not like how she was with Angela, which was actual dislike. While affection towards him rationed, Judy, on the other hand, got it all. Now knowing what he did, their relationship made more sense. Judy, like Angela, was her biological daughter, whereas he was not her son. The question he wanted an answer to was; did she know that he wasn't Lennie's either?

*

Opening the door, Angela ushered Cassie and Mark into her flat. Taking their coats, she tried not to let her excitement spill over.

'Interesting,' her brother said as he looked around.

Cassie elbowed him in the ribs. Angela, too pumped up to care what he meant, indicated that they should sit.

'How do you feel?' she asked.

Mark laughed as she grinned back at him. Cassie stared at them both.

'This is serious.'

'We know,' said Mark and Angela as they broke into another round of laughter for once in sync, breaking the ice between them.

Shrugging her shoulders in annoyance, Cassie told them, 'I have explained to Mark about the house, and he also had never heard of anything ever said about it. I have continued to search for any details of Elaine's whereabouts but have come up blank. Although, if Mark hadn't had a middle name of Carson, I would still be looking for his birth certificate, as there were other Mark Stubbs born on the same day as him. The fact that it was also his grandfather's and great-grandfather's name makes me confident that Elaine is his mother.

'Mark's birth certificate shows us the details. His DNA results flesh their relationship out. I have also done a more thorough search on the ancestry site, confirming that some of the distant cousins who are showing up as related to Mark are also related to Elaine. It would be better if we could find her and ask. But with no idea what has happened to her, Mark has to decide what he wants to do. Confront your parents or leave it.

'We need more information from both of them. My searches show that in Lennie's family tree, which is small, I'll admit, I can find no cross-over between either of you. If we could get a sample from him, it would definitively show whether or not you are related.'

'I want to know what they have both been playing at,' Angela demanded. With a growl of frustration, she asked, 'so, who is my father? If Mark is not my brother, is Judy my or his sister? I have to admit that when I saw the results. I was disappointed. I thought if I weren't mum's daughter, it would make some sense why we never got on. To find out I am hers and not likely to be Lennie's raises more questions. Was I the result of a one-night stand, or did she have a proper affair? I keep thinking about their circle of friends and hoping it is not any of those spineless wonders.'

Mark heard the anger but also sadness in Angela's voice, she'd always tried to maintain a hard shell around herself, yet since all this had come out, he had started to see another side to her. The thought, he liked her, had popped into his head while shaving. Once embedded, Mark realised that although not related, they were similar. Something he would never have given credence to before. Mark had never spent so much time in her company, disgusted with himself not to have taken the time to visit her at home or taken any interest in how she may feel. Somehow not being related had freed him from – hard to put into words, freedom though, he thought, best summed up how he was feeling.

Placing the tray down onto the table, Angela, like Mark, was feeling happy for once in his company. Letting him pour the wine, she sat back with a satisfied sigh.

Taking a sip of her drink, she announced, 'I think I may have hit the jackpot.' Laughing at their expressions, she explained, 'because Byford's attic was too much to sort through alone. I decided to raid mum and dads. As you would expect, theirs was chaotic, and thinking that if either of them had hidden something, it must be in the further reaches. I went exploring. Nothing. Nada. To say I was disappointed would be an understatement. Clumsy is sometimes my middle name. I hadn't brought a torch with me, and with the lighting dim and flickering, I got annoyed, and in my usual imitable way, I knocked off a box which started a chain reaction.

'Once the dust settled, there it was; the ubiquitous old shabby suitcase tied up with string, and like something out of a film shoved into the crawl space. I have no idea why it had the string when it also had a padlock. I went to fetch a crowbar to prise it open. It was worth it. Ta la.'

Laying an old stained envelope onto the table, Angela sat back and waited. Cassie was the first to snatch the papers. Her eyes went wide as she stared at Mark.

'What is it? What have you found? Let me see,' he exclaimed impatiently.

Expecting to see something about himself, he could not comprehend what the old newspaper showed him. Angela chuckled, earning her a pained look.

'I may be acting a bit thick. But I don't understand. What am I supposed to be looking at?'

'Look at the headline Mark. Mother commits suicide in baby snatch case. Why would our, sorry my mum, have kept this? Perhaps Cassie can tell us? She is, after all, related to the woman and the child.' Seeing Cassie's face blanch, Angela added. 'We can all do research. I wondered why you were keen on keeping Judy out of the loop. It didn't make sense to me, especially when we found out Mark and I wasn't related. The odds of Judy being our sister also seemed unlikely.'

'I ... My mother told me about Rose before she died. She knew that I was continuing her research on our family history, and her last request was I try to find out what had happened to the baby.' Looking at Mark, Cassie blushed. 'I am sorry. It started when I was at the same restaurant as your family. I saw Judy and couldn't believe my eyes. She was the spit of Rose. Coincidence or serendipity. I do not know. I knew that I had to find out who she was. The next time I saw you, I ...'

'You used me,' Mark interrupted. 'All this time. *You!* I knew it was something to do with Judy. She needs to know. Mum and dad, don't. Not until we are all ready to confront them.'

'We need her to do a test, make sure,' Cassie handed them each a picture, 'take a look. I am pretty sure that I am right.'

*

'**N**ot today, mum,' said Judy, for what felt like the umpteenth time. 'I told you yesterday when you rang that I am going away for the weekend. No, Paul is not back yet from his seminar, and he will not be until Tuesday at the earliest. Whether he will mind me going isn't your concern, is it?' Judy snapped out before she could stop, thinking, why does my mother always have to have an opinion about every little thing I do?

'Oh, don't be like that. I am going to be with friends. No, you do not know them. *Mum*, will you stop?'

The phone went down with a bang as her mother hung up. She was getting too much, thought Judy, it was only nine in the morning, and she was already slurring her words. The packed suitcase stared at her from the hall. What the hell am I doing? She had been at a loss for words when Mark had left her a message.

'Hi, Cassie and I wondered if you'd like to come and see a house we are thinking of buying.'

Since becoming adults, any time spent in each other's company generally only happened at family get-togethers. Mark asking her to go anywhere immediately made her suspect his motives. Even if she hadn't been feeling so low, she would probably tell him to get lost. However, in this instance, Judy decided that a day away was what she needed. As if aware of her decision, Cassie phoned.

'Mark forgot to tell you to pack a bag, as the trip is for the weekend. The house is unoccupied, and the owners are happy for us to stay in the house to help us decide on whether or not to buy it.'

Judy had listened in disbelief and subsequently phoned Angela intending to ask if the estate agents where she worked ever did the same thing as it all sounded a bit suspect.

'I've also been invited. I can't wait. Do you want to drive down together? I can pick you up.'

So shocked was Judy by her proposal that she had forgotten to ask the question.

Now waiting for Angela to arrive, she again had doubts about what they were doing. Hearing the toot of a horn, she looked out of the window to see Angela beaming at her. Still unsure of what she was getting into, Judy closed and locked the door. And in a moment of defiance switched her phone off. Putting her case into the boot, she jumped inside.

'Ready?' Angela asked.

'Is this okay?' Judy replied. 'Only I have never heard of anyone trying out a house before buying it.'

Angela chuckled. Checking her mirror before pulling away, she pompously announced, 'don't worry, sis. All will soon become clear. Think of it as an adventure. A voyage of discovery. The path to a new life.'

Judy's anxiety went up a gear. Glancing at Angela, it was easy to see that she was nervy and on edge. The jolting of the car did not help, never having been driven by Angela, she had no idea what type of driver she was. Judy's question of where are we going? Had been ignored by Angela as she sang along to the radio. Wondering what she had gotten herself into, Judy slumped down into her seat and closed her eyes, letting the sound of Angela's caterwauling lull her to sleep.

The car jolted, making Angela swear. Judy sat up as the house came into view. Angela laughed at her reaction.

'Wait until you see inside. It is huge.'

Mark and Cassie appeared at the front door as they pulled up, waving unnecessarily.

'You are thinking of buying this?' Judy asked, unable to hide her astonishment, as Mark opened the car door. 'Not being funny, but how can you even afford it?'

Angela and Cassie grinned as they collected the bags from the car. Judy's anger flared, telling herself. I should not have come. Mark surprised her by kissing her cheek.

Taking her arm, he led her inside, explaining, 'don't look so mad. It isn't you that they are laughing at, but the situation. We have lots to tell you. Come into the kitchen.'

The silence stretched as they concentrated on eating and drinking, each wondering who would speak first. Cassie took up the baton and turned to face Judy.

'Before you jump in with any questions, will you let me say my peace in full? Only it is difficult to know where …'

Cassie could get no further as her emotions exploded and tears coursed down her face. Judy looked at Mark and Angela, and both shrugged.

'Sorry,' sniffed Cassie, wiping her eyes.

Angela muttered, 'for fucks *sake*, we should get on with it. The sooner Judy knows, the sooner we can make a plan of action. This business all started with you, Mark. Perhaps you should go first?'

'Well, it didn't, did it? Cassie was the one who stumbled on our family, intending to root out our secrets. She should do it.'

'What the hell is going on?' shouted Judy. Banging the table in frustration, thinking again, I wish I'd never come.

Taking a deep breath, Cassie laid a photo on the table. She tapped it with her finger. 'This is my mother's cousin Rose who killed herself. My mother took an interest in researching our family history. And she passed that love onto me. All the online access available today has made gathering information much easier. It also throws up long-hidden secrets many people would rather not have exposed. Before my mother died, she asked if I would try and find out what happened to Rose's baby.'

Cassie placed a copy of the newspaper cutting that Angela had found beside it and continued. 'As you can read, Rose's baby was snatched when only a few months old. Rose blamed herself. She had left Dawn outside a chemist's shop, and when she came out a few moments later, the baby had gone. Worry and anxiety about the missing baby wore her down, culminating in her suicide. She left a note stating that it was all her fault and that she couldn't live anymore with the guilt.'

Judy's face flamed, and her body felt as cold as ice. The picture could have been of her, the likeness uncanny. She heard what Cassie was telling her but could not take it in. Glancing at Mark and Angela, their faces looked fearful as they waited for her reaction. Her first thought was why are you showing me this? Hearing more about Rose's story, something inside her clicked into place. Words she remembered hearing her mother say. But could never fathom, now had new meaning.

Picking up the clipping, she asked, 'Are you saying Rose is my mother and Wendy is not? How can you be sure? I may look like Rose but so probably do a lot of other people. There are only so many face types to go around. It all sounds – well – farfetched.'

'We have both taken a DNA test,' explained Mark. 'Mother, sorry, Wendy said something to me which made me think. Thanks to Cassie's online research into our family history. It turns out not only am I not her son, but I am not Lennie's.' At a nod from Angela, he added, 'Lennie also appears not to be Angela's father, but unfortunately for her, Wendy is her mother.'

Seeing Judy's confusion, Angela explained, 'Cassie has taken a DNA test. If you do the same, it will show if you are related to each other. We are pretty certain who Mark's mother is but have no idea who his father might be. As for mine, who knows? We have all seen how mum can get when drink gets inside her, it could be anyone. At least your DNA can be tested with Cassie's. Without confirmation from either of our so-called parents, Mark and I can only guess who we are related to.'

'Why don't I put the kettle on,' said Mark. 'Or shall we have something stronger?'

'Not for me,' murmured Judy. 'I need a walk. My head is ready to explode with information.'

Leaving the others inside, she donned her coat and headed out. The house had extensive grounds, mostly unkempt but a raggedy path led down to a small wood. Judy wanted to clear her head and sift through the words spoken. One part of her brain was unconvinced that what she'd heard was true. Knowing that paperwork could easily be forged. Yet, it all made a kind of mad sense.

They had all racked their brains to think how Lennie could have gotten Elaine to sign over her property to him. Without confirmation from him that he hadn't forged her signature. They could only surmise that they were legitimate.

The cool of the trees was like a balm to her soul. Judy realised that taking the DNA test may confirm her heritage, but it would not change anything about her biological mother being dead or her pseudo-one still living. For Judy, though, everything had changed. As Cassie spoke, the shackles that Wendy had woven around her had fallen away. Unbeknown to her husband, Paul, the ones he was putting in place made his time also at an end. If honest, Judy had known right from the start of their relationship that she should never have said yes to getting married. She should have trusted her instincts. And regardless of the outcome of all that Judy had heard today. She and Paul's marriage was over. It was time to take back control.

9

SEPTEMBER

'*Lennie*,' screeched Wendy. 'Have you put the bunting up? Set the tables out? Lennie, where are you? There you are. What have you been doing? They will be here soon, and nothing is ready.'

'Perhaps if you put your glass down for a minute, you would get more done,' Lennie suggested, sarcasm dripping from his voice as he nodded to her full glass of wine. He had counted three top-ups at least since they had started the preparations, let alone those she had sneaked while he wasn't looking.

Wendy's face turned puce. Anger flew out of her mouth like an arrow seeking its mark.

'You are nothing but a lying bastard and an adulterer. It's your fault that I drink. I need it to be able to even look at you. A waste of space is what you are. Remember, I know what you have done, and don't you forget it. Your precious son Mark, the stuck-up little shit, would not take too kindly to knowing. It would spoil the façade he wears of being someone special.'

The blow slammed against her face as Lennie's fist connected, making her drink fly out of her hand, glass shattering against the wall. Wendy fell onto the floor. Lennie held a handful of her hair, pulled her head up, and growled close to her face.

'Keep your bloody mouth *shut* if you know what's good for you, or I will make you regret it.'

Wendy rocked herself in pity as Lennie kicked her legs, making her cry in pain and anger. The alcohol she had drunk; had been quickly wiped away by hate. Stone-cold sober, she forced herself to stand, as dizziness made her wobble. Putting a hand to her face, Wendy grimaced to feel the heat. As she had stood, Lennie had backed off, his face set, yet she could see in his eyes real fear. He knew he had gone too far. She had pushed him many times in the past, once before Lennie had lashed out. The words he'd spat at her following his punch were something he had since regretted. Recognising that by speaking out, he had given Wendy the perfect weapon to hold over him.

Flinching as she bathed her face, Wendy wished it was possible to cancel her birthday party. But, their friends saw it as the highlight of their year and knew that she would pull out all the stops to make the night special, the drink would flow, and the catered food would be superb, taxis arranged so that no one had to drive home, people would soon start to arrive, it was too late to stop.

Walking down the stairs, she felt like some doddering old lady as she gripped tightly onto the rail and decided she needed a large drink to settle her nerves and play the dutiful wife.

Although her face had calmed down and the make-up she

had applied had largely covered the bruise, Wendy still felt as if she wore a sign around her neck, saying, been punched.

Thankfully, Lennie kept out of her way, and she hoped he would stay away from her for the remainder of the night. Wendy had more interest in seeing Judy, she was always able to make her feel good, and the closeness between them eased her loneliness. A shame that Angela would also be there. It was a real pity that she wasn't still going out with Gary, because he at least had kept her from making too many of her sarcastic remarks. Wendy was hardly surprised to hear that they had split up and had always felt that Gary was way above Angela's pay grade. Hearing Lennie booming out a welcome, Wendy glowered as she looked out the window to see Mark and Cassie appear in the garden. Here they are, she thought, Mr up himself and his sidekick, Miss drippy. Downing her wine, she straightened her shoulders, and checked her face one more time while telling herself, let battle commence.

*

'**H**ello mum, happy birthday,' Judy muttered to herself like a mantra. Be normal, Angela had said, don't forget she'll expect a hug and a kiss, and remember not to stray too far from her; you know how she likes to keep you in her sights. She glanced across at Paul, since coming back from her stay in Byford House, she knew she had been on edge and snappy with him. His puppy dog ways, Judy found even more irritating than usual, like a blanket his love smothered. When Mark suggested that she tell him, Judy was horrified.

'If you mention anything, even overtly to Paul, I will bring the whole fiasco out into the open and see how you liked having everything picked to pieces.'

Paul did not know it yet, but their marriage was over. For now, she would use him as a shield in helping her to deflect

Wendy's attention. The thought of calling her – mum; made Judy feel physically sick. All of them had insisted that she carry on as she usually would, and her behaviour was to stay the same. Both Carrie and Angela reiterated to her that until her test came back, she should hold fire before saying anything. Judy though had no doubts. It was they who needed the official confirmation.

Her mother swooped, and Judy pushed Paul forwards, pretending to juggle with the presents. Kissing her on both cheeks, he told her that she hardly looked a day over thirty. Mark mimed being sick; while Carrie giggled. Passing over the gifts, Judy leaned forwards and air-kissed her mother, mumbling. 'Lovely day.'

Lennie bounced over and pulled her into a hug, and Judy could feel herself stiffen up. Another mantra, relax, relax, entered her head as she saw Angela arrive and, like a demented child, let rip.

'Happy birthday to you. Dear mummy. Happy …'

Scowling at Angela was enough to distract them from Judy, and she stepped away.

'Looking good, mother, my dear,' crowed Angela, still in a sing-song voice before peering closer and asking, 'what have you done to your face?'

'Do you have to shout?' cried Wendy. 'For your and anybody else's information, I fell over, and no, I wasn't drunk, and you can take that sanctimonious look off your face.'

'What are you all having to drink,' interrupted Lennie, wanting to steer everyone away from Wendy's injury. 'Come on, Mark; you can pour them out while I get the barbeque going. It's supposed to be a party. Not a wake. Enjoy!'

Judy sidled up to Cassie, and with a shake of her head, she understood that the test wasn't back yet. Taking a drink from Mark, they clinked glasses. Angela, sauntered over, unable to control her grin. Cassie whispered so only they could hear that she needed to move away. Wendy, Judy could see, was throwing puzzled glances her way to see her standing with Angela and Cassie. Unable; to get away from Peter and Betty's clutches, she waved Judy over.

Ignoring her, Judy knew, was not an option, the word mother still sticking in her throat. Wendy's arm snaked around her waist and pulled her close.

'Here is my girl. Doesn't she get prettier every day?'

Judy forced herself to lean in and relax, surprised that her voice sounded normal as she asked, 'how are you both?'

Betty grimaced as Peter leaned in to kiss Judy. She wished he wouldn't. She loved Judy like the daughter she never had, and the thought of Peter having mucky thoughts about her was the one thing guaranteed to make her angry with him. Angela was a different matter. Betty hated Angela; her birth had threatened to spoil her relationship with Wendy. So caught up in the dislike of her new baby, Wendy wanted to farm her out to Betty the way she had done to Judy. Betty had refused. She wanted nothing to do with the child and didn't want her in her home.

Every time they met, the urge to pinch Angela made Betty squirm. She would be left in her cot to cry. Betty used to watch as Angela shook her tiny fists, her face red with hunger, stopping as she loomed over the cot, Betty, would grab her arm or leg and twist. Angela would scream, but no one came. Wendy was too drunk to care.

Hearing that the barbeque was ready, Peter dragged Betty away; their love of food was as bad as Wendy's love of drinking, thought Judy.

'Are you alright, love? Only you seem a bit distracted. You are not ... Only if you are, that would make me so happy. I promise I will not tell anyone, not even your father.'

Anger suffused Judy's face, this *woman!* She raged inside her head. Who the hell does she think she is? I hate her. I wish she were dead. As the thought took shape and her fists clenched, Angela barrelled her way in front of them.

'You alright, sis?' She sneered loudly. 'Only you're not looking your usual put-together self, a bit on the rough side. Watch out, or you'll start looking like mum, and no one wants that to happen.'

Wendy reared back. 'Why do you always have to be so horrible and spoil everything?'

'*Huh!* Look who's talking. If only you could hear yourself, mummy dear. There is only one person to blame for all this, and that is …'

'Angela,' roared Mark from across the garden. Making heads turn as everyone stared to see another family conflict erupt between Wendy and her daughter.

*

Finally, things had calmed down. Cassie sipped her drink and watched Wendy as her eyes followed Judy's progress around the garden. She had made out that the test had not yet come back, but it had. Since then, Cassie had been working hard on their shared ancestry. Finding out she was right made Cassie feel vindicated for all the long hours she had sat in front of her laptop trying to figure out what had happened. Glancing over to Wendy and Lennie, they acted as if butter wouldn't melt. Even without what she knew, Cassie thought they were both despicable human beings. Wendy had seen Dawn as she was then and took her wanting a daughter, giving no thought to her mother and what she would feel at losing her child.

Cassie was pleased that Mark had finally admitted that her research skills were second to none, realising at the same time that if she could not find anything of Elaine's whereabouts, no one could. Convinced that the only option, apart from witness protection – and that was unlikely – was that Lennie must have killed her. They had talked long into the night, and if he had, how on earth were they going to prove it? A confession would be the only way, and they both realised; that wouldn't happen. A body; if she was dead, then she could be anywhere.

Angela favoured somewhere in the grounds of Byford House, believing that is why Lennie has never said anything about it and why he still owns it. If so, they would still be unable to find her. The grounds were extensive; no way could they dig them all up.

'Once we have confronted Lennie,' Cassie had assured Mark. 'With what they knew and suspected, he would crumble. He and Wendy are bullies. Okay, while in control, but once they lost it and their world tumbled, she was sure they would find out what had happened to Elaine.'

Poor Judy thought Angela, this party, was going to be hard on her to keep up a front. For her, pretending to be something she wasn't; had always come easy to Angela. Mark was acting as if on drugs, hyper and strung out. Shouting at her earlier, he had sounded like a sergeant major on parade. Judy at least had been grateful for the interruption, and easy to see that she was struggling to keep up the pretence. Angela had no intention of blubbing; besides, she liked winding her mother up. Mark had changed his stance and was all for wading in and telling Wendy and Lennie what they had found. Cassie was the only one who could seem to put a brake on his actions. When Judy's, DNA test results, have been confirmed as Cassie expected them to be, then and only then would they sit down and discuss what they were going to do. Angela had been at great pains to say that she wasn't bothered by who her father was. But it wasn't true. She wanted to know. Sure that it must be one of her mother's sycophantic friends. But who? Angela could bear some of them, but others, even the thought that she may be related to them, made her feel queasy.

Going to Judy's rescue and upsetting her mother had tasted all the sweeter with the knowledge they all held. Finding it strange that she was the daughter shoved to the side and always left one step behind, and yet she and her mother were related, whereas she, Judy, Mark, and Lennie weren't. Looking at all their disgusting friends, the men lolling about, some with bellies so big they looked pregnant, while the women with their plastic-looking skin stared vacantly at the men they had managed to capture. Angela wondered what would happen when the revelations were public and what will everyone think. After all, both are criminals, mum for sure, and if Lennie hadn't had a hand in killing Elaine, questions needed an answer as to why, if not coerced, she had signed over so much property to him.

*

Mark took a deep breath; the party was the last place he wanted to be, which made it the place he had to be. Lennie was buzzing around like a fly as if he could sense something was wrong. Wendy had her usual sneer in place when spotting him and Cassie. She tried to hide her feelings, but as the drink took hold, it became increasingly difficult for her to do so. Judy looked like a deer caught in the headlights, and if any of us cracked, he thought, it would be her. Although he now recognised how much Cassie's investigations had found, he was again getting fed up with her cackling on about trees, families, and ancestry. He was bored with her findings and bored with her.

His distrust grew when he realised how she had used him to get closer to Judy because all she had to go on was a photo and a gut feeling. Although everyone around them thought of them as a couple, it was laughable. As to his relationship with Cassie, Lennie wouldn't understand that at all. As a red-blooded male – his words when describing himself; Lennie would expect that any son of his would be the same. A gay son is not something he would expect to have. Mark could not wait to point out that he was not his son. And therefore, it didn't matter.

Once all this was over and, everything was out in the open, he intended to finish with Cassie. She would have to move out; the pretence was over. There was no way he could out his so-called parents and keep his true self hidden; he would be a hypocrite.

*

Lennie had not meant to hit her. Usually, it was he who had to duck. She was the one to let rip. Throwing anything she could pick up while screaming obscenities. Today, she had gone too far, and he had lost his temper. Lately, their rows had gotten more vocal, their words stabbing into each other, their intent to rip and wound. Wendy had convinced herself that Judy was pulling away from her. Lennie had tried to say that now married, of course, they would not be as close, and after all, she had a husband to put first.

Shooting him down in flames, she'd replied mockingly. 'I have always put her first, and being married to you never changed that. You have always been second best and always will be.'

Upset at first, but if honest, he knew she spoke the truth. The only time he had ever known her to put him before Judy was when they had first started seeing each other and after Elaine disappeared. He can remember asking to see her daughter, telling her often to bring Judy along, that it would be good for Mark. But Wendy was adamant that she stay with her friend Betty, citing that she did not want to confuse her, especially if their relationship did not work out. Lennie was happy to have her company and help and tried not to push it. Sometimes though, he wondered how much time Wendy spent with her daughter; if she was not with him, she was working.

'Betty must be very understanding,' he'd said.

'She doesn't have any children of her own, so looking after Judy is the highlight of her day, and it would be cruel to stop.'

He could tell she had not wanted to discuss it further, and he dropped the subject.

It was only a few weeks before getting married that he finally had the chance to meet Judy. She was bundled up against the cold her face perpetually smiling made him like her straight away. He remembered how Wendy had gasped in fright as he leaned into the pram and swooped Judy up, swinging her around before showing her to Mark as his new sister. Wendy hovered around them as if Lennie had no idea how to hold a baby and was not happy until he had laid her back down again.

And still, after all these years, she hovered. Easy to see that Judy found it claustrophobic and when younger, she had even taken to hiding in his home office to get some respite from her mother's attention. Wendy would come looking, and he would try to keep a smile off his face at her worried look as Judy hid under his desk, a finger to her lips. It made him sad to think those happy days were long gone. The secrets they shared had worn away at both of them. The shell left behind bumbled along as the pointed barbs they sent each other's way pushed them further apart.

*

Mark's suggestion that they all meet at the house was met with enthusiasm. Judy saw it as another weekend away from Wendy's endless questions of, 'what's wrong?' To Paul's constant buzzing around, wanting them to do things together.

Angela, though, was feeling at a bit of a low ebb, seeing Gary with curvy blonde had thrown her. His laugh had been what she had heard, and recognising the sound, she had looked up and wished she had not. Arms around each other as they looked adoringly into each other's eyes – or at least that is what she saw – made her yearn for him back, even at the same time, knowing they were not suited. The trouble was Angela was drowning in her sorrows after another disastrous relationship had floundered within weeks. Since finishing with Gary, she had found it hard to maintain being with someone else. Her friend Maureen had admonished her before regaling her pompously.

'Don't forget that you are free to do what you want. You can have your best life while living alone.'

Maureen's pronouncements on life were usually quite astute, but her words sounded like something said more to impress than mean. Angela reminded Maureen that as someone now engaged to be married, she would soon have to learn the art of compromise and that the words free and alone would have no more relevance in her life.

Cassie was once more happy to be in Judy's company and had brought with her some more family pictures to show her, hoping that it would help Judy gain a sense of herself, sure that she must be feeling out of sorts. She was still annoyed with Mark, who stressed that Judy was not the wimp that Wendy made her out to be. She was strong and did not need a babysitter. Since the reveal of Mark's parenthood, they had begun drifting apart. Both had different reasons for being in their relationship, and now that Judy knew the truth, Cassie had no more reason to stay with him. Asking why he was acting so mean to her, usually kept at bay, he had yelled at her like a madman, showing his nasty side. Deriding her efforts, belittling her while calling her a stalker; for the way she had hunted down his family. Acid remarks poured out as he stomped around the flat like a child with a temper. Even with the knowledge that it was because of his insecurities he was acting up, Cassie blocked her ears to his tantrum, looking forward to the day when she and Judy were a family of two.

Sitting around the kitchen table, for the first time in her life, Angela felt as if she belonged. The fact that none of them were related somehow brought them closer together. Although she could not stop the thought that Cassie was now the odd one out. Knowing Mark as she did, it was easy for Angela to see that he and Cassie had once again had words, which was happening a lot lately. The emerging lies and secrets within their so-called family meant that Cassie was moving away from Mark. Instead, like a moth to a flame, she was drawn to Judy, unaware that Judy was not interested. Judy had told Angela that she'd had her fill of families and other people's wants and dreams and was craving peace and time to think.

'When are we going to confront them?' demanded Cassie. 'They have to be made to pay for what they've done to us. To be able to move forwards with our new lives, we have to deal with the situation. The police also have to be told. Wendy has to face punishment for what she put Rose and Judy through, not to mention my mother and her family. I can't wait to see her face! That will wipe the smile and snide remarks off it. Lennie, at best, is only a thief, and with Elaine nowhere to be found, it looks as if he may also be a murderer.' Oblivious to their silence, she continued with relish. 'I can't wait for my family to meet Judy.' Glancing at Angela and Mark, she added, 'thanks to my research, you now have families you can get in touch with, and they may even be able to fill in any of the gaps I have missed.'

Sitting back with a self-satisfied look on her face made Judy want to smack her. Pushing her chair back, she banged the table with her fists. Looming over Cassie, she enunciated each word slowly and clearly.

'I do not want any more family. I am up to here with family. I wish they were both dead.'

Cassie opened her mouth.

'Shut up. You have had your say.' Turning to Angela and Mark, she asked, 'what about you two? How do you think we should deal with them?'

For a second, Angela's mind went blank; at the start of the year, even though her thoughts had turned to murder, she had known that it was more a dream than a reality, a way of blowing off steam. Now, something stirred inside her, and she recognised it as freedom. With both her parents out of the way, no more would she have to put up with their put-downs and snide remarks, the constant reinforcement by her mother of being unwanted. With no close family to worry about, she would be free to start a new life, reinvent herself if she so wished, even her past. She could wipe them out of her life for good.

All of them could walk away, which Angela knew would not be enough. Her mother would do everything she could to persuade Judy to stay, and if she left, her mother was sure to try and follow. Lennie would probably do the same with Mark. She, the only one to be related, would be waved off without a backwards glance.

'I feel the same,' interjected Mark. 'Wendy may have been nicer to me than she ever was to Angela; even so, from a young age, I have always known that something was missing between us. I used to think it was because Lennie and I were so close

– a bit of parent rivalry. Now that I know I am not related by birth to either of them and the possibility that Lennie killed my mother. I want them punished.'

While Mark had been talking, Judy had been thinking. What she wanted more than anything; was answers that only Lennie and Wendy could give. Plus, glancing around the kitchen, another thought entered her head, none of them had known about this place. What else were they both hiding, and who benefited from their wills? Before they did anything that they could not come back from, these questions needed answering. How they could get them to tell the truth, though, was the problem. When cornered, both were capable of saying anything to save their skin.

*

Angela had been pleased to hear that her mother and Lennie were going away and taking Judy and Mark with them. The thought; when they are dead. Popped into Angela's head, quickly followed by, I won't have to listen to their constant rows anymore. Something that had been happening a lot lately, and Judy and Mark, saying the same thing kept happening to them.

Judy told her that she kept zoning out when listening to Paul drone on about his fishing trips, letting her imagination run riot on how her life could be, only to be brought back by him clicking his fingers in front of her face as if trying to wake her from a trance.

Poor Mark had Cassie to contend with, telling Angela.

'She won't stop talking about it. Finding Judy seems to have been her main aim in life.'

Meeting him for lunch had been a surreal experience. Never had either of them invited each other out. Angela stifled a laugh as his rant continued.

'Even in her sleep, Cassie was still muttering about the niceness of it all. On waking, it would be the same old refrain, how if it wasn't for her …'

'She still seems pretty obsessed. I know Judy finds her intensity frightening.'

'I want Cassie to move out, but I daren't suggest it. She's so volatile, and I'm not sure; how she will take it.'

Angela used all her skills to convince him that this mustn't happen. He had to act the same around Cassie as they all had to around her mother and Lennie. They were all outsiders. Reiterating that even though she, Mark, and Judy may not be related, in the literal sense, they were, even so, a sort of family, even if Judy did not want one.

The lunch had been a pleasant experience, both realising that they had much in common and that their sense of humour was very similar. Judy had managed to join them for coffee making, their unrelated triangle complete, a name Angela had started calling them, much to Cassie's annoyance, another thing Mark relayed that she could not let go.

Her phone calls, Judy exclaimed, were becoming a nuisance. She had been letting Paul answer, able to bore the pants off most people even if he could not put Cassie off wanting to speak to her. Judy's excuses were getting thinner by the day. Instead of feeling closer to Cassie as the only actual member of her family that she knew, Judy explained that she was finding it stifling to be around her. It was as if Cassie appeared to believe they were both destined for some utopian paradise together, where she would introduce Judy to all their long-lost relatives. Her latest thing was trying to convince Judy to visit their mother's graves. Sure for some reason, she would want to. Unable to understand that she did not. Judy exploded with anger.

'Do not try and manipulate me into doing something I don't want to.'

Making them laugh when she'd said that to do so, she had channelled her inner Angela and let rip.

*

Angela let herself in. The house, empty for once of any shouting, felt like stepping into a void, as if it was holding its breath. Determined to be more thorough and careful, she headed upstairs. This time she had come prepared with a torch. The last time she had entered the attic, Angela found the suitcase, and the lights kept flickering on and off before plunging her into total darkness. Pulling down the step ladder, she could not stop a shudder. Angela had never liked dark places and had a real fear of spiders. Be methodical, she thought, and tidy. The last thing Mark had said was to make sure she put everything back in the same place as it should be. Just in case Wendy or Lennie wanted something from the attic.

When she had mentioned what he had said to Judy, she had grinned like a loon.

'Lennie's far too fat to fit through the gap in the ceiling, and unless Wendy has a stash of booze hidden up there, the likelihood of either of them wanting to visit would be a million to one.'

Nevertheless, Angela was making sure to be careful. The dust, though, once again was making her choke. If anything screamed, someone was here, was the trails she was leaving as she moved apart the boxes. Pulling an old chair into the middle of the room where the light was brighter, she unpacked each box and scanned each bit of paper before putting it back. After hours of fruitless searching, Angela went back down the ladder. Stretching out her neck and back, the thought of a long hot bath and a glass of wine was the only thing that kept her going.

Wearing her mother's bathrobe, Angela sat on her bed. Her parents had slept apart for years and she'd overheard her mother telling the lovely Betty that the habit once formed was hard to stop. Glancing around the room, Angela realised that it held no personality. Bland was her first thought. The curtains were the only colour in the room. The array of drinks on the dressing table added to the feeling of being a drunk's lair. She had already found a few forgotten empty bottles; hidden at the back of the wardrobe. Everyone knew that her mother drank, it wasn't a secret, and she never hid it. Angela often thought she liked to revel in the notoriety that it brought her.

Her mind wandered to the problem they faced. Angela thought perhaps her mother's drinking was the solution. As her eyes alighted again onto the wardrobe, she had a brainwave. The bottles stacked inside looked odd and made no sense. What if they were a decoy, she thought?

Taking a picture of how they looked, Angela began carefully taking them out. A wooden box, hidden at the back, was now revealed. Punching the air with excitement, she pulled it out and saw the padlock. I need a crowbar was her first thought before deciding that she had better not break it. Her mother could not know that she had been searching. Angela was sure there must be a key hidden somewhere, but where?

Angela smiled. Next to the bottles on the dressing table was a silver cocktail shaker grabbing hold of it she gave it a shake. The rattle inside made her laugh. Her mother had never been the one to mix or drink cocktails, telling anyone who would listen that she liked her drinks, unshaken or stirred.

Lifting the lid, Angela thought all her Christmases had come at once. Angela's phone pinged with a text, making her jump. Judy's face filled the screen. With her fingers stumbling over the letters, she texted back, all good, and used a whole line of thumbs-up emoji's.

This time they all travelled together in Mark's car to Byford House.

'Cassie,' he told them. 'Is thankfully away on a course. The questions she keeps asking of late are getting on my nerves. Because she has a connection to Judy, she feels that everything we discuss and decide has to include her.'

'The holiday with Lennie and Wendy had been a nightmare to walk,' said Judy. 'Cassie, nearly letting the cat out of the bag after being wound up by Wendy, was only stopped from telling all by me pretending to faint. Talk about dramatics; it was like a scene from a soap opera. Wendy was shouting for help, all while not letting go of her glass. Lennie had tried to stop me from slumping to the floor and put his back out while Cassie was wailing; that everything was all her fault. As for Paul, he was useless; all anyone could hear was him squeaking, 'Judy, Judy, are you alright,' his voice was getting more anxious as he said it.'

Angela grinned. 'Sounds like fun. Not! For once, I am glad; I hadn't gone with you. Spending time with them both is becoming harder and harder. As for Cassie, she is becoming a liability.'

'Tell me about it,' barked Judy. 'Sorry, I never meant to snap at you. But she is doing my head in; bad enough Wendy fawning over me, now Cassie has started. It is becoming like a competition between them on who can have more of my attention. So much so that I kept on trying to hide in my room. Paul, the idiot he is, kept on coming to get me. Booming out for all to hear, 'here she is.'

They all laughed, happy to be in each other's company. Safe, in the knowledge they all wanted the same thing and had each other's backs. Naming them the Unrelated Triangle,

Angela had made it clear that everyone else involved was surplus to requirements. Pulling up in front of the house, all three sighed with pleasure.

Angela stated what they were all thinking. 'Isn't it funny? Although we have never lived here; but, each time we come back, it feels more and more like home.'

For the hundredth time, Angela told Mark that after photocopying the paperwork, she had put everything back where it had come from, and her mother and Lennie would have no idea that she had been searching.

'Before I sorted through the box I found in mum's room. I went into Lennie's. Applying the same reasoning to hers, I sat on his bed and let my gaze land where it will. Golf was one of Lennie's passions, and it made sense like mum's bottles; if he wanted to hide something, it would be with them.'

Angela told them how she was stumped; she had emptied his golf bag and had done the same with the clubs, expecting that one of the heads would twist off and reveal something hidden inside. Nothing. She had even gone through the old ones he kept in the garage, screaming as a spider fell out and scuttled over her foot. Shaken and swearing, she had bumped into his tool cupboard and set everything inside shaking. Like a light bulb moment, she thought, shed. She knew it would be locked and bolted, always a joke at their parties, to what he had inside. Many a drunken guest had tried to prise it open. Lennie had not played ball, and she could remember him pushing Peter out of the way as he had taken a hammer and tried to knock the lock off. Snatching it from his hand, he had squared up to his friend, red-faced, eyes bulging, only Peter's wife Betty stepping between them to stay his hand. Lennie had tried to brush it off as a laugh, but they had all seen his face and stance change.

Once again, she needed a key. Not as predictable as her mother, Angela had to give Lennie's hiding place more thought. Deciding to have something to eat, she headed inside and stopped. Stifling her giggles, she ran back into the garage. Golf was not Lennie's only passion; his first love was his old car. Lifting its cover, Angela remembered when she was younger, overhearing him tell Mark his car had a secret hiding place. Even though the vintage car spent more time covered up than it did on the road, Lennie would never get rid of it. When missing from the house, he often sat inside it, lost in his thoughts while listening to the radio. Tucked out of sight – for no purpose that Lennie could ever explain – was a small opening underneath the radio, and that is where Angela was sure she would find the key. Pushed right to the back, and with not much room, she about managed to get her fingers inside the slot. Dropping the key onto the floor, she grabbed it in triumph and headed for the shed.

Angela's mouth gaped open as she stepped inside. Two walls; were lined with a collage of pictures depicting them all. Taken without them realising they had captured each of them at times when they were not at their best. Her mother featured a lot, obviously the worst for wear in most of them, a bottle and glass not far from her hands. Mark was shown either as a child throwing a tantrum or as an adult shouting. Judy's pictures were of her looking either vacant, serious, or annoyed. In respect of some women, including Cassie, he had mainly focused his attention on their busts or legs. The word sleaze popped into Angela's head. Unsurprised to see that she had not featured in many, those that she did, her expression captured was a cross between a grumpy baby and a furious toddler.

Angela used her phone to take pictures. She had no idea what the others would make of the collage. It creeped Angela out. She asked herself why Lennie had hidden it away and did her mother know it was there. Angela suspected not. Turning away from the collage, she scanned the rest of the shed.

An old chair she recognised from the dining room was pushed up against a metal filing cabinet. Inside was a long metal box. Another bloody key to find, thought Angela, looking to see if Lennie had put it somewhere accessible. Angela was losing her temper, she had to open the box, but at the same time, she could not damage it. Exasperated, she looked again at the collage and found a photo of Lennie with Mark as a baby and what could only be his mother. As an adult, he was so similar in looks to her that there could be no mistaking their relationship. Angela desperately wanted to take it. A photo on her phone she knew for Mark would never be enough, and only the real thing would do. So predictable Lennie, she crowed. A small picture of Mark in his pram was the only photo not to lie flat. Stuck on the back was the key.

*

'This house and everything that Lennie owns, on his death, will go to Mark, and Judy inherits everything from my mother on her death. I, of course, am not mentioned in either will,' Angela explained, handing Mark and Judy copies of all the documents she had found.

'What is surprising is the extent of what both of them own and the money they have. Not only does Lennie own this house, but he also owns the five shops on South Street, including the overgrown plot of land behind them. As to money. The paperwork with the wills and deeds seems to show that when written – which appears to be about a year before he and my mother got married, Lennie could draw on funds over a hundred thousand pounds. As to my mother, she also has access to a considerable sum of money – considering to the best of my knowledge, she has hardly worked a day in her life. Half a million, to be exact. The best bit, though, is she also owns the property, the flats where I live, well she owns all eight of them, including mine. Which means I pay rent to my mother!'

'I know, as a family, we have never wanted for anything,' said Mark. 'What I do not understand though is why with all that they both have, we never moved somewhere more expensive. Do you think each of them knows what the other has?'

'I would be surprised; they are both secretive. We have all seen it or experienced it first-hand,' chuckled Angela. 'What? Do you think, Judy? Lennie hasn't said anything to Mark. Did my mother say or hint at anything to you of any of this?'

Listening to her explain the documentation had made Judy's headache with tension. Angela had turned herself into a detective, finding paperwork hidden in various nooks and crannies, copying it, and at the same time making sure to cover her tracks. Who'd have thought that she could be so resourceful? Judy could understand Lennie not leaving anything in his will to Angela, but her mother ignoring her as if she did not even exist, was too much to bear. They had all tried to figure out why Wendy loved Judy, who was not even her biological child, and disliked, even hated, Angela, who was. It did not make sense, and now that Judy knew she and Wendy were not even related, it made her feel even more uncomfortable.

The holiday had been a bind from day one. Small talk about all she could manage, and that dragged from her. Several times Paul had wanted to know if she was coming down with something, while Wendy, ever hopeful that she may be pregnant, kept on dropping hints about being a grandmother. All Judy wanted to do was scream at all of them. Mark tried his best, but as they couldn't look to be getting on too well, his efforts had to be kept low-key. Even though Cassie stepped in on several occasions to turn the conversation to safer topics, Judy found her constant presence cloying. Pulling herself back to the present, she could not stop a sigh from escaping; she wanted it all over.

'Never,' she told them. 'About the only thing she ever mentioned was that if anything happened to her, I would be okay. I always took it with a pinch of salt. If I were a better person, I would say I do not want anything from her. But I am not. She owes me, as she does to you, Angela. They both do to all of us, and I intend to take everything they have away from them.'

'Cassie,' said Mark. 'Will not let it go, to hear her talk Wendy has ruined her life. I am not sure how. Like a mantra, she keeps saying she needs to pay. I agree. I shut her down, though. I told her that even so, she should not be talking about it, especially when we are out or in their company.'

Angela's head ached; they had somehow gone through a bottle of wine with only nibbles to eat. Each of them threw into the ring their ideas, no matter how outlandish the ways Wendy and Lennie could be punished. Each; was held up, dissected, and dismissed as unworkable. Killing them had also been thrown into the conversation. After a moment's silence, they all laughed.

'If you don't mind going to prison, simple then,' Angela muttered.

Neither Judy nor Mark had laughed, though when she had suggested that if they did decide on a frontal attack could they make their wills out in her favour before doing so?

With no agreement on how to get them to talk, they had gone to bed. Tossing and turning, Judy could not let the problem go; she had even gone so far as to wonder if they should involve Cassie. After all, she felt as strongly as them that Lennie and Wendy should be paying for what they had done. Cassie; couldn't be trusted not to do something stupid and annoying Judy did not want to see her arrested either.

Deciding to get up and make a drink, she drifted down the stairs, her thoughts still muddled. Taking out a cup from the cupboard, her hand held in mid-air, Judy gazed at the glasses stacked next to them. Sitting down, she let her mind have its way as the twists and turns of what it was proposing flashed in front of her. It could work, she thought. The opportunity would have to present itself, and if it did, would any of them be up for the challenge? Wendy's drinking may be well known. Even so, Judy had never seen her lose control. Drunk, but not incapable, is how she would describe her, whereas Angela and Mark thought of her more as a functioning alcoholic. Would a few well-chosen words be enough to tip her over the edge?

10

OCTOBER

With the party in full swing, Judy tried not to let her nerves show. Starting a row with Wendy would not be easy. The timing was everything. If very drunk, it wouldn't work; not drunk enough, though, meant that she might not react the way they wanted her to. Fortunately, Lennie was being particularly obnoxious, brought on by the fact that the barbeque was not working, and everyone was voicing their opinion on what he should do to fix it. Giving up, he resorted to ordering takeaway for everyone instead, swearing and shouting as, once again, arguments started, as they all kept changing their minds on what to have. With him and everyone else occupied, Judy nodded to Angela and Mark. Cassie, the first to enter the fray, sidled up to Wendy and whispered.

'Baby snatcher.'

Wendy pulled away, and her eyes; immediately went to Judy while her face drained of colour. Downing her wine, she ignored Cassie as if she hadn't spoken.

Angela stepped forwards into her line of sight. As she drew near, she pointed her finger and hissed.

'I am your only real daughter,' before glancing meaningfully at Judy.

Wendy staggered, her mind whirling as she tried to make sense of what she had heard.

Mark loomed over her, asking, 'are you okay, mum? Only you look like you've seen a ghost.'

Clutching his arm, Wendy shook her head; her brain felt fogged, and grabbing a chair, she sat holding out her glass for a refill. Cassie brought over a bottle. Wendy flinched as she poured out the wine, unsure seeing Cassie's smile if she had imagined what she had said.

'Here you go, Wendy, have a top-up. Great party as always,' Cassie chuckled. 'Lennie, though, seems to be in a bad mood. Have you upset him again? What does he think about it all? Or doesn't he know?'

Wendy's heart banged against her chest; she felt faint, her lungs tight as if her breathing would stop. Mark was laughing as Cassie spoke. Before she could say anything to either of them, Angela appeared beside Cassie, looking at her for an answer. The timing thought Angela could not have been better. Paul had lost sight of Judy and wanted to know if they had seen her.

'I think she went inside,' Cassie told him, adding with relish as she stared at Wendy. 'She looked upset.'

Both Wendy and Paul's eyes swung towards the house. Wendy stood, her eyes unfocused and wet. Making heads turn, she shouted at Paul that he was to stay outside and that she would go and find out if anything was wrong.

Shivering with nerves, Judy waited for Wendy to find her. She sat on the bed; the bedroom had been left untouched as if in a shrine to her. As soon as Mark and Angela had moved out of their bedrooms, Wendy had gutted them. Everything was sold or given away. Judy felt weary; now that she knew, she wanted to go and leave everything behind. The only thing keeping her here was her need for vengeance. She also knew that even though Mark and Angela felt the same, she was unconvinced their need was as strong as hers. They wanted them punished, whereas she wanted them dead.

Seeing Judy sitting on the bed, Wendy stilled herself not to worry. 'Here you are. Paul was wondering where you were.'

'He will not have to for much longer. I will be leaving him. I should never have married him in the first place, and when I do not have to look at or be anywhere near you anymore. I shall start a new life; that is not built on lies and betrayals as you and Lennie have done.'

Wendy's legs collapsed beneath her, and she slid down the wall rocking backwards and forwards.

'I don't understand. What is it you think I have done? What have those bitches been saying?'

Judy stood up, looking down at Wendy, her face smeared with tears. All her feelings of betrayal showed on her face. Grabbing Wendy by the front of her dress, she hauled her upright before slamming her against the wall. The overwhelming desire to kill burnt inside her like a furnace. Wendy's eyes widened at the look on her daughter's face, and before she could utter a word. Judy flung her aside.

'Mark is not mine or Angela's brother, is he? Lennie was married before. A woman called Elaine Gibson is his mother. Not you. Why did neither of you tell us? Why keep it a secret?'

Wendy's brain felt ready to explode, finding it hard to understand. Sure that both Cassie and Angela were talking about Judy, and yet here she was talking about Mark. She wanted peace to sort out her thoughts. How do they know? Does Mark? Questions she would love to ask but daren't without speaking to Lennie first. But then, if told, he may let spill what he knows about her, something Wendy did not want to happen. Sure she must have imagined what had been said earlier, too much drink as usual. Her befuddled brain had once again betrayed her.

Judy watched Wendy as her thought processes played out on her face. If only she knew how transparent she was, she'd think twice about letting her guard down. With the seeds sown, it was time to make her exit.

'You make me *sick*,' cried Judy, 'I can't be around you anymore.'

Running down the stairs, she turned at the bottom, waiting for Wendy to appear before yelling at the top of her voice, hurling words like daggers.

'*I hate you*. Stay away from me; I never want to see you again.'

Pushing through those who had gathered behind her, Judy glanced at Angela and Mark before slamming the front door as hard as she could. With her whole body shaking, she jumped into her car, accelerated away with a screech of tyres, and ignored Paul as he shot out in front of her waving his hands.

*

'**H**ave you spoken to Mark since the party? Lennie, I am talking to you,' exasperated, Wendy threw down her magazine. 'Do not ignore me.'

Lennie opened one eye. He had been deep in a lovely dream. His face was in the shade, and his body was in the sun. Wendy blocking the light, had that look on her face of. She to be obeyed. Sitting up, he reached for his drink, aware of her impatience.

'Well? Are you going to answer me or stare at me like an imbecile?'

'What's it to you if I have spoken to Mark? After all, you are never usually interested in any of our conversations. What sleight have you imagined he has said about you this time?'

Wendy glanced across at Lennie, letting her eyes rake his body, and she realised, not for the first time, that he was showing his age. When younger, he used to be proud of his toned body, owning a six-pack well before they were fashionable. Now his stomach protruded over his shorts, looking like a creature trying to escape. His skin, in places, was the colour of strong tea, and the white parts stood out in sharp relief. Wendy had been churning over in her head; the question, who knows what? She had tried to decide if what she thought she had heard Cassie and Angela say was real or something her drunken brain had made up. If so, she could not understand why now. What to tell Lennie or to tell Lennie anything had also been filling her thoughts. Every time he started a conversation, she had felt herself flinch, and the worry that it was all going to unravel was wearing her out.

'I know somethings not right though,' Lennie told her, 'maybe he has had enough of Cassie. I've noticed that she is a bit clingy at times.'

'Yeah, and all we know, the part of her you would like to cling to, don't we?' Wendy retorted.

'If you are going to be like that, you can bugger off. I was having a nice kip before you plonked yourself next to me. Why don't you go? Bother your darling Judy and leave me alone.'

Before she could stop, Wendy told him, 'she knows I am not Mark's mother. She also knows about Elaine.'

Lennie felt the breath leave his body. His heart sped up, threatening to jump out of his chest. He flexed his fists, wanting to strike Wendy, thinking somehow that it must be her fault.

'You told her? Why would you do that? Are you mad? Perhaps I should let her know your secret. See how you like that.'

'Of course, I never told her. It must have been Cassie. She is the one interested in our family history. She asked us once, don't you remember, if she could poke around in ours. I soon gave Cassie her marching orders. The last thing either of us wants is for anyone to be nosing around in our past. Judy didn't say if she was going to tell Mark. What are you going to do?'

'I need a drink,' stalking off, Lennie could barely contain his anger. Mark meant everything to him. Perhaps he should have told him. Too young to remember Elaine, Wendy instead became his accepted mother. The last thing Lennie wanted to do was talk to Mark about her. His questions would require answers, something; that he would rather not have to find.

Pouring himself a large scotch, for once in his life, he didn't know what to do. Usually, when faced with problems, he was always able to find a way out. Unsure whether he should wait for Judy to tell Mark or him himself. Deal with the fallout or cause it to happen. Not a choice that he had ever expected to make.

'So,' Wendy asked as she reached into the fridge for a bottle of wine. 'What are you going to do?'

Downing the first glass, she poured another and raised it as if in a toast before knocking it back and pouring herself another.

'Thinking about it, this is your problem, not mine. Mark and I have never been close, whereas the two of you have. Finding out will affect your relationship with him more than mine.'

'Why not state the bloody obvious,' mocked Lennie. 'You are not exactly blameless in all this. It suited you to go along with the charade. Look at you; you are hardly mother-of-the-year material. You hate Angela and overcompensate with Judy. Have you seen how she looks at you lately? I think your days of tracking her every move have ended. And as to that wimp you encouraged her to marry, it will not be long before she dumps him. And before you say anything. I sometimes play him and Mark off against each other. Stirring the pot is what I do. I don't mean anything by it. Mark knows that. I love him.'

Wendy laughed, filling her glass to the brim, she pointed the bottle at Lennie.

'*Love!* You do not even know the meaning of the word. When we first met, you were like a breath of fresh air after all the other creeps I had dated. The first years of our marriage were also bliss until you started worrying about whether Elaine would put in an appearance and spoil everything. You did not marry her; you married me. What could she have done; she left you and Mark. No court in the land would let her take him after doing that. They may not though have been so happy to hear you had been fleecing her money and transferring some of her portfolios to yourself. I don't expect it will go down well with Mark either.'

Hate flooded Lennie's face, and his fist shot out and connected with Wendy's chin, snapping her head back and throwing her into the cupboards. With an ooh, she fell to the floor and curled into a foetal position to protect her body. He kicked and made her moan. Grabbing her by her hair, he hauled her upright. Wendy spat into his face. As he flinched backwards, her hand snaked towards the half-empty bottle of wine, and she brought it down onto his head. Blood ran down his face and into his eyes as she pushed him out of the way. His turn now to fall. Hitting his head on the corner of the island, he fell to the floor like a dead weight. Wendy nudged him gently with her foot, but he didn't move, so she tapped him on the nose expecting his eyes to open. His breath was ragged and weak, and blood lay like a pool under his face where it rested on the floor. I have killed him, she thought, placing her fingers against his neck. She could feel nothing.

Her legs wobbled as dizziness took hold. Holding onto the worktop, she splashed her face with water. Still, Lennie did not move. The thought, she should call someone, flited into her head, quickly replaced by who? An ambulance on one side of her brain told her, the other told her to wait, what's the rush; he is dead.

Judy? Before dismissing the thought, she did not want her involved. Angela, I will call Angela, she'd know what to do. But first, she needed a drink. Calling her daughter out of the blue would be tricky. Angela may not come. What then? Should she leave, let someone else find him. That was no good; her logical side said it was an accident, and if you left him. Deliberate. No one would know that it was her fault, she argued. The police might think an intruder did it or even that Lennie fell. Repeatedly she topped up her glass as her thoughts went backwards and forwards on what she should do.

*

'Hi, it's me, Angela. I have had a very garbled phone call from mum, and from what I could understand, she and Lennie have had a row, and there has been an accident.'

'Is that all she said?' Exclaimed Judy. 'Not being funny, but why did she call you?'

Angela snorted. 'Who knows, can you come and pick me up? My car is in for its service. When we get near to it, don't go straight to the house. Park behind the old rectory, and we will go through the back.'

'A bit cloak and dagger.'

'We may be able to use whatever has happened to our advantage, and if so, I would rather no one knew that we were there.'

Angela tried not to giggle. Glancing at Judy, she could see that she felt the same. As kids, they had often sneaked home using the old hidden path behind the house. With no usage, it had overgrown, brambles and nettles trying their best to block their way. The silence, unnoticed when they were children, now felt creepy. The abundant overhanging trees that hid them from view blocked the sunlight and gave the path a sinister feel. Climbing over the fence as children had been a breeze, but as adults and not so flexible, it took Judy two attempts and Angela three. Dressed in black, by the time they pulled themselves out of the bushes, they both looked bedraggled. Grinning at their state, Angela led the way.

Pushing open the back door, she put a finger to her lips as Judy went to call out. Shaking her head, she pointed towards the kitchen where the radio was playing. Hearing a moan, they rushed forwards; and both stopped in the doorway. Lennie lay on his side in a pool of blood. Judy gagged. Angela's head whipped around; the moaning was coming from upstairs. Creeping up the stairs, it got louder. Wendy lay across her bed, surrounded by pill bottles.

'I will see to her,' Judy whispered. 'You go and check on Lennie.'

Steeling herself to enter, Judy bent over and lifted Wendy's head.

'Mum, what have you done? How many have you taken?'

Wendy tried to focus, the drink sloshing about in her stomach combined with Lennie's punch, making her feel drowsy. Wendy was sure it was Angela she had called, and could not understand why Judy was talking to her.

'I told him,' she muttered. 'He did not like it, and he hit me.' Wendy giggled. 'Not allowed. So I killed him.' Pushing herself up the bed, she smiled at Judy. 'Hello love, I am having a bit of a nap. I don't feel so good.' Her eyes closed as she started to sink back down into sleep.

Grabbing her shoulders, Judy shook her.

'Mum, wake up. I want the truth. Did you …'

Wendy's eyes snapped open, 'I need a drink,' she slurred while trying to get off the bed.

'Stay there. I will get you something.'

Judy ran down the stairs to find Angela sitting at the kitchen table with Lennie, still on the floor. Not wanting him to hear, she whispered, 'have you checked him? She said she had killed him.'

'He is unconscious but breathing,' Angela whispered back. 'What about mum?'

Grabbing a couple of bottles of red wine from the rack, Judy donned a pair of rubber gloves.

'She wants a drink, and I want answers.'

Wendy somehow managed to get herself off the bed before toppling onto the floor. Pulling her up and propping her up against it, Judy felt overwhelming revulsion about what she was about to do. Opening both bottles, Judy reached for the rest of the pills scattered over the bed and piled them on the floor next to Wendy. Filling up a glass, she crushed a handful into the liquid.

'Mum, drink this. You will feel better.'

Wendy opened her eyes and tried to smile, but her mouth would not obey and instead gaped open, making her look like a fish. Judy held her head, tipping up the glass carefully; though she wanted nothing more than to ram the drink and drugs down Wendy's throat, she was still conscious that she had to be gentle so as not to show any force.

'*Mum*,' she snapped. 'Tell me, did you ...'

Wendy grabbed Judy's arm, gabbling.

'He took her money ... He loves Mark. Lennie says it was for me so we could be together. He killed Elaine. She won't like that; Lennie was drunk ... Never going to happen, he said. It is nothing but nonsense, wishful thinking ... Why would he? Now he is dead. Mark doesn't have to know. You won't tell him, will you? Please don't let on that I have said anything. If he finds out, I have said anything. He'll ...'

Filling a glass with drink, Judy was determined to get to the truth.

'Mum, look at me. Am I your daughter?' Slapping Wendy across the face as her eyes flew open, Judy raged. 'Tell me. For once in your miserable life, tell the truth. Did you take me? Am I somebody else's child?'

Tears slid down Wendy's face; her life was unravelling in front of her. She loved Judy. Wendy chose her to be her daughter, unlike Angela, who had been thrust on her by circumstances. She had to make her understand ... Her head was so fuddled, pushing away the glass Judy held, she attempted to pull herself up. Judy's eyes followed her progress, flopping back down, the effort too much. Wendy mumbled.

'Your mother made it seem like she did not want you. I saw her leave you outside the shops while she chattered away inside. You smiled at me, and I was lost. I picked you up and walked away. You snuggled into me and slept. I saw it as a sign that everything would be okay. I love you. You are my child.'

'Did Lennie know?'

Wendy shook her head; once, she had nearly told him but knew that she could not take the chance that he would make her give Judy back. It had been bad enough when he'd found out that she had changed her name so that no one could find her. Mrs. Took, whose inheritance she had received, had been expected by her family to leave it to them. They had wanted to contest the will saying that she had coerced Evelyn into giving everything to her. They had no proof, her lawyer assuring them that it was all above board and that Evelyn had been in sound mind, and her death might have been unexpected but was explainable.

After a friend of hers had died in childbirth, the thought of being pregnant was something Wendy determined she would never be. Taking Judy had made her life complete. She had been an adorable baby. Meeting Lennie, who already had a son, was like a dream come true. The only blight on the horizon was Elaine standing in her way of having a proper family, and then she wasn't. Wendy realised early in their relationship that Lennie was playing fast and loose with Elaine's property and money. He had been indiscreet after a particularly drunken afternoon that they had spent in bed.

'Money. Lots of money. Shush … I haven't taken it all, a few properties, and she'll never miss what she doesn't know she has.'

'Who? Lennie, what do you mean? Have you been stealing?

As Lennie fell into a stupor, Wendy filed away the information for the future and never mentioned anything about what was said. When she started looking after Mark, she searched his house and found paperwork showing that he had been practicing Elaine's signature. From her background, Wendy knew precisely; what that meant. When Elaine left, Wendy had doubts, but as it was what she had wanted, she pushed them to the back of her mind and went along with what Lennie told her, and was a mother to Mark as she was to Judy, building their lives together until Angela came along and spoilt it all.

She had known Peter and Betty for years and that Peter fancied her even when he knew she was going out with Lennie. Constantly saying he loved her and that Betty meant nothing to him and that he would do anything for Wendy, she only had to ask.

Peter would corner her with his regrets. His words were always the same.

'Say the word, and I will dump Betty in a heartbeat. It's you I love, and I always have.'

Who would have thought a one-night stand would get you pregnant it was the sort of thing you read about happening in books, not real life. It happened after a few bad months when the rows between her and Lennie had reached war status. They had met by chance in a hotel lobby, Wendy staying to meet up with an old friend and Peter for a business meeting. Disappointed the evening was cancelled when Janice, her friend, had been taken ill and at a loose end, Wendy was heading to the bar when she heard her name called. Her first thought of seeing Peter was, oh Christ, with no Betty in tow, she had let her guard down and allowed him to take her to dinner. The drink had flowed, and the rest, as they say, is history.

Wendy could not shift her. Angela had clung on, no matter what she did. Sure that Lennie suspected when he began to look elsewhere for his entertainment. Peter had no idea he might be her father, and more importantly, neither did Betty. Angela was the image of Wendy, and nothing of either Lennie or Peter's looks marred her features.

Wendy's head flopped forwards as she slid down onto the floor. Judy checked her pulse, which was now fluttering and weak. She filled another glass to the brim and knocked it over into some pills, leaving Wendy among the mess.

Angela heard Judy come down the stairs closing the kitchen door, she whispered, 'I have managed to keep out of his eye line, but I think he may be coming round. What about mum?'

'Let's go,' Judy answered, pulling Angela towards the back door. 'She's drunk enough wine and downed enough pills to drop an elephant. We'll come back. Find them and then report them. Perhaps for once, they will do us all a favour and die. If they do, then it could not have worked out better. It takes the risk out of killing them ourselves.' Seeing Angela's look, she snapped, 'why pretend?'

Arriving back at the house this time, they pulled the car onto the drive; Judy and Angela were surprised to see a car they did not recognise blocking their way. They could see that the keys were still in the ignition, and the front door was open. Puzzled as to who it could be, they entered the hall.

'Mum, dad,' shouted Judy.

'In here.' A voice replied from the kitchen.

Betty was bending over Lennie while speaking on her phone.

'Thank god you are here. I only came to pick up some paperwork. I was not expecting to find anyone home. That is why I used my key. They were supposed to be away. Your father is hurt, and your mum is. Oh, Judy, I am so sorry. I think … she is dead. I have called an ambulance, and the police are also on their way.'

Lost for words, both Angela and Judy stared at Betty. Taking it for the shock, she took Judy into the lounge and made her sit down. Angela expected to follow.

Speaking to Judy while excluding Angela, she said, 'best wait in here, love. Let the professionals deal with … Wendy. Your mother … has been drinking, and I think she may have … they're … Wait here. I will go and speak to them.'

'Should we call Mark,' whispered Judy as the paramedics pounded up the stairs, hearing another lot in the kitchen talking to Lennie.

'Christ, it's all going to come out, and I can see the headline; Killer dad and child snatcher mum; I wish Cassie hadn't been so thorough with her research and had let the past stay buried.'

Angela was glad it would all come out, and what did she care? Lennie didn't love her, and her mother hated her. Like a wild beast, her mother directed her fury toward Angela, and what was to miss about that? She glared at Betty hovering in the door, staring at her Angela drawled.

'You found them, so the police will want to speak to you, and I hope you have an alibi.'

She laughed to see Betty blush at the insinuation.

'Your father's injured, and your mother is dead. Why do you have to be so nasty? I have only been trying to help.'

'I will text Cassie,' said Judy. 'Let her tell Mark in person.'

'Good idea,' interjected Betty. 'Better that way. Mark will be so upset. What with him and Lennie being so close.' Glancing over to Angela, her expression equally hard, she added, 'as was Judy also to Wendy.'

With the arrival of the police, Betty became flustered, as if she had guilty written onto her forehead. Trying not to look amused, Angela and Judy were glad when Mark turned up, Cassie dragging behind, the questions she dearly wanted to ask written large across her face.

As the ambulance paramedics took Lennie out by stretcher, Angela nudged Mark in the ribs and nodded.

Patting Lennie's shoulder, he muttered.

'You'll be fine, dad.' Looking up to see everyone staring, he made his face crumble, 'I love you.'

Cassie wrapped her arms around him.

'They will look after him. We can follow them to the hospital.' Turning to the policeman, she asked, 'I take it we can go?' Before he could answer, she glanced at Angela and Judy. 'Are you coming?'

'Once mum has left, we will follow,' Judy replied, her voice breaking. 'We want …'

'Of course, you do, Judy.' Betty trilled, pulling her into a hug. 'You go with Mark,' she told Cassie, 'I will stay with Judy until. Well …'

Finally, they could leave, thought Angela, Betty going to the police station to make a statement had wanted first to come with Judy to the hospital, still convinced she was in shock. Waving her away, Judy felt that, at last, she could breathe. Sitting in the car, they let the silence between them calm their nerves.

'That was a bit of luck,' said Angela. 'Usually seeing Betty always sets my teeth on edge, today though she saved us from a wealth of questions. I wonder if she would act differently towards you if she knew that you and mum aren't related.' Glancing across at Judy, smelling the tension coming off her, she asked, 'did you kill her? Mum, I mean not Betty.'

Judy's heart had not stopped hammering since she had walked into the bedroom. Sure that her actions; had certainly helped Wendy to die. Did her intervention tip Wendy over the edge into death; Judy had no idea. The pills, scattered over the bed, could be Wendy opening the boxes, not necessarily because she had been taking them. Something Judy would never know and, if honest, didn't care to know. When Betty had told them that Wendy was dead, she had felt a weight lift from her shoulders. The last few weeks had been particularly hard. The more she pulled away, the more Wendy clung on. Now all she had to do was leave Paul, another who thought everything required picking over. That was for another day, though phoning him to say what had happened meant he was already rushing to the hospital, telling her not to worry and that he would look after everything.

'In answer to your question,' Judy told Angela, 'I don't know, maybe. She was pretty drunk when we got there, and whether she had taken any pills, who knows? How can you be so calm about it?'

When Angela found out they weren't sisters, dislike of Judy had been at the forefront of her mind. Loved by the mother who should have loved Angela, jealousy reared its ugly head. Now though, she was glad. With her mother dead, she was not related to anyone. The relations Cassie had found she didn't count because Angela had no intention of ever getting in touch with them. They had been a means to an end. Her mother's death felt like a release and a beginning.

'Mum often threw pills about and threatened to kill herself, usually after a blow-up with Lennie. But I am pretty sure that she never took any. I think she liked the theatre of making him think that she would. I caught them arguing about it once. Lennie was goading her to do it, and she was screaming at him that one day she would, and then he would be sorry. Lennie laughed, which made her screech all the more.'

*

Lennie could hear muttering as if from a distance, and his eyes felt sticky as he opened them, his voice croaking as he asked for a drink.

'Dad, thank god you're awake. I'll get you some water.'

Mark's hands shook as he lifted the carafe, supporting Lennie's head, and gently held the glass to his lips.

'What happened?' asked Lennie, shocked to see the concerned faces peering down at him.

Mark indicated that they should all sit.

Angela nudged Mark and murmured, 'hold his hand.'

Judy stifled a giggle, feeling that it was all a bit surreal. Cassie clamped her hand onto her arm and shook her head. Shaking her off, she leaned forwards to peer at Lennie, thinking, a pity Wendy did such a useless job. With him dead, it would all be over. Instead, because of his injury, they would have to wait a bit longer before dealing with him.

'Mum is dead,' stated Angela bluntly before glancing at Judy. 'The police think she took her life thinking she had killed you.'

Lennie stared. 'That's not possible. We argued, and I'll admit I hit her, and she retaliated. Nothing new there, so why take her life? It does not make any sense.'

'Well, it is too late now to ask her,' said Angela. 'I wish we had been able to sort out our differences, and I will never now find out why she did not like me,' Head down in remorse, she let Cassie draw her into a hug.

The door opened and in bustled a nurse.

'Time to go, Lennie; need's his rest. You can come back tomorrow.'

'Bye,' they all said together while at the same time trying not to look eager to leave.

'Dad, I know you must feel bad. Don't blame yourself. I'm sure it wasn't your fault. Concentrate on getting better.'

'Thanks, Judy. That means the world to me.'

Judy grinned as she closed the door. *Thinking you won't be thanking me when you get your just desserts.*

As they left the hospital, Mark asked, 'so what happened?' looking to Angela and Judy for answers.

Throwing the question back at him, Judy asked, 'how would we know? When Angela and I arrived at the house, Betty was already there, and she told us what happened.'

'So it was suicide then,' exclaimed Cassie. 'You … I thought maybe you had …'

Angela laughed.

'That was only ever meant as a joke. Neither of us killed mum. Mind you, Betty, may have, for all their supposed friendship, sarcastic remarks often flew between them. They shared a secret, of that I'm sure, but I have no idea what. Honestly, do you think either of us could have gone through with it? You heard Lennie say that one of their fights had gotten out of hand. I agree it seems strange that mum would take her life. I can only imagine that she must have truly thought she had killed Lennie. Which I'll admit still seems strange as it was obvious that she didn't like him.'

Cassie heard the words but was unsure if she believed them. Angela may have been hesitant to help Wendy on her way. She was her mother, but Judy was a different matter. Cassie had seen how Judy had acted towards Wendy even before they had found out what she had done. Since then, she'd been trying to move further away from Wendy's influence. Something which she didn't understand, so Wendy clung to her more. Plus, Judy had been the one adamant on more than one occasion heard to say they would all be better off if both Wendy and Lennie were dead. As the hairs on her neck stood up, Cassie realised she did not trust either of them.

Shaking the thoughts of what they may be capable of out of her head, she said, 'when Lennie comes home, I think one of you may have to move in to look after him, especially for the first few weeks. Do you think it should be you, Mark? If so, I don't mind helping. Plus, there will also be Wendy's funeral to arrange. Do you know if she wanted to be buried or cremated?'

At the words funeral, Mark flinched. He had no idea what either Wendy or Lennie wanted to happen to them after their death. Nothing in the paperwork they had found mentioned anything about funerals by either of them. Mark thought, as her daughter, it would be up to Angela to sort it out. He certainly did not want to do it, bad enough when Lennie went, they would expect him to deal with his one.

Mark dearly wanted to walk away from all of them. Like Cassie, he was unsure about the facts of Wendy's death. Something niggled. Betty had told Mark the police had determined nothing wrong with the picture she had presented in her statement to them. She had phoned once home to find out if he was okay and wanted to know how Judy was coping. Reminding him that if either of them needed anything, she and Peter would be only too happy to help; all they had to do was call. As usual, no mention of help for Angela was given.

11

NOVEMBER

It hadn't taken long for Lennie to bounce back from his injuries, thought Angela, as she got herself ready for her mother's funeral. When he had first come home from the hospital, she had caught him on the odd occasion looking at her with a puzzled expression; his face scrunched up as if trying to figure something out. The few times Lennie had looked as if about to say something, her sixth sense made her beat a hasty retreat. Sure that if he spoke about what was on his mind, it would set off a chain reaction that she was unsure about letting play out. Angela remained convinced that Judy had killed her mother but was unable to prove it and had gone along with the suicide theory. The autopsy had determined that Wendy's blood alcohol results were through the roof, and her system flooded with paracetamol, known for her love of drink, the state of her liver added even more weight to the findings that her death was a suicide.

When Angela had asked for help in arranging the funeral, Mark laughed. His only offer was; to burn the *bitch*.

'I'm happy to take her money,' said Judy. 'But I can't help you. Because of her, I don't know who I am, and I cannot forgive her that.'

Angela understood her sister's anger and the emotions stirred up since the revelations came to light, but her refusal to help with any arrangements annoyed her.

Cassie was also no help. She flitted about, still moaning that Wendy had escaped punishment for her crimes.

Now that the day was here, Angela could admit, if only to herself, that she felt a bit sad. Even though she and her mother had never gotten on, Angela still felt a thread of something connecting them as mother and daughter. Convinced her feelings were not as simple as blind love or hate; if asked to articulate, Angela wouldn't be able to give a clear answer. Sorry that her mother was dead one minute, and the next, glad that she was.

'The last time we were in this church,' whispered Angela to Judy, 'was for your wedding.'

'And like then, this lot have only turned up for the party,' Judy retorted, glancing round at the filled church full of Wendy's friends.

She would have loved being the centre of attention – even if it was at her funeral, thought Judy, she would have seen it as a fitting send-off. With no help from herself or Mark, Angela had gone all out regarding the wake. Judy would have preferred to have stayed home. Only turning up due to Mark's persistence in telling her that if she wanted to lay Wendy's ghost to rest, she needed to be there at the finish.

Angela smirked. Like black crows, her mother's friends left the church and made a beeline toward the three of them; as they offered their condolences, tissues patting away pretend tears, careful not to smudge their make-up, they clucked together like geese.

'We shall miss your mother's parties. Nobody could party like Wendy.'

Lennie was equally surrounded, widows and even some of their younger friends fluttering around him, offering their support while their husbands and boyfriends looked on with amusement. Paul and Cassie stood off to the side like spare parts. Paul kept his eyes focused on Judy tracking each person who came near her. While Cassie's foot-tapping impatience was doing nothing to stem the tide of her anger towards Wendy, seething still, even though she was now dead and buried.

Back at the house, it didn't take long before a party atmosphere prevailed. Lennie busied himself, pouring drinks and filling the glasses to the brim, his smile though, for once, more like a grimace as he did the rounds, Wendy's absence duly commented on by all. Mark quickly retreated to a corner and placed a bottle of whiskey on the floor beside him, the look on his face making sure he was left alone. Even Cassie read the signs correctly and gave him a wide berth. She had tried to initiate a conversation with Judy and had been given the brush off. Another one, she thought, with a face like thunder, scowling at everyone who dared to approach her.

Everyone had heard Judy bite Paul's head off when he had tried to take her arm, and now he stood morosely watching her from the side-lines. Betty had also cornered Judy.

'Oh, Judy, you must miss your mum so much. She loved you. I'm sure she took her life by mistake. Wendy would never do anything to hurt you. I'm here if you need me. Please call me. You're like a daughter …'

Betty had gotten a mouthful for her troubles, making others mutter that Judy was distressed because of how close she had been to Wendy.

Angela was the only one who appeared to be taking on her mother's mantel and having a good time doing so. Her loud laughter and wild gestures made her appear as drunk as her mother used to be. Aware of the glances thrown her way, Angela became more outlandish in her actions. She was not drunk but stone-cold sober. Between her bouts of rowdiness, Angela had seen everyone's eyes roaming between her and her family, and with the tension in the air, none wanted to miss anything if it kicked off.

Lennie was the first to break. Terry was braying that they needed Wendy back to liven up the party.

'This is dull. Crank up the music and get some dancing going.'

Taking exception at this being her wake and not a party, Lennie punched him. Terry fell against the table with the food on and sent it flying. Everything stopped. Lennie stood red-faced and panting. All eyes swung towards him, accusations like arrows splaying forth from each one.

Peter helped Terry to get up as a couple of other men squared up to Lennie, shouting at him to get a grip.

Mark, pushing himself away from the corner where he had taken up his refuge, roared. 'Enough,' and stepped between them. 'Can't you all for once fucking behave?'

'Time to go,' shouted Angela, clapping her hands to make the point, trying not to giggle at the smell of testosterone flooding the room.

'Thank you all for coming. It has been a long day.'

Angela herded everyone like sheep towards the door. Betty and Peter wanted to stay.

'No chance. Now be good fatties and piss off.'

Slamming the door on their cries of outrage, she turned to look at Lennie.

'Still handy with your fists, I see. Mother told me that you used to hit her. It's because of you that she is dead. Pity, it was not you instead.'

Lennie exploded, amazed at her outburst. He retorted, 'why are you defending her? You know she never liked you. As to hitting her, let me tell you, she gave as good as she got. Do not forget I ended up in the hospital; she could have killed me. So before you start casting blame, you should get your facts straight.'

Angela's first instinct was to retaliate, the words bubbling up in her mouth, ready to let fly. Think, she told herself. Remember to play the long game.

Keeping her voice steady, she replied, 'I am well aware that I was not mother's favourite. We all know that Judy was. But I still loved her.' Trying to look sad, she added, 'I am upset because ... Well, she told me that she was going to let me into a big secret. Now, I will never know what she meant.'

Angela worked hard to keep her face immobile aware that she had thrown a grenade into the mix.

'Her secret or someone else's?' demanded Lennie. 'You are lying. Wendy might tell Judy something. I do not believe that she would ever tell you. I think you are making it up. Do any of you know what she is on about?'

'Tell us about Elaine?' Cassie blurted out.

Lennie's eyes flew to Mark's.

'Yes, tell us about my mother. Did you use your fists on her as you did on Wendy? Is that why she left? And me? Why did she not take me with her?'

Lennie felt like a caged animal looking for a way out. His first thought was, how do they know? Sure that Wendy would never have said anything as she had more than enough of her secrets to hide. None that she would have liked Judy to know. What to say? How much did they know? Cassie looked smug, Mark furious, while Judy looked bored – a look that she had been wearing a lot lately, and Angela looked even smugger than Cassie. His main concern was losing his son. That could not happen.

'Mark, would you come with me to my office? So I can talk to you in private.'

'You want to fob him off,' yelled Cassie. 'Tell us, how is it that not only is Wendy, not Mark's mother, but that you are not even his father either.'

Lennie launched himself at Cassie, his roar galvanising them all to act. Before he could reach her, Mark had blocked his path, and Judy had pulled her out of the way. Angela was trying hard not to grin; this was much better than she had hoped.

'Am I your son? My birth certificate shows the column for my father as unknown. I'd never seen it until Cassie ordered me a copy. Is that why you always dealt with anything requiring one? Because you knew that I would ask questions.'

Seeing a chink of light, Lennie grabbed it, explaining to Mark, 'we had a row, and Elaine may not have put my name on it as a punishment. I am your father.'

Angela clapped, Judy swore, and Cassie snorted.

'What a liar. I tracked your ancestors, and there is no crossover anywhere with Mark's. DNA is a wonderful thing. It doesn't lie, unlike you.'

'My name may not be on it, but I am and have always been a father to Mark,' Lennie pleaded. 'Remember, it was Elaine, his mother, who left him. I did not. Why would I have taken care of Mark? If he isn't my child and why would Elaine leave him with me? Because I am his father.'

'So where is she?' Cassie flung back at him. 'Where did she go? After she left you both, she and her money appear to have disappeared. Why have you never tried to find her? Have you never wondered what had happened to her? Or is there another reason why you did not? Or could not, because …?'

Judy, who had kept silent, suddenly piped up, 'you took her money and property and stole it the same way mother did. Was finding out that she was a thief what gave you the idea to do the same to Elaine, or had you done it before to someone else?'

Lennie poured himself a drink, his hands shaking as he lifted the glass. His thoughts were in turmoil. How the hell have they found all this out? Deciding to come clean and tell the truth, well, his version of it, might mean that he could salvage his relationship with his son.

*

Betty put the phone down. Lennie's assurances that all was well didn't ring true. She had known him long enough to know when he was lying. Peter was worse than useless. She had sent him around to find out what was happening. Instead, he returned home drunk. Usually, she would have helped him to bed and brought him a coffee and a bucket. This time, though, she had lost her temper and flew at him. Unable to defend himself, she'd pushed him backwards onto the sofa. Never had she looked at him with such disdain and hatred? Peter turned over from her death stare and let sleep claim him.

Betty didn't sleep; she paced and remembered her last conversation with Wendy...

'They know something.'

Distracted by her knitting, Betty hadn't replied.

'Listen to me,' shouted Wendy. 'The children they know, and I think ... What if they tell Lennie? I blame Cassie; her meddling has unsettled everything.'

Betty froze. She knew all of Wendy and Lennie's secrets accumulated over the years. Only one of them bothered her coming out, and that was not going to happen.

'What's been said? Are you sure you weren't drunk and imagined it? What have you told them?'

Wendy had clammed up, and nothing Betty did could get her to open up. When she had left, like now, she paced. Her anger swelled. She knew that all everyone saw when they looked at her was a fat, middle age woman, completely lacking any sense of style. Hair permed tight to her head, her round face making it look like a halo of fuzz. Inside though, she was a different person. Not meek. Like she showed the world. She acted the way she did for Peter. Betty loved him and wanted to be the opposite of Wendy, who she knew he truly loved. When younger, she had never been jealous of how he felt, but the older she got though, the years wasted; hung heavy on her heart.

Wendy, she loved and hated in equal measure. She had gloried having a friend like her, their closeness, no one could understand. Their look was so different. Betty was safe and was no competition to Wendy, and she would never outshine her, and that had always been the basis of their friendship. For Betty, being in Wendy's orbit meant she stayed out of the shadows; and was part of the group, not forgotten.

She knew that Peter only married her because he couldn't have Wendy and that she wasn't a second choice; or even third. It didn't matter.

It was what she had overheard at Wendy's funeral that had made her frightened. She had to stop Cassie's investigations. And if Lennie would not do it, then it would be up to her. Once again, she would have to clear up the mess that others made.

She remembered how finding Lennie hurt had made her feel powerful. Usually larger than life, to see him inert, his breath laboured, had thrilled her. She would have left him, but she heard a noise and realised they weren't alone. As she mounted the stairs, she called out to Wendy, and only a groan returned. She lay on the floor surrounded by drink and pills. She'd vomited, and it lay pool-like beside her. Betty had jumped when her eyes opened and rolled backwards. Shaking her, she shouted.

'Wendy, what have you taken? Come on, enough now. Lennie's hurt. He needs you.'

'He's dead. I've killed him.'

Betty let Wendy fall. Indecision made her shake. Lennie wasn't dead yet, but he still might die. Perhaps she could … If both of them were gone, then the truth need never come out. She and Peter would be safe.

'Wendy, my love. Let me help you sit, sip this, and you will feel better.'

'You are the only one I can trust,' slurred Wendy. 'You need to …'

'I'll see to everything, now drink.'

Betty looked back at her friend. Wendy's face looked slack, ugly, and blotchy from the drink. Her eyes roamed around the room, smelling sickness and alcohol like a sleazy pub, her gaze alighted on the address book – Wendy always thought of herself as modern – when in fact, she was more old-fashioned in some ways than Betty. Picking it up, she flicked through its pages, stilling as she heard a car pull onto the drive. Kneeling beside Lennie and fixing a caring expression on her face, Betty had to suppress a grimace when Angela entered the kitchen but smiled when her eyes alighted on Judy. With Wendy gone, she hoped to step into her shoes, sure that she could be a better mother to her than Wendy had ever been.

*

Mark opened the door to the house and closed it with a sigh. The last few days had drained him. When Lennie had asked to talk to him privately, his expectations were low of hearing anything worthwhile. Lennie surprised him by getting straight to the point.

'I admit that before Elaine left us, I transferred some of her property and money into my name. When she asked me to look into her finances, she had no idea of her worth or what she had in her portfolio.'

'How is that possible?' Mark asked.

'The subject of finances bored her. Her father had always taken care of the family business and was disinterested as long as she could buy what she liked. Handing it all over to me to sort was nothing more than what she was used to doing.'

The temptation was too great for him to resist, especially as Elaine would never ask what they were and didn't want to read them. Expecting that with having a baby, they would stay together, and it helped to ease his conscious about deceiving her.

'When you were born,' said Lennie, 'I was over the moon, so happy. I thought Elaine was too. However, it hadn't taken her long before she showed signs of having the baby blues, a catchall term used back in the day to describe mothers who were not coping. Mostly they showed themselves by her moping about the house still in her pyjamas, unwashed and unkempt. Then things changed.

'I worked out of my office at home and could hear her shouting at you to be quiet. Returning home from visiting a client, I found the front door unlocked, you in the garden, and Elaine was asleep upstairs. I will admit that I lost my temper and hit her, a glancing blow, enough to give her a black eye. By this time, you were in a state, balling at the top of your lungs, nappy wet, and desperate for a feed. Elaine was indifferent to your needs, more intent on making herself a cup of coffee, yelling at me that if I was that bothered, I should see to you myself. After that, I was wary every time I left the house as to what I would find when coming home.

'My hitting acted as a catalyst, and she started to be in the present more and aware of what you needed when you cried. Cleaning the house and taking care of herself all improved she became a different person. The only blip was when I suggested that we get married. She worried over it for days, and I thought she would slide back into her old ways. She didn't. She also made it clear that she did not want to get married. If I'm being honest, I had only asked because of you, and it wasn't something that bothered me. Then she left.'

Mark had tried to listen with an open mind. They all wanted to hear the truth, but none believed that Lennie was doing so. The question.

'Were you seeing Wendy before my mother disappeared?'

Had soon made Lennie pause, and it was easy to see the cogs in his head turning as he thought of what best to say in reply. Admitting that he had, appeared to make Lennie deflate. Mark suggested that perhaps this was why his mother had gone.

'No!' he had exclaimed. 'Elaine believed that Wendy was a client. I gave her no reason to think anything other than that.'

'You can't be sure of that! Whatever the real reason, I still do not understand why she did not take me with her. No offence to you, but usually a child goes with the mother, especially as there may be some doubt that I am even your son.'

'You are mine,' shouted Lennie, 'no matter what Cassie thinks, she has or has not found out. Elaine was probably being Elaine by not putting my name on your birth certificate. You are my son. I have no doubts.'

'The problem for you is that I do not believe I am. The evidence stacks up against me being so, and Cassie's research supports that fact.'

His suggestion that he take a DNA test made Lennie blanch giving Mark all the answers; he needed. Lennie had pleaded with him before raging about everyone else, asking Mark if they could put it all behind them. After all, he had raised him, and he loved him. Lennie cried.

'If I knew where Elaine had gone, I would tell you, but I don't.'

Playing on his sympathy, he told Mark that even though he and Wendy may have rowed, he was grieving for her and needed time to come to terms with not only her death; but the revelations that Mark was putting to him.

Deliberately bringing the conversation back to the properties that Lennie had taken from his mother, Mark asked if Lennie still retained them. He mentioned every property sold in his name except Byford House, yet it was still very much owned by him. More than anything, this convinced Mark that he was not telling all the truth if any. Why mention everything else but not that? Determined to find out, Mark told Lennie he also needed time to clear his head and come to terms with Wendy's death, because although she may not have been his mother, she had brought him up as if she was.

They had agreed to give each other space to sort out how they felt. Hearing what they had discussed, Angela and Judy said they all needed to come to terms with what had happened. As soon as he had gotten home Mark packed a bag, Cassie had wanted to go away with him, but he had declined her offer.

'I need some time alone. There is a lot to take in and process.'

*

'We should confront him, find out what he knows,' whined Cassie, not for the first time. 'Does he even know that you and Angela are not his children? I feel that Mark is going to let him off too lightly. He has holed himself up in Byford House. He says that Lennie made no mention of owning it. Surely that must mean something. Wendy may have been your mother, Angela, yet, I cannot help but feel that by committing suicide, she has gotten off lightly. I wanted her punished, someone has to be, so it might as well be Lennie.'

Judy was numb and fed up listening to Cassie as she droned on for the best part of the day. The three of them had been holed up in Angela's flat while they figured out what to do. They wanted to talk about Lennie and hadn't told Mark they were meeting, worried that Lennie could sway Mark into letting him get away with what he had done. If he knew what Wendy had said to her, it might make him think differently.

Was it true? She was still coming to terms with the part she had played in Wendy's death. Angela, she knew, suspected that she had, if not killed her mother, then at least she helped her on her way. What did it matter? Thought Judy for the hundredth time, she had wanted her dead, and she was.

She was not so uptight about Lennie not being her father, which Judy saw as a bonus. But she would like to know if he knew she had been taken by Wendy and wasn't her child. Angela, she had found in the last few days even harder to understand, the only one of them who should by rights be genuinely grieving and yet the only one not seeming to be bothered.

At the reading of the will, Angela, at first, kept her face blank and her demeanour calm. The explosion came when the solicitor told them that the estate belonging to her mother was to go to Judy, and Angela shouted.

'The *bitch* hated me, and the feeling was mutual. I am glad she is dead, and you are welcome to her tainted money,' before picking up her bag and slamming the door as she stormed out.

Judy did not feel bad about taking her inheritance from Wendy; the only part that made her uncomfortable was when Mark informed them of what Lennie had told him. How Wendy had changed her surname from Jones to Page after inheriting the estate of a Mrs. Took to keep one step ahead of her family, who believed that she had defrauded their aunt. Somehow Mark told them Lennie was under the impression that bringing Wendy's past to light made his defrauding of Elaine not so bad. His words that they were as bad as each other had not gone down well. Mark declared that Lennie might think it was okay to treat people that way, but Mark did not.

If Lennie killed Elaine, then not acknowledging the ownership of Byford House may mean that is where he has buried her. Surely though, Judy thought, if he had, he would have made plans that the house was not left vacant. Squatters could move in, or someone could have trashed the place, and with a possibility of police involvement, Lennie would be taking a chance on someone finding her. The grounds were huge, and it would take some doing to find out if he had buried her somewhere in them, but using modern technology, it was a possibility.

Breaking into her thoughts, Angela stated, 'don't you think that it has all been a bit of an anti-climax? Mother's death and Lennie coming clean. Where do we go with what we know? Now that my mother is dead, whatever we accuse her of is irrelevant. Lennie is doing his best to ingratiate himself with us all. Although the only one who matters to him and he has to win over is Mark. In Lennie's eyes, we do not count. We never have.'

Without thinking, Judy replied, 'Lennie killed Elaine. That is what Wendy told me.'

'*What*?' Screeched Cassie, jumping up. 'When did she tell you that? How long have you known? Why have you not told us before?'

Angela stared at Judy. Aware of her gaze, Judy blushed with shame.

You utter fucking cow, thought Angela. Knowing that the only time her mother was likely to have said something like that was when Judy was with her before she died. This god-forsaken family and their secrets whirled through her head. Even at the very end, it had to be Judy that got the gossip. Judy the one to be trusted. Even the one to kill. Convinced at the time that she had done it, now she was sure that Judy had killed her mother. Angela waited with interest to see what she said.

'Well? Are you not going to tell us?' demanded Cassie, all the anger she felt at Judy coming to the fore.

Her thoughts had been churning for days. Once the revelations had begun tearing the family apart, Judy had pulled further away from Cassie, and her dream of them starting a new life together and making their own little family of two; was disappearing. Instead, Judy was planning a new life abroad and had no idea Cassie had seen the brochures. Unable to reach Judy by phone Cassie called around to their house on the off chance of speaking to her. Paul had answered the door, telling her she was out, before enthusiastically inviting Cassie in. He had wanted to talk.

Boring, she had thought, had reached a whole new level. Paul had gone on and on about Judy and how since they had married, she'd changed. How he wanted children, but she did not. They hardly talked or laughed, how she was lost and in another place in her head, often not hearing him when he spoke to her. Cassie had to keep on stifling a giggle that threatened to break through. Finally, pausing for breath to ask her if she would like a drink, and while he was in the kitchen, she took the opportunity to have a nose around. She recognised the leather tote bag belonging to Judy pushed behind the settee and wondered why it was there. Cassie took a peek inside to see a brochure entitled. How to resettle in another country? Her pulse raced. Putting it back inside, she sat down as Paul brought the drinks.

Cassie could feel a headache coming on as she asked him, 'Any holidays coming up? Are you and Judy thinking of going abroad this year?'

Paul laughed.

'Not so likely. Judy does not like flying. Our honeymoon flight was a real trauma. I have never seen anyone look or be so sick. It was much worse than when we went to France, which had been bad enough. You and Mark were lucky to have gone ahead with Wendy and Lennie; believe me, the sight of Judy retching through the flight; was not one I wish to contemplate anytime soon.'

*

Judy sighed and wished all of her family would go away, and once they had dealt with everything to do with Lennie and Wendy, it was what she intended to do, get as far as possible and not come back. She had been driven mad by Cassie, who would not let it rest until she had squeezed every little nugget of information out in her quest to avenge the death of Rose. Pretending to care about Judy, Cassie's obsession was becoming frightening. Following Judy, her new occupation. Like a spy in a movie, Judy had nipped in and out of shops trying to shake her off. Looking in the windows to see if anyone was behind her, glancing over her shoulder as she hurried away.

Turning her head quickly when her name was called, her friend Sarah waving from across the road, Judy saw Cassie turn sharply away. Ignoring her, she continued on her way home, and sure she could feel her eyes on the back of her neck. Each time she went out, her constant looking over her shoulder had drawn Paul unusually for him to snap at her. Judy realised that she did not care and let her follow. What was there to see her life was boring, and Cassie was more than welcome to have it.

'I am not sure I believe what she said,' replied Judy, ignoring Cassie's glare. 'If she thought he had killed Elaine, why on earth would she stay living with him? Especially if she thought he was going to do the same to her. It does not make any sense.'

'It does, kind of,' Angela mused. 'If mum thought that there was even a small chance that Lennie would make public how she had gotten the money to pay for her garden parties, she would have stayed and kept quiet. Even more so if he threatened to tell you, and I bet if he did kill Elaine, he buried her within the grounds of Byford House. It makes sense Lennie hasn't said anything about it, even when speaking to Mark. I do not understand why he had to kill her in the first place. He had already taken money and property, which she was unaware she had. So to all intense and purposes, his fraud, if they had stayed together, would never have been found out.'

'When her parents died apart from Elaine, they had no other children,' explained Cassie. 'Her death would be the end of their family line. Perhaps the house belonged to her grandparents, and that's how she inherited it. If you think about it, the inside is old-fashioned, and there is no central heating for a start, only fireplaces. I bet no one has lived there for years. Yet the utilities are still connected. Do you think that Lennie did visit? Perhaps on the anniversary when he …'

'Do not be so stupid,' Angela laughed. 'Why? Would he want to remember? Besides, when I first looked inside the house, everything had a layer of dust. No one had been inside for years, and it smelt damp. As to her family owning it, my boss said it had been a rental for years before being taken off the market. As to the utilities, who knows why Lennie kept them connected, and who knows why he does anything? Without telling him that we know about it, we cannot ask him. It would be funny if he turned up while we were there. I am not sure who would be the more shocked.'

Mark, on his return from the house, had listened in disbelief as Judy told him what Wendy had said, each word uttered, his head filled with murderous thoughts of what he would like to do to Lennie. They told him they had all debated the truth, especially as Wendy was prone to lying and exaggeration. It felt right, and it explained a lot. He gained comfort from the fact that his mother did not abandon him with Lennie. He wanted the truth, whatever the consequences of hearing it may be. Lennie had to come to the Byford House. If this is where he buried Elaine, Mark wanted to know where on the grounds she was. How to get him there without alerting him would be the tricky part. Since Wendy's death, he danced around on tenterhooks, frightened to push Mark too far. He had tried to find out from Judy and Angela what Mark was feeling or how he and Lennie's relationship would work going forwards. Fed up with being pestered, Angela had left him a voicemail.

'Mark's gone away for a few days to sort himself out, and we have no idea where even Cassie doesn't know.'

'I am going to call him,' said Mark. 'And invite him to dinner, take him to that new restaurant that has opened in Aldeburgh. I want you to join us and make it a fun evening. Get him to relax, get him drunk. When we leave the restaurant, we bring him back to the house, which is only about a half-hour drive away from it. Once here, we sober him up and then make him tell us what happened to my mother.'

'And Cassie?' asked Angela. 'Only if she gets wind of what we are doing, she'll want to be involved. I think she is getting even more obsessed. Poor old Judy is getting worn out trying to avoid her. Aren't you?'

'Cassie has been following me for weeks. I am getting so used to seeing her pop up out of nowhere that I am more surprised when I do not see her. I don't think she is all there. I know what we have found out is weird by anyone's standards. But it is our weird and not hers. A distant relation of hers happens to be my mother, who killed herself after losing me. It seems to be a very tenuous link. She also seems to forget that I was only a baby. All I have ever known is Wendy. If Elaine was still alive, I might feel differently about having Cassie as a relative.

'No offence to you two, but I have had my fill of families. Wendy took me for her own while disliking Angela, her actual daughter. That, I can't get my head around. I am also not sorry in the least that she is dead. Her clinginess was becoming a problem, let alone her drinking, and none of us knew what she would say when full of it. I do not want what has happened shouted from the rooftops as Cassie would have us do or Wendy may have done when in one of her drunken rages.'

'You did kill her, didn't you? I know for a fact that she would not take pills.'

Judy gazed at Angela, aware also of Mark's questioning stare.

'I crushed several of them into her drink which she drank. Coupled with the drink already inside her. I think so.'

'Does that mean that I should kill Lennie,' blurted Mark.

Angela giggled.

'I feel a bit left out. To even it up, perhaps, I had better make plans to kill Cassie.'

At her words, all three went silent, their thoughts turning inwards as each contemplated what killing Lennie and Cassie would mean to them. Wendy's death had felt like a weight lifting from the three of them. For Judy, the smothering she had been feeling, the constant wanting to know where she was

217

and what she was doing, coupled with the same from Paul had worn her down for weeks. Angela, even though never close to her mother, had mixed feelings about her death. One part of her was glad she was dead, while another side still wanted a mother-daughter relationship to have been possible between them. She also felt a degree of animosity towards Judy; for her closeness to Wendy and because she had killed Angela's mother without seemingly a second thought.

Wendy's death for Mark had also been a release. When he had thought she was his mother, he had always been aware of the distance between them. Finding out she was not his mother added a sense of relief that they were not related. His relationship with Lennie was more complicated. When he believed that he was his father, Mark had thought the world of him until the competition between them morphed into something a bit darker once he had turned a teenager. As an adult, it was easy to see the flaws that made Lennie who he was. Now that he knew they were not related, coupled with the fact that they had proof that he had stolen from Elaine and with the possibility that he may have also killed her. Mark's feelings were all over the place.

*

'This is nice,' said Lennie, settling back into the seat. When Mark suggested going out to dinner with the girls, he had been beside himself. Hoping that it meant that things would soon be back on track and that they could move on from Wendy's death and all the questions and feelings it had stirred up. Listening to the three of them chatter made him think of how life could have been if Wendy had not been so wrapped up in Judy, pushing Mark and especially Angela away. For a moment, his part in Angela's treatment flared, making him blush at how he had treated her. That is all behind us, Lennie told himself, new beginnings, fresh start.

'Here we are,' pointed Mark. 'Looks good, do you not think? And more importantly, it has had plenty of good reviews. So it should be a good night.'

Lennie opened the door and ushered the three of them inside, and Mark told the receptionist they had a table booked. Her smile at his son lifted Lennie's heart to see. He wished that Mark would dump Cassie and find someone more suitable. When Mark introduced her to the family, she appeared to fit in mainly because she hung on every word he uttered and agreed with everything Wendy said. Lennie had found her intenseness wearing and, if honest frightening. The term "Bunny boiler" often came to mind when he heard her name mentioned.

Taking their seats, the waiter handed Lennie the wine menu, which he then passed to Mark. 'You chose. I am sure you'll choose a good one.'

Angela snorted. 'He will pick Merlot. After all, that is all he knows.' Turning to the waiter, she told him, 'I will have a large glass of Malbec, thank you very much! Raising her eyebrows at Judy, she asked, 'you?'

Judy nodded her agreement, thinking, I do not care. Seeing Lennie's smile each time his eyes landed on Mark was riling her. It didn't make sense. Mark had always been his favourite, and she had been Wendy's. Yet, she was feeling jealous. Angela appeared to be amused rather than angry. She certainly, was not jealous. If Judy had to sum up Angela's attitude, it would be indifferent.

Even though she had never met her biological mother, the thought that Lennie may have killed Mark's mother, she was finding for some reason hard to get over. Her feelings were at odds with her possible responsibility for the death of Wendy. The pills she had given her contributed, if not caused, her death, and Judy could not even find a flicker of angst that she may have committed murder.

Mark knew the evening was proceeding just how he had hoped as soon as Lennie began his usual one-upmanship. As the drink kicked in and the whiskey flowed, his words became more slurred, his finger pointing more extreme. Making him aware early on in the evening that the meal was on him, Lennie had laughed as he patted his pocket.

Telling Mark with a chuckle. 'My old pad; won't be needed.'

Mark had laughed along with him while Angela and Judy had gone to the toilet.

Watching them go, Lennie had smirked.

'Girls, huh. Always have to go in twos. Speaking of girls, where's Cassie? She's usually stuck to you like glue. Haven't fallen out, have you?' he asked hopefully.

'Cassie's not well,' said Angela as she and Judy sat down. 'Shall we get the bill, Mark? Take the scenic route home. Show Lennie what Paul is proposing on buying next?'

'You are moving? Why?'

Angela interrupted. 'We all know what Paul is like, always trying to climb the greasy ladder. Bigger is better as far as he is concerned. Poor old Judy has no say in the matter. This place is enormous. Mother will be livid that she cannot interfere.' At their looks, she grinned. 'Oops, a bit of a gaffe; forgot for a minute that she is dead.'

Silence greeted her words.

'Don't pretend that you all miss her. Be honest for once.' Glugging the last of her wine down, she pointed the glass at the three of them, 'that is not going to happen any time soon. This family is incapable of telling the truth.'

'Angela,' exclaimed Mark. 'That is enough. You do not have to spoil the evening. Judy, you bring the car around while

I pay the bill. Dad, you go with her. You had better keep hold of him he is a bit worse for wear. Angela can wait for me.'

Once Lennie and Judy were out of earshot. Mark grabbed Angela's arm.

'You have drunk most of the wine and are beginning to sound like your mother. What are you trying to do? Can you at least wait until we are at the house before sounding off? Fortunately, Lennie has done the same to the whiskey. Hopefully, that means he is not with it enough to understand what you were talking about.'

Lennie had fallen asleep and was snuffling. Locked inside their thoughts, Judy, Mark, and Angela stayed silent on the drive to the house. As the lights swept across the driveway, Lennie began to stir. Mark got him out of the car before he could have a chance to question where they were and frogmarched him inside. Angela headed to the kitchen to put the kettle on while Judy lit the fire in the lounge. Pushing Lennie down onto a sofa, Mark's heart hammered inside his chest. Still feeling lightheaded from the whiskey, Lennie's head fell back, snapping forwards as Angela breezed into the room.

'Coffees up, and more importantly, there is cake.'

Placing the tray down onto the table, Angela asked, 'shall I be the mother?' before collapsing into giggles. 'Sorry, it's the wine. It is making me feel a bit silly.'

'Where are we?' asked Lennie as his gaze travelled around the room, his memory piqued.

Three avid faces stared at him, waiting for him to realise.

'What?' he snapped, for some reason feeling cornered. Taking the cup from Angela, Lennie's hand shook, dismissing her offer of a piece of cake with a shake of his head. He felt strange, something was not right, and fear swept over him, and he could almost taste it.

'We brought you here so you could tell us the truth about what happened to my mother.'

Puzzled, Lennie looked to Angela and Judy for help, replying, 'I don't understand what you mean. Wendy killed herself.'

'*Not her.*' Mark snapped angrily. 'My real mother, Elaine. Before Wendy died, she told Judy that you had killed her. Saying you did it for her so the two of you could be together. Do not look away. Tell me, did you kill her, and if so, where? Is she buried?'

Lennie stood up, 'I do not have to listen to this. How could my son accuse me of murder? She has poisoned your minds. How do you know she did not do it? Wendy was more than capable. I have worn the bruises to prove it.'

'But that is it. I am not your son, am I? Besides, I am gay, and we all know that such a macho man as you could never have a homosexual for a son. Oh no, that would never happen, a red-blooded male like you with women falling at your feet. Bet I am not your son now, am I? Look at your face; it's a picture of horror at the thought. Before you ask, Cassie does know because she has been playing a part, giving me a front to hide behind, and I, well, she has her reasons for being with me.'

Lennie flopped down onto the sofa. His thoughts scrambled; Mark was wrong. Mark being gay didn't bother him so much – it did a little bit, more than a bit if he was being honest. It was more the hatred Mark felt for Lennie that hurt the most.

When Lennie found he would be unable to father any children, it was a killer blow to his self-esteem as a man. Meeting Elaine and finding out that she was pregnant had been like all his Christmases had come at once. He never said anything to her but worked hard to assure her he was happy and couldn't wait to hold his son in his arms. As her pregnancy progressed, she had endeavoured several times to say something to him, but he wouldn't listen. As far as he was concerned, the baby was his and no one else's. To hear Mark talk to him with so much venom was too much to bear. He had loved him from the moment he was born.

Making sure to speak clearly, Lennie looked at each of them in turn and said, 'I did not kill Elaine. However, I will admit I took …'

'You are lying,' interrupted Angela. 'You've always been shifty, looking out for number one. Why take Elaine's money, this house, and other property; if you intended to marry her, it could all have been yours anyway. Cassie's research has been extensive in her quest to find Elaine's whereabouts. Nothing. She has no footprint anywhere. I will grant you she may have changed her name or even gone abroad. Her searches; came to nothing, meaning Elaine must be dead. You are the only one at the time to benefit from that happening. Did you bury her here? Is that why you haven't sold it, scared in case someone starts digging and finds her?'

'I have had enough of this,' Lennie heaved himself up off the sofa. 'You can all think what you like. I can only repeat. I did not kill her. As to this place, it goes on the market tomorrow. That should shut you all up about buried bodies. Now I would like to go home.'

As the cab pulled away, Angela turned to Mark, 'what do you think? Is he telling the truth?'

'I am loath to say it, but I think he is,' said Judy. Sighing as she felt a headache coming on. 'It all seems to be getting a bit out of control. Yet, we are no nearer to knowing what has happened to Elaine. Unless she's living as a hermit somewhere, I do not see how she can still be alive.'

*

Once home, Lennie, his brain still fizzing after his words with Mark, hoped he had managed to convince him that he was telling the truth. Selling the house should have been done years ago. Every time Lennie had gotten nearer to selling Byford House, he never let the sale go through. Long before Elaine had owned the property, it already had a dark reputation for a body buried in its grounds. The ground dug, ready for a pool to be fitted, revealed a grisly find, and the thought of someone digging up a body brought him out in a cold sweat. He had lied to Mark. Helped by Peter and Betty, they had buried Elaine at Byford.

They had fought, still convinced that it was an accident, all being one that he had hidden up. Lennie did not want Mark to find out. Their relationship was fragile enough, and if he wanted it to become stronger, Lennie knew that he would have to go through with it and put the house on the market. Cassie, he could cheerfully murder. If she had minded her own business, then none of this need come out. Looking into his finances and past without permission made him so angry he could strangle her with his bare hands. If Wendy were alive, she would no doubt laugh at the situation. Lennie wished that he hadn't ignored Betty's warnings at the funeral.

'What's going on? I've just heard Cassie telling Mary that she is researching your and Wendy's family history. Surely that can't be possible. You have to stop her. You're not the only one who will be in trouble if the truth comes out.'

Caught up feeling sorry for his situation, he had dismissed what Betty said out of hand.

Whenever Lennie's conscience pricked, he often convinced himself that Elaine had left, even going so far as to search online for clues to her whereabouts and even wondering if he should tell Mark of her existence. Whenever he was in this mood, Wendy would get angry and remind him that Elaine had walked out on him and Mark. Now with Cassie's help, Mark was finding long-lost relatives he never knew he had. Lennie felt rejected every time she mentioned a new one she'd found. Perhaps, he thought, that is what Mark needs; a physical connexion to his mother, and owning Byford House would fit the bill. Sure that he would never sell his mother's inheritance, Lennie could make the house over to Mark, which should also go a long way to healing the rift between them and keeping the burial ground of Elaine safe and undisturbed

12

DECEMBER

Betty still smarted from Judy's brush-off and Angela's nasty comments at the funeral. Lennie had dismissed her worries over what Cassie was doing out of hand. She could tell he knew more than what he was telling her and seemed unconcerned that his secrets were about to be dragged into the open. The trouble was, she told him, they weren't just his. Peter was worse than useless. Betty had tried to talk to him about her worries, and like Lennie, he had dismissed her fears. With Wendy dead, she thought everything would settle down. Instead, Cassie was still digging. The thought of Peter finding out that Angela was his daughter was too much to bear. That couldn't happen. She had to stop Cassie from finding out. Taking a deep breath, she picked up the telephone and punched in her number.

'Cassie, hi, it's Betty.'

'Sorry. Who?'

Betty squeezed the receiver as anger rose through her.

'Peter's wife, Wendy's friend. Could you help me? Lennie told me that you like researching family history. I was hoping that you could look into mine for me. I have lots of photos and old letters.'

Cassie didn't know what to say; she hardly knew the woman. As to her husband, the thought of being anywhere near him, made her shudder. However, unable to resist the lure of looking through old photos and letters made her decision for her.

'Yes, why not. I am busy this week, so it will have to be next week.'

That was not what Betty wanted to hear. Time she felt was running out.

'Perhaps you could pop in today and take the paperwork, look through it, and see what you think? Then we could get together when you have more time.'

Cassie waited; when she had rung Betty back to tell her that her car wouldn't start and that she was stuck in Sainsbury's car park and couldn't pop by, her silence had been unnerving before snapping.

'I'll come and pick you up.'

As the car stopped beside her, her skin prickled with unease, and Cassie wanted nothing more than to run away.

'We'll sort your car out later. Jump in,' shouted Betty through the window.

As soon as Cassie closed the door, they were away. Betty clutched the steering wheel and hummed. Turning her head, she glanced at Cassie.

'You like digging up the past, don't you? Lennie has told me that you have been delving into his and Wendy's. Of course, what you should have done was ask me. I know all their secrets and lies. Oh yes. They both liked nothing better than to offload them. Wendy was my friend, I loved her, but I also hated her. Peter loved her too. He and her they… That doesn't matter now that she's dead. I thought Lennie would die, but he managed to bounce back. Too handy with his fists. That is what he is. I'd stay away from him if I were you.'

Cassie flinched at Betty's tone, it wasn't in the least friendly, and her sideways looks were making the hairs stand up on the back of her neck, making her wish that she had never gotten into the car.

Pulling up in front of the house, Betty cut the engine and turned to face Cassie. Her smile; not reaching her eyes.

'We have a dog, he is friendly, but sometimes… I'll just go and put him in the kitchen.'

Betty jumped out of the car and dashed to the front door. Opening it, she called out something Cassie couldn't hear before closing it with a bang. Cassie hesitated, the door opened, and Betty ushered her inside.

As her arm swept up, Betty brought the hammer down onto Cassie's head. She crumpled and fell to the floor. It wasn't enough. Her arm rose and fell, the rhythm mesmerising her. Betty stopped. This time her smile reached her eyes.

As her heartbeat settled and the red mist cleared, Betty sighed. Cassie lay bloodied and broken. Also covered in blood, Betty pulled her dress over her head and grabbed another from her wardrobe. As she sat on the bed, her muddled thoughts gave her a headache.

She needed Peter; he could bury Cassie like he buried Elaine. But he would want to know why she had killed her. She would have to leave, go far away. What to do?

Betty walked slowly down the stairs; she ignored Cassie, her mind already blanking out what she had done. As she drove away, tears began to fall, and her mind groped for someone to blame. Like Wendy, her thoughts immediately turned to Angela, and there she was. Without a care in the world, Angela was walking along the pavement. It was too much for Betty, she pushed her foot flat down onto the accelerator, and the car surged forwards. Betty felt the force of hitting Angela shudder through the car. Angela flew over the car's bonnet, her body twisted in mid-air. Betty looked in her mirror to see Angela fall. Now, she thought, things could get back to normal. With Angela dead, I don't have to leave home.

Cassie lay where she had left her. Betty stood in the hall, her mind once again floating free. Unaware of the blue lights flashing through the windows, like a statue, she gazed at the bloodied mess before her, only brought out of her fugue state upon hearing Peter's voice.

'What have you done? Betty, look at me.'

A police constable on either side of her, he could only stare as he watched her taken away.

*

'**H**ello, sleepy head, keep still, don't try and move. The doctor has said that you are to keep lying flat. You have been unconscious and have only just come around.'

Angela's eyes felt as if she had a film clouding her vision. Blinking cleared them, and then she became aware of the banging in her head, wincing as the pain raced around her skull.

'What happened?'

'What hasn't,' tears fell down Judy's face as Angela become more aware of her surroundings. 'We thought that she had killed you, like …'

Judy sobbed as Mark held her. Calm again, she wiped her face with a tissue and blew her nose.

'Sorry. It has all been a bit too much to take in. Mark, you tell her.'

Angela looked from one to another and tried to sit up, making her aware of how much her ribs hurt.

'Ouch.'

'Are you okay? Should we call the nurse?'

'Mark, never mind the bloody nurse. Tell me what's happened and why I am in the hospital and feeling like shit.'

Diving straight in, he told her. 'It was Betty. She ran you down in her car. After she had killed Cassie.'

Angela stared, trying to make sense of what he had said. She remembered turning into a side street and passing a garden just as a small dog defending its territory attacked the gate, the manic barking distracting her as she felt a shove from behind and had a feeling of flying before it all went black.

'I don't understand. It doesn't make any sense, I know Betty doesn't like me, but I wouldn't have thought enough to try and kill me.'

Judy helped Angela take a sip of a drink and placed her arm around her shoulders to lift her, her body trembling.

'Better?'

Plumping her pillows, she smiled, pushing Angela's hair off her face, and kissed her forehead.

'You are safe now, and Betty is in police custody.' Holding her hand, she nodded to Mark. 'Tell her from the beginning.'

'Betty and Peter have known Wendy since they hung out together as teenagers and never strayed far from her orbit. Betty was Wendy's shadow and would never be far from her. Peter, had always fancied Wendy; well aware of this, she blew hot and cold. She promised him the earth and delivered nothing. Betty loved him with a passion. She comes across as feeble, Peter the one that rules the roost. It was an act. She thought acting submissive would make him like her more. How? Betty came to that conclusion when Wendy, who he hunkered after, was the opposite; we will never know. Perhaps she thought she could not compete with her more outgoing nature and went the other way.

'Peter and Lennie became friends, boys together, they got up to all sorts. Lennie, as we know, is a charmer, and Peter is nothing but a creep. Betty, of course, puts up with their shenanigans. Wendy didn't and came down hard on both of them, and, for a while, they behaved themselves. When Wendy and Lennie got together, Betty and Peter sort of fell into marriage because of it. Betty felt she was losing her best friend and Peter his chance to be with her. Both their lives have been on the periphery of Wendy's.

'Lennie did kill Elaine, and Betty knew all about it, he had called Peter in a panic, and she answered the phone. He and Elaine had rowed, and as is often the case with Lennie, it had gotten violent. Elaine struck the first blow, a glancing one, and Lennie retaliated.

'Unfortunately, he was holding a knife at the time, and she died instantly. When they arrived, Betty could see that Lennie was in no fit state to deal with the situation, and she took charge. As we suspected, they buried her in the grounds of Byford House. All committed to not speaking about it to anyone, even between themselves.

'Surprisingly, it was not the only secret she was keeping. Betty knew all about Wendy taking Judy. She also knew about the money and property Wendy had embezzled. It seems that neither of them gave her a thought seeing her as some bank where they could offload their crimes, knowing Betty would keep their secrets. There was only one that she was concerned about, and she saw the danger of it being dragged into the light when Cassie started digging. Betty and Peter could not have children, something that Betty always wanted. He finally got his chance with Wendy, a one-night stand, and you were the result.'

'What?' Angela roared. 'You have got to be joking. The pervert. Is my father? How can you be sure? Betty could be lying.'

'She is not,' said Judy. 'Wendy intimated to me. Before she took her life, I didn't say anything; because, well, she was very drunk, and she could be hateful. I knew if true, you would hate it. I know he came on to you. Peter did the same to me. Angela, I am sorry. I should have said something before.'

'Fucking hell, could it get any worse, and does he know?'

'After knocking you down and speeding off, the police tracked her number plate, and when they turned up at her house, they found more than they bargained for,' explained Judy. 'Peter is dead. He drove himself into a tree and was killed outright. The police believe that with Betty arrested, he knew the game was up and that his involvement in helping Lennie cover up a crime would all come out. Wendy was not the only one to think that her life was over when you were born. Though you don't look anything like Peter, Betty saw the resemblance to his mother's sister. She confronted Wendy. Rather than hate either of them, she could not. Betty loved them, and so she hated you instead.'

'When I was younger,' muttered Angela, 'she used to pinch me when no one was looking. I remember telling mother, who laughed, not believing a word of it, and as for him! Ugh, I feel sick at the thought.'

'You were on the pavement, and witnesses say that Betty drove straight at you before driving away. The only reason the doctors believe that you are alive is that you landed in a hedge which helped to break your fall. You got knocked out when you bounced off. She told the police that she had not been planning to kill you. Like you, the barking dog drew her attention, and she saw you and reacted.

'Earlier, Betty had arranged to meet Cassie, telling her that she wanted her to do research into her family history. When she stepped over the threshold of Betty's house, she hit Cassie with a hammer. Betty intended to kill her. The reasons she gave to the police were that it was Cassie's fault for poking around in things that did not concern her by stirring up the past. The main worry for Betty was Peter finding out about you. She felt that if he did, he would leave her. Betty also admitted to killing Wendy. When she found Lennie in the kitchen, she heard a thump from upstairs and found Wendy. Booze and pills were everywhere, and Betty acted on autopilot. Crushing them into a powder, she filled Wendy's glass with wine and poured it down her throat. Hearing your car in the drive sent her into a panic. Betty left Wendy to her fate and went to help Lennie, who was drifting in and out of consciousness.'

When Judy first heard what Betty had done, she realised that perhaps, after all, she wasn't responsible for Wendy's death. Judging by Angela's face and the squeeze of her hand, she had the same thoughts.

'So where does Lennie fit into all this?' asked Angela.

'He has been arrested for the murder of Elaine. With Peter dead, Betty does not care anymore, telling the police about Wendy and Lennie's embezzlements and the taking of Judy. The papers are having a field day. Be glad that you are in here.'

*

Nestling as it did into the landscape of Yoxford helped the house withstand the worst of the rain and sleet. It had been pounding down outside since Angela arrived, and both the roof and windows had taken a battering. With the fires lit in the lounge and dining room, the inside had begun to feel warm and cosy. Given her carte blanche to get it ready, after a week of cleaning it from top to bottom, the house gleamed. Brought back to life, she could not wait for Judy and Mark to see it. Left out of the celebrations last year, Angela determined that this Christmas would be different.

Her New Year resolution hung like a reminder before her, and all week it had intruded on her thoughts when she had least expected it. Taking a swig from her glass of Malbec, she smacked her lips together in delight.

The turkey was resting; she had slow-cooked it overnight. The last of the potatoes were peeled and ready to go in. As the music from the dining room wafted along the hall, her thoughts swirled. What a year it had been, Angela chuckled. At the start, she had a family, and now she was an orphan. Her mother's best friend killed her, and the man thought to be Angela's father; was also dead. At the same time, her biological one – someone she did not even want – had killed himself, and to top it all off, Mark and Judy were not even related to her.

Raising her glass, she shouted to the empty room, 'to new beginnings.'

Hearing a car pull up, she opened the front door, 'good journey? Here let me help. Christ, what have you got in here?' Angela laughed. 'My presents?' she asked, as she helped to take the bags out of the boot.

They sat in the lounge, the fire roaring in the grate, all drinking brandy, Judy's let her eyes roam around the room. Angela had gone all out to decorate. Mark, unable to put a damper on her enthusiasm for Christmas, let her have full reign, and she had taken him at his word. After the year they had all been through, Judy was grateful that she and they had survived, and with Paul sent packing out of her life, free at last. The future is something to look forward to rather than fear. Stretching out her legs, Judy gave a satisfied sigh.

'Dinner was smashing, thanks, Angela. I had no idea that

you were such a good cook. My belly is so full I may need a crane to get me up the stairs.'

'Me too,' said Mark, enjoying the peace as the three of them chatted.

No dramas occurred as they usually did when the family had gotten together. Mark had been ignoring the phone calls from Lennie's solicitor and emails to get in touch. Two weeks before Christmas, he had received a letter informing him that Lennie had suffered a heart attack and had sadly died. This time he rang back and told the solicitor he was not interested. Lennie was no relation and not his problem. You are, however, the solicitor told him pompously his beneficiary, and to claim your inheritance, you need to sign some paperwork.

Looking around the room, Mark decided to put the house up for sale in January. With his mother's body removed, there was nothing to stop him. Angela would not be pleased as she loved the place. When he suggested doing so after Lennie had made it over to him, she had shouted at him before begging him not to. Saying at least let's have one Christmas together there. Why so fixed on doing it here, he could not imagine. He would be happy with a bottle of wine and a plate of sandwiches. When he had seen the table laid as if for a banquet, he had dearly wanted to laugh. Nudged in the ribs by Judy, he had about managed to keep his expression blank as he congratulated Angela on all her efforts, her smile warming his heart. Her words brought him out of his reverie.

'I know you want to sell. Thank you for holding off. I wanted to have this time together before we leave, to go our separate ways. Celebrate the year. I know that may sound daft, considering all that has happened. If you remember, though, we started it barely able to talk to each other without being sarcastic or nasty, especially you, Mark.'

'Agreed,' he grinned.

'Before we go to our beds, I'd like to make a toast.' Filling their glasses, Angela raised hers and chuckled, 'here's to not being any relation.'

As Mark and Judy prepared for bed, drawing the curtains closed, Angela checked that the windows were shut and; securely locked. With the temperatures plummeting, she double-checked that the ancient boiler – temperamental at the best of times – was set correctly to come on well before any of them were likely to get up in the morning before locking the back door and slipping the key into her pocket. Making her way up the stairs, she knocked gently at Judy's door.

'Cocoa?'

Hearing her voice, Mark opened his door.

'I haven't had one of these for years,' taking the proffered mug, he took a sip. 'Yum, that is so good.'

'I have added a drop of brandy. It is so cold I thought it would help us sleep. There are extra blankets in the boxes at the end of your beds. If the temperature keeps dropping, you may need them. Have a good sleep, and I will see you both in the morning.'

Waiting for their doors to close, Angela paused before hers. As they did earlier, her thoughts once again began to swirl. Shaking her shoulders, she admonished herself; too late to back out. The worst part was the waiting. She found herself tapping her watch every few seconds, as if doing so, she could move time forwards. Angela thought, would four hours be enough?

Carefully opening her bedroom door, stepping over the creaky floorboard, she opened Judy's door. Laying stretched across the bed, she looked like she had been fighting some unseen opponent. The covers and pillows were all on the floor and the sheet wrapped around her body. She had vomited, the smell making Angela cover her mouth. Her heart hammered as she reached and placed her fingers on Judy's neck. Snatching them back, Angela stood like a statue and only moved when giggles threatened to bubble up. Clasping her hand to her mouth to stifle them, she quietly closed the door. One down, she thought, one to go.

Unsure what she would do if Mark were still alive. She placed her ear against the door and listened. Pulling her hand away from the handle, she stayed still. Telling herself, you have to know. Make sure. Taking a deep breath, she opened the door, and like Judy, Mark had been thrashing about the bed. Unlike her, his eyes were open and staring right at Angela, making her step back in fear before whispering.

'Mark, are you all right?'

She waited, breath held, conscious of the time bleeding away. Plucking up the courage, she bent over the bed and touched her fingers to Mark's neck. Flinching, she thought she felt a pulse. His eyes didn't blink, and like Judy, he'd vomited, the stench again making her want to gag. Angela leaned against the door and waited for her heartbeat to slow down. Checking that all was in good order, she gave the reflection of herself in her bedroom mirror a nod and pulled it shut.

Returning to the kitchen, Angela stood in front of the cooker, and her mind went blank. Shaking her head to clear her thoughts, she turned on the rings and opened the oven door. The smell of gas immediately began wafting through the house. Pulling the inner door closed, she dragged a small hall cabinet across to block before closing and locking the front door.

Driving away, Angela felt no remorse. Once out of the hospital, it had not taken her long to realise nothing had changed. She was still the odd one out. All through her life, her family, at one time or another, had excluded her. Even now, after everything that had happened, Judy and Mark had been making plans to move away and start new lives with no thought given to how their words may make her feel. Both had offered her money, which she had refused. Telling Judy that if her mother had wanted her to have any inheritance from her, Wendy would have named Angela in her will and told Mark the same, and wanted nothing from Lennie.

In truth, she did not need their handouts. When trashing Gary's flat, she had also found a hidden stash of money, which he had failed to mention to his friends or the police. It was not a fortune by any means, but it was enough for her to leave the country and make a fresh start. Where no one knew her and where she could be free of the past and take hold of her future.

With her thoughts taken up thinking about her new life, and the plans she had put in place, she neither saw nor heard the lorry. Angela was broad-sided by the fully loaded artic. Her car rolled like a child's toy before being flipped onto its roof. Scraping along the road as it rolled over, the metal sending sparks flying up into the sky, lighting it up like a fireworks display. The car finally came to a halt after ramming itself into the side of a brick wall. As it stopped rocking, silence and darkness surrounded her, and Angela moaned. Hanging upside down, unable to feel her body, and with blood gushing from her arms and legs, Angela desperately wanted to laugh at the waste of all her plans but only managed a strangled croak.

A voice shouted, inches from her face, 'she's alive. Don't move, my lovely.'

In any other circumstances, Angela would have raged at the stupidity of it all. Killing Judy and Mark, she thought, would set her free instead, she, like them would die.

'I've called an ambulance, and the police are on their way. What's your name?'

She could hear people shouting as something exploded. The car jolted with the backwash from it. The emergency services were getting nearer, the sirens louder, fluid filled her lungs to strangle her breath, and the thought exploded through her head, if only …